Displa

Dan Hook

First Edition

Edited by Liminal Pages

Proofread by Alexa Tewkesbury

ISBN: 978-1-8380389-0-8

www.danhook.co.uk

Book design by Veradia

DISPLACED

BOOK 1 OF
The Dark Array Series

Dan Hook

NEW WORLD MAP

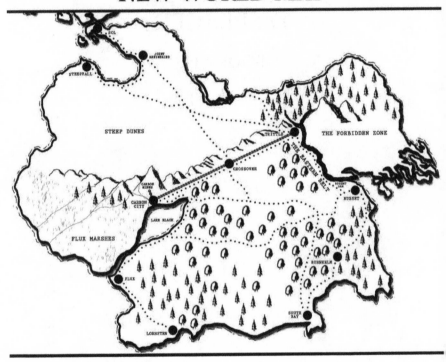

PROLOGUE

A foul wind pushed up from the south with a smear of cloud as Arlo tried to get ahead, leaving the crumpled roads of a forgotten world behind him. He rushed into a decaying forest, the concrete beneath his feet turning to dirt. There were screams among the gunfire, the sounds joined by a deep rumbling that vibrated the earth. The ground sloped sharply in front of him. He slowed his pace to avoid falling.

The screaming grew louder, followed by a gurgled screech. Arlo stumbled down the slope, finding a splintered tree stump to hide behind to catch his breath. The sun had hardly risen, making it difficult for him to see his surroundings. He heard the crunch of footsteps moving closer, eventually coming to a halt.

Pulling out his knife, Arlo glanced back up the hill now that the screaming and gunfire had started to settle. Several metres up the hill, a woman stepped into view, wearing a thick black trench coat and holding a rifle. She aimed into the forest, away from him.

He could approach her from behind, grab her gun. Arlo hesitated, and moved back out of view. He rubbed his rough, worn face. Attacking from such a distance would be foolish.

The dead silence made him curious, and he placed a hand on the tree trunk to lever himself into a better view. A sudden loud crack sounded and his hand fell through the rotten wood. The woman ahead turned in one swift motion, aiming at the tree he hid behind. A few moments of quiet passed before Arlo took another peek. The woman still faced in his direction.

Bubbled screeching erupted from the forest behind the woman and a pale-yellow figure of drooping flesh jumped onto her. Bullets rattled off into the air from the gun, followed by another shriek coming from the forest. Arlo jumped up and stepped backwards, watching the woman struggle against the creature as it sank its teeth and nails into her.

Behind them, a thick cloud of yellow haze blew through the forest, shrouding the creature and woman and hiding them from view. Arlo turned, grasping for the mask that clung to his belt, and hurried down the hill, attempting to keep ahead of the haze while putting the mask on. He placed the straps over his hair and tightened the seal, slowing his descent as the haze engulfed him.

****

Two weeks had passed. Arlo had met back with his family, the idea of escaping at the forefront of his mind once again. It was different this time, now having witnessed the danger himself. Explaining it to his partner and daughter had been difficult; they were still unconvinced about what he had seen. To him, there was no longer a choice. They needed to leave and find safety.

The family of three carefully made their way down through the rocky remains of a dead woodland, the ground uneven and steep. Rotting trees gave no support, an honest reflection of the surrounding wasteland. The branches and trunks snapped and crumbled each time they dared to lay a hand on them, reminding Arlo of the events in the forest two weeks prior.

'Over there, Evaline.' Arlo pointed to a shape between the trees. 'Grimsfoot.'

On the horizon stood an immense rocky ridge that hollowed into a cavern beneath itself. The overhang curved into a blade-like point, touching down into the ground.

'Sure we're welcome?' Evaline eyed the cold and uninviting shape as she moved down the slope with their daughter, Kiera.

'They welcome anyone inside who won't give them trouble.' Arlo smiled. 'We'll be fine.'

All three of them moved down the hillside, hastening towards the ominous rock face. Both parents glanced behind them every so often.

Several figures appeared, encircling the family.

'Hands in the air,' a voice growled. 'Including the child.'

With slight reluctance, the family raised their hands and moved closer together.

'Just checking you over, is all.' The voice had softened.

One figure approached and started to pat down their tattered clothing.

'Bags,' a woman barked after searching them.

All three of them removed their backpacks and held them open.

'Been here before?' A man ahead of them stepped closer, holding a crossbow.

'No, first time,' Arlo said. He kept his attention on the woman rummaging through their belongings.

'Alright. Well, if you hear a low hum and the lights cut out, keep your mouths shut. Routine patrols pass by every so often, and we might be due one today.' The man looked westwards before turning back. Arlo watched him scan over them. He knew how tired they looked, their dark skin dried and scarred.

'So, reason for entering?' The man stared at him.

'Looking for a way out,' Arlo said. He glanced at his daughter.

'A couple of blades, but they're clear otherwise,' the woman said, returning to the formation around them.

'In that case, head to Matteo's on the second floor. He'll have some info for you. Keep moving ahead and you'll find your way. Now, no violence. We've got zero tolerance for it.' The man backed away with the others, disappearing from sight.

They dropped their arms and Arlo nodded towards Evaline. 'It'll be alright, trust me this time.'

All three of them moved under the vast rocky overhang into the cavern, following the dim yellow lights that hung along the damp stone walls. After a minute of walking, the walls opened out into a cave. They passed over some vents in the floor in line with two huge metal doors that stood on either side. Ahead, a rusted cage came into view with a man wearing a top hat leaning against the wall beside it.

'Where can I drop ya?' The bloke gave a yellowed smile and turned to open the front of the cage.

'Matteo's,' replied Arlo.

'Matteo's it is.' The man gestured to the cage. 'It's a little bumpy but does the job.' He closed the front and pulled a lever. 'Well, usually.' He let out a laugh, disappearing from view now that the cage had started lowering.

Darkness surrounded the family, with only the deafening clank and rattle of chains keeping them company, along with the occasional jolt.

Minutes passed before the cage came to a stop, the family now being able to see two dim yellow lights on the walls opposite. A woman stepped out in front, opening the cage door. Ahead they could see a narrow passageway with noise and light bleeding in from the other end.

'Matteo's?' the woman grumbled.

'Uh, yeah, yes,' Arlo confirmed.

'Second turning on the right,' she said, stepping behind them and shutting the cage door with a clang.

The family huddled together and moved down the walkway, following the yellow lights on the wall once again. Eventually, the passage opened up to reveal an underground street ahead of them. The ceiling was low and dotted with more lights but high enough to accommodate the small buildings that lined either side of the wide pedestrian pathways. Dozens of people filled the street, roaming, drinking, shopping and talking among themselves.

The sight of them made the parents freeze and glance at each other. They gripped each other's hands and cautiously made their way through, uncomfortable at the sight of so many people.

Arlo and Evaline warned Kiera not to make eye contact when passing the bars, shops and various merchants; some of whom attempted to gain their attention.

Eventually, they reached Matteo's, a small shop with barred windows on the front, wedged between a gas mask shop and clothing merchant.

'Wait here,' Arlo said, before entering the shop.

'Where's Dad going?' Kiera pulled her mother by the hand towards the door he disappeared behind.

'He's gonna get us someplace safe, apparently.' Evaline twitched at the words, pulling her daughter back. 'Away from all this. Out of here completely.' She smiled briefly.

'Can't we go with him?' Kiera took a step towards the door, wanting to see inside.

'We are going with him.' Evaline turned to face her. 'He's just finding out how we're gonna get there, my darling, that's all. We'll be together like always.' She pulled her daughter in for a tight hug, her eyes still focused on the passing strangers. 'Regardless of what dream your father's on again.'

Shouting flared up down the street as two women attacked each other. Evaline stepped closer to the shop door with Kiera, keeping an eye on the two people fighting.

Bystanders formed a wide berth around the dispute, keen to avoid involvement but still wanting to witness the fight. A few seconds later, guards appeared and split the women up, forcing them to their knees before cuffing them and dragging them away. Within moments the street noise returned to normal.

Arlo emerged from the shop holding a scrap of paper, glancing over to where the commotion had occurred.

'Well, the man knows of two ways currently used.' He spoke slowly and cautiously. He turned to Evaline. 'The first one is heading north around the mountains, which is what we've heard before. It's both slow and dangerous. The other route is west and much faster, though still dangerous.'

'Your idea, you choose,' Evaline said sharply. 'Quicker is surely better, though?'

'I would say the same. However, it would mean crossing—'

A low rumble echoed through the ceiling followed by the lights switching off, making everyone fall silent. Only a few lanterns and luminous rocks remained to light the place.

'They must be near,' Arlo whispered. Both he and Evaline took their daughter's hands and slowly headed back towards the exit.

They reached the small area where the rusted cage swayed.

'No use of the lift for the time being. Patrols nearby,' the woman stated, standing in front of it with a rifle in her hand.

'Happen often?' Evaline hoped it was a usual affair with little to worry about.

'For the past couple weeks, it's been almost daily. Used to be once a fortnight but something's stirred the hornets' nest,' the woman replied, now staring up above. 'They haven't spotted us yet.'

The lights flickered back on, followed by the distant noise of people continuing with their dealings in the street. The woman opened the cage door, gesturing the family in.

It wasn't long until they emerged out into the open from the same cavern they had entered through. A dark smudge of grey filled the sky. None of the figures that had appeared on their arrival were anywhere in sight.

The wind still blew harshly from the west, making them hurry up the hill and sigh with relief at the sun still shining, even if it was only for another hour.

'A bridge, far north-west,' Arlo said between heavy breaths. 'That's our way out.'

'Is it really good on the other side?' the daughter asked.

'Apparently so.' Evaline sighed. 'At least that's what your dad would have us believe.' She flicked a glare towards him.

Behind them, Arlo could see a large plume of yellow haze fast approaching and filling up the sky.

'Masks on now,' he called out.

All three faced away from the haze and strapped their gas masks on. Evaline checked her daughter's twice over to make sure the straps were tight and the mask sealed.

'It's on.' Kiera brushed her mother's hands away, stepping back to watch the haze thunder across the landscape towards them.

'Gotta make sure,' Evaline replied, now checking over her own mask and tightening the straps.

'It's getting denser,' Arlo warned from inside his mask, but he doubted Evaline heard.

They stood holding their hands out for one another, waiting for the yellow mist to arrive and bring their visibility down to several feet around them. Once in the thick of it, the family stepped forwards, continuing up the hill.

****

The haze began to clear after an hour of walking, though little daylight remained. They followed along the edge of an old forest, looking for a place to spend the night. All three had spent the time in silence, the masks making it too difficult to talk without shouting.

Evaline took off her mask. 'I won't do it.'

'What? Why?' Arlo pulled his mask off, turning to her. 'This is for the better, for all of us, and especially for her. You know that. Particularly after what we've seen this time, it's not just some tale any longer.' He glanced towards his daughter who still held their hands between them. 'You promised this time, Eve.'

'What we've seen? I've seen none of the things you talk about,' hastened Evaline. 'What was it again besides some sick starving person attacking those Legion soldiers?' She sharpened her tone. 'We do the same damn thing!'

'Evaline, I've told you. It wasn't... wasn't a person.' Arlo shook his head. 'Their teeth were far too long... and their skin looked sickly... melted...'

'Yeah, well, some people get it worse, and they often end up doing worse. We've seen plenty of mangled things, I know it. But who's to say where we're heading won't be more dangerous? Huh?

I'm bettin' we'll get shot at before we come close to this bridge of yours,' Evaline spat.

'It'll be worth it,' Arlo said, raising his voice. 'We can deal with the danger if we take it slow. And the haze, it's been far more frequent and thicker than it usually is.'

'No.' Evaline froze. 'It won't be worth it.'

'It will.' He stopped moving and turned to their daughter. 'What do you think, my love?'

Kiera removed her mask and ruffled her matted hair. Arlo thought she looked like the spitting image of her mother, sharing her same deep brown eyes and thick black hair, though he was thankful she lacked her stubbornness.

'I want to leave,' Kiera replied quietly, avoiding her mother's stare.

'She is a child. She doesn't know. You don't even know,' Evaline snapped, making her daughter flinch.

'And you do?' Arlo challenged, keeping his volume low. 'Now come on.' He turned with his daughter to continue walking, pulling Kiera and her mother's hands apart.

After several paces, Arlo and Kiera turned back to find Evaline still standing in the same spot.

'Come on, Mum.' Kiera held her hand out, her eyes filling with tears. 'Please?'

'Now you just come here, my love. Come here.' Evaline beckoned her daughter over, but Kiera resisted.

'You really want to do this again?' Arlo's voice became brittle. He felt a lump form in his throat. 'Just come on already.' The strain worsened. 'Why are you doing this again? After what we've seen?' He stopped, attempting to hold in his tears. 'You know it's for the best. Those things, they aren't natural. I don't want our girl near them, or us either. Trust me on this.'

'I don't care. This is my home. Our home. How do ya know what you saw? You said you were in the haze. It coulda been some animal or just someone like us, desperate to survive. This ain't no reason to go walking into some sorta trap. These stories of a better place, they ain't true. How can you believe them? You trust the words of a stranger.' Anger filled Evaline's voice and she choked back tears. 'Who knows what this Matteo guy has waiting for us? It's where everyone's been heading, right? Lady knew where we were going before you even said it. So why choose them over us? Why this Matteo? He could be the one laying out some rotten bodies and spreading crazy stories. Getting people all riled up to go!'

'Alright, it's alright,' Arlo said. Evaline had worked herself up into a panic. He paused, unsure what to say. After a minute of silence, he moved towards her. Fighting head-on would only make the situation worse.

'We'll stay,' he muttered, putting his arms around her.

Evaline's eyes narrowed at him for a moment. 'We are doing fine just here, the three of us.' Her words were bitter. 'We know this world. Our world. It's real, and nothing needs changing, we do just fine by it. Whatever you think is out there, ain't. We can deal with it just fine, the haze and all.'

Arlo let out a quiet sigh and gestured for Kiera to join him in hugging her mother.

'Now, let's get some food sorted so we can rest our eyes. It's getting too dark to travel.' Arlo dropped his rucksack on the floor beside a row of old tree trunks that marked a clear edge to the forest.

'We'll all think better on a full stomach.' He smiled, taking out a tin and some dried meat. 'I'll take the first watch.'

****

The night had been peaceful. Evaline woke up to the same usual smudge of greys in the sky and stretched, her eyes adjusting to the light.

'Morning,' she mumbled, before realising what she had said. The sun had risen already, yet she had not done her watch. Only silence met her ears.

Bolting upright, she turned and scanned the ground beside her. Neither Arlo nor Kiera were anywhere in sight. She searched around the trees and stared at the floor for any sign of them, finding only a few dead leaves and broken branches.

Then she caught sight of a smear of charcoal on a tree stump reading, 'Sorry'.

Her mind crumbled at attempting to piece together what was happening, a scream failing to escape from her throat. Evaline fell to her knees, still scanning for Arlo and her daughter, but only the charcoal word remained. She hid under her arms for a second before letting out a coarse shriek. Her family was gone.

TWENTY-ONE YEARS LATER

CHAPTER 1 - ZARA

'Did it work then?' Zara sighed, leaning against the metal wall. She winced at the cold metal touching her skin and reluctantly stood up. Since arriving, regret had slowly taken hold of her. She shouldn't have taken a job so different to her usual responsibilities back home.

Zara rested one hand on the back of her neck, brushing through her short black hair. Her small frame and younger age, compared to Trent, meant she was often crawling around in the small passages of the dam when parts needed repairing. Tonight had been full of it and her back was beginning to feel strained.

Both of them stared up at the ceiling expecting a noise, but all they heard was the quiet hum of a generator on the floor above. The faint sound had been a worthwhile trade for decent lighting within the windowless structure.

Trent had told Zara the dam could provide an endless amount of electricity when functional, using the energy of the ocean passing through it and out into the ravine. She knew the value of it to the nearby town of Russet and why they were keen to get it operating again, even though it went against the wishes of those who now patrolled the area. This patrol was the reason she and Trent had both agreed to work nights, though Delia, the local who had organised the job, insisted they return each morning to bring her updates.

'Oi.' Zara snapped her fingers. 'Did it work then?'

'I... I'm not sure. Let me check the upper level.' Trent broke his gaze from the ceiling, pushing the lever back up into its previous position. He moved towards the door, running his fingers through the faded patch of hair left on his head. 'I'll figure it out. Delia will just have to wait a little longer.' He glanced back towards her, presenting a thin smile.

'Trent, why are you doing this?' Zara asked, preparing for him to dismiss the question. She knew of the hostile relations between her city and Russet, though she doubted Carbon City would ever find out they were helping a rival settlement. It still felt odd to her that Trent, in his old age, still wanted to work. Zara knew he earnt more than his share of money from rebuilding and maintaining steam trains; a job few could do.

He paused at the comment. 'Apparently, I look knowledgeable enough for them to ask... Must be the wrinkles.' Trent shrugged before he rubbed his chin and chuckled.

'Well, if knowledge hides in wrinkles then you're far smarter than I realised,' she joked. 'No need to be modest here. But seriously, Trent, why?' Zara questioned more sharply.

'A year's worth of salary, now that's good pay. And money is money, can't have too much of it. Though we gotta get it running before any of that.' Trent raised his eyebrows.

'Think it's really possible?' Zara murmured. She felt disinterested by his reply, even though it rang true for why she had come.

'Sure. It was running once and it'll run again. Don't see a reason why not… Delia knows the information she's given us isn't enough and is aware of how complicated this all is. Why else would I be here?' He grinned. 'I'm one of the best around.'

'Ha, did I just call you modest? My mistake.' She smirked.

Trent gave back a smile more genuine than his last, something that had become less frequent over the years.

'Right, I'll check to see what's happened upstairs and I think we'll call it a night. The sun will soon be rising.' Trent left the room, accompanied by the echo of his boots against the grilled metal flooring.

Zara had suggested getting more lights working inside the place, which would enable them to work easier and faster, but it had turned into a project of its own.

To have a job in a place off-limits and surrounded by patrols meant neither of them were fully relaxed. Her clothes were getting dirtier than usual, too, with smears of coal, oil and grease staining the reds of her top and darkening the greys of her trousers. The jacket of hers, currently thrown on the floor, had put up more of a fight in its old age and the dirt was less noticeable against the blackened leather. She struggled with knowing Trent continuously lived in his overalls, even when at home.

Her parents had never been keen on Trent, accusing him of leading her astray and giving her dangerous ideas. Zara missed them more than she would admit, with it being her first time out of the city. Saying goodbye had been messier than she planned. And her parents weren't the only ones she missed. The damp chill of the coastal air made her ache for home and the touch of Heather's warm skin against her own.

The lights cut out, followed by the halt of the generator's hum. Zara shook her head, confused by the unexpected darkness while trying to put her jacket on.

'Trent?' Zara called out, rummaging for a torch.

'Someone's here.' Trent's silhouette appeared in the doorway. 'They're here.' His voice trembled between each breath. 'We need to hide.'

'What?' His sudden panic startled her. Delia had been applying pressure, but the woman was hardly a threatening figure. The thud of heavy steps above interrupted her thoughts. 'Delia? How would *she* sneak past th—'

'They aren't from Russet.' Trent closed the door behind him and eased the heavy handle down into the locked position, sealing them both in the room. Zara stood motionless with her torch in hand, staring at the ceiling and following the echo of boots.

'Did you not hear me?' Trent grabbed both their bags, chucking Zara's at her. 'It isn't anyone we know,' he snapped.

The pit of her stomach dropped with the realisation of whose footsteps they were. She slung the bag over her shoulder and moved to Trent, who was kneeling on the floor.

'Here.' He pointed to a service hatch underneath the grilled flooring. They both lifted the panel and placed it to one side, giving access to the hatch door, which looked identical to the grilled flooring. The corroded handle resisted Trent's efforts to open it. He reached for his hammer and hit the handle free, making Zara wince at the sudden noise.

She could hear the footsteps thump against the metal as the patrol made its way down the stairs on the opposite side of the door. Zara kept glancing towards the closed door and then back at the floor hatch as Trent gently pulled it open.

'You first,' he whispered, holding it up.

Zara lowered herself down onto the ladder with her bag. The metal was cold and rough on her hands, accompanied by a bitter breeze that sent a chill through her. She reached the floor and stared back up at Trent, who hesitated, leaning over the edge. He put the hammer back into his bag and closed it.

'Catch.' Trent dropped his bag down to her and sighed. 'Sorry I got you into this, Zara.'

Before Zara realised what Trent was doing, he'd closed the hatch door and locked the handle back.

'Wh… what?' she fumbled. 'What are you doing? Trent?' She wanted to shout but forced her voice down to a whisper. Zara put the bags down and climbed back up the ladder with her torch in hand, the hatch only a metre above.

'They might not know how many of us are here. If they find me, well…' Trent stopped, listening to the sound of the boots in front of the doorway. 'They won't come looking for you. Meet me back in Russet if I'm taken.' He edged the metal floor panel back into place and stood up.

'Trent, don't—' A loud metal bang broke her sentence, vibrating the ground. The door unlatched with a clunk and swung open. Zara stepped off the ladder and switched off the torch.

'I'm in here,' Trent announced in a clear but shaky voice. 'I am unarmed and understand this area is off-limits. I will cooperate fully.'

Through the holes in the hatch, Zara saw only darkness. She moved away in fear of being seen. Footsteps started to pace the room, breaking the solemn silence.

'Please d—' A low thud followed by a rip then the weight of something hitting the ground echoed down into the hatchway.

With one hand over her mouth, Zara stifled her cry. She held still, waiting for the footsteps above to move again, hearing only faint muffled breath. Above the hatch, Zara could see a yellow glow linger before it disappeared with the footsteps back upstairs.

When the sound of movement finally subsided, Zara reached out to climb back up the ladder, her hands trembling. She dismissed the unusual gluey texture now on the metal. At the top, she went to push the hatch up with both hands above her head but something dripped down, making her lose her balance and almost slip. She tried pushing up a few more times, but the hatch resisted.

'Trent… please,' Zara sobbed, unable to see anything but darkness. She climbed back down the ladder and found her torch. The light flashed onto her hand, revealing what had been dripping down onto her.

'No… no, no, no,' she whispered, failing to wipe off the blood that started to congeal and smear on her. Zara flashed the torch upwards, quickly switching it off at the sight of more blood dripping down in front of her. She retched, moving to lean against the wall as her legs started to weaken.

'Breathe, keep breathing,' she assured herself, before a surge of fear made her heave and throw up onto the floor. She straightened, attempting to compose herself. Staying in the same spot would only make matters worse.

A warm breeze hit her further on down the corridor. Zara held the torch in one hand and both her and Trent's bags in the other. The passage went straight before sloping downwards, where she was careful not to slip on the wet soles of her boots. Then it split; one path opened into a generator room, and the other led to the ventilation systems. Zara took the latter. Leaving the dam through a vent was far safer than attempting to escape via the main entrance, if they suspected anyone else was in the building.

Zara eventually came across a large enough vent and followed it, squeezing past a large metal fan and breaking through several old filters. The vent proved big enough for her to crawl through and twist around in. Fortunately for Zara, the end of the vent was in a poor state. The metal was a brownish red, rusted and exposed to the elements. There was a foul dampness in the air, most likely from the ocean, but no sounds of waves nor hint of sunlight. The continual bitter breeze from the coast felt warm and stagnant.

She thought back to when she and Trent had arrived in Russet. She'd been so excited to see the ocean for the first time. Now, the thought of travelling alone and finding her way into Russet by herself made her nauseous; she had relied on Trent to know the way. *Trent... I need you.*

Twisting around, Zara placed her feet in front and pushed on the vent face, but the sharp metal grills were stubborn, remaining in place. Though it was still dark outside, she refused to hit it any harder, fearing someone might hear. Zara thought for a moment, remembering Trent's bag. She ignored the bloodstains and found his pliers, knowing they would easily break the corroded metal. With them in hand, she broke each horizontal bar on the grill down the left side, bending them back into the vent. Zara placed her bag and Trent's past the sharp metal and onto the narrow vent edge, then climbed through. She rested on the lip of the vent and twisted around to pull the grills back into place. The last thing she needed was for someone to see they had been tampered with.

As she moved the last spoke to its original position, the metal snapped in her hands. Zara lost her balance, grasping in a desperate attempt to save herself from falling. Her fingers found something to grab onto, bringing a breath of relief before she realised it was Trent's bag, which was now being brought down with her. She fell from the vent, plunging into the darkness below.

****

Hard rock met her feet before Zara collapsed onto her back. Pain shot through her spine while she lay winded on the rocky surface. Struggling to gasp for air, her body throbbed in agony. For a minute, Zara was unsure of what was happening. She squirmed at the aches plaguing her, failing to focus on the surrounding blur. Zara closed her eyes, taking in a deep breath. The sharp pain had focused down onto her legs. Each breath brought renewed agony, forcing her to take shallow, gentle breaths and minimise her movements.

After a few minutes, the pain began to subside. Still lying on the ground, Zara noticed her bag overhanging the vent above. Thankfully, the drop had only been a few metres. Her eyes traced the rusted metal to the faint outline of the dam that seemed far higher than it should have been. Confused, she closed them, only to taste something metallic on her tongue. *Blood.* Zara leant to one side and spat onto the rock.

Sitting up carefully, she wiped her mouth and looked down at the bloodstains that covered her pale skin and clothing. She stared up towards the vent again, unsure whether to feel lucky about surviving the fall – that it hadn't been much further. She was more thankful that she had somehow avoided screaming.

Zara dragged herself over to a large rock and rested against it, still lying on the ground. She attempted to look behind her for the town of Russet, but discovered a new pain in her neck.

The sky brightened, yet Zara remained in darkness. She focused her eyes and began pushing herself up from the ground, eventually able to stand. She supported herself against the rock and turned away from the dam. Zara's heart dropped when the sunrise was nowhere to be seen. The smell in the air was far more pungent than she'd first realised, and the sight of waves crashing against the shore was non-existent. She had fallen into the ravine on the opposite side of the dam where water once flowed. The town of Russet and the coastline were on the other side.

CHAPTER 2 – SHELBY

Shelby prepared breakfast on the porch table as usual. The sun poured into the sky and across the ocean in front of him. He knew such a clear and calm day was ideal for travelling into Lornsten to trade and start buying supplies for winter.

Living remotely meant Shelby continuously worked around the clock to provide for his two children, alongside his older neighbours, Frank and Lorel, who helped when possible.

'Time to get up,' Shelby called into the house. 'Breakfast is on the table. You've got two each this morning, so don't let them get cold.' He caught a glimpse of himself in the reflection of the front window, his olive skin worn and eyes tired. Shelby's morning of skinning deer and chopping wood had exhausted him before the day had begun.

'We're coming,' a small voice replied, followed by a clatter of noise and groans.

After a few seconds Mia, his eldest at fifteen, appeared at the door. Shelby often put her in charge of Kai, her younger brother, while he carried out his daily routines around home.

'Two, Dad?' Kai exclaimed, shooting past his sister. 'We never have that many.' He gawked at his plate on the table in disbelief. Aged eleven and a handful, Kai needed continuous distractions if Shelby intended on doing his work.

Usually, the chickens only laid enough for one egg each in the mornings to go along with their slice of bread. Any extra collected he sold or saved, depending on the season. Shelby never struggled too much for food but rationed when possible. Today, they could spare the extra, having filled up some egg cartons already for a decent sale.

All three of them sat down at the table on the porch and watched the sun continue to rise over the sea.

'I know. Let's hope they keep it up.' Shelby smiled at Kai before taking a mouthful of oatmeal. 'Reckon you can keep an eye on them for me today?'

'Me?' Kai jumped from his seat. 'I can look after them, yes I can.'

'You're off to town?' Mia asked.

'The weather's clear and calm, so I was thinking about heading in, yes.' Shelby rubbed his stubble, knowing her knack for seeing through his words. 'I'm pretty sure Lornsten will have new stock, considering how lucky we've been with the weather. Some feed wouldn't be a bad idea either now summer's coming to an end.' He attempted to shift the conversation elsewhere. 'The last thing we'd want is Maisy suffering. We won't do well without her milk in the winter.'

'You'll need Frank's cart then, right?' Mia stood up from the table, quickly finishing her breakfast. 'I'll go see if they're about.' She stepped off the porch with a mouthful of food.

The lack of arguing made Shelby suspicious as he watched her disappear behind the house to run further up the hill. Mia often attempted to convince him that she was capable of heading into town herself, with a cart or bicycle. He refused to give in; the idea of her going alone always put him on edge. Even when he travelled in with Frank or Lorel, they each armed themselves with a rifle.

Kai wiped the crust of his bread around the plate, soaking up any remaining yolk.

'Full?' Shelby asked.

'Yep.' Kai nodded, before jumping up from his chair.

Shelby put his hand on his son's shoulder, halting him for a second.

'Good. Now don't go winding up your sister while I'm gone, alright? She's got her own things to be getting on with.' He ruffled Kai's hair before taking another mouthful of oatmeal.

'She's a liar, I never do that!' Kai yelled.

'Oh, really?' Shelby stared at him. 'Lying is bad, Kai. Especially lying to your family, you know that.'

Kai let out a small laugh before turning as stern as an eleven-year-old could. 'I know, Dad. Mia lies too.' He scrunched his face.

'I'm sure she does. Mia should know better than that. It doesn't make it right for you to do it back, though, does it?' Kai began to tear up; something not easily settled. 'Would you like to come with me to Lornsten?'

Shelby wasn't keen on leaving either of his children when he made the trip into town, considering theirs was only one of two houses that sat alone here, with little protection. Neither Lornsten nor home was completely safe, but knowing his neighbours also kept an eye on the children was a comfort. Mia would be okay at home with Frank or Lorel nearby, and Shelby hoped the offer would distract Kai from his approaching tantrum.

Kai looked down at his hands before eventually answering. 'What about the chickens? I was going to look after them today, I was.' His voice wobbled.

'They'll be alright, they've got each other to keep themselves company, haven't they?' Shelby assured him.

'I... I guess so.' Kai seemed puzzled. 'We don't speak chicken, do we, so how do we know if they're happy?'

'Well, they lay eggs if they are happy, and today they laid more than usual.' Shelby smiled.

'So they are very happy?' Kai's voice rose in excitement.

'Yes, very happy. They won't mind if you go into town today. Mia will be here anyway in case they need something,' he replied. 'Now, we'll be leaving soon, so you go get ready for town.'

Kai sprinted back into the house, leaving Shelby seated. He let out a sigh of relief and took another mouthful of his breakfast in silence, feeling himself tire before the day properly began.

A minute passed, then Mia ran back around the corner, in a far happier state.

'Lorel's just coming around with Frank, and she's offered to—'

'Frank? You're joking.' Shelby ran a hand through his thick waves of hair. If both neighbours headed into town, it meant he would have to stay at home and keep an eye on the animals and area. 'I've just told your brother he could...' He realised Mia might not take kindly to the plans of Kai going. It fell quiet between them for a second until Frank and Lorel pulled around the corner, seated in their horse and cart, stopping by the porch.

'Morning,' Frank announced, giving a wave. 'Making the most of the day, I see. We had the same idea.' He jumped down from the wooden cart.

'Morning,' Shelby replied. He was always surprised at how agile the old man kept.

'Lorel!' Kai screamed, bolting out of the front door and jumping up into their cart. He hugged Lorel, forcing her to let go of the reins.

Shelby grimaced over deflating Kai's mood. One of the children would have to stay home with him, and knowing how chaotic his son could be, it would have to be Kai. He'd be too much of a handful for Frank and Lorel.

'Well, you're full of it this morning, Kai,' Lorel said softly. 'Had a good breakfast, so I hear?'

'Town. Lorelsten...' Kai hesitated at the name.

'Lornsten.' Lorel laughed and raised an eyebrow at Shelby.

'Sorry, I didn't realise you'd both be going up.' Shelby stepped towards the cart. 'So I'm afraid, Kai...' His son's face dropped at the impending news. 'You'll have t—'

'NO!' Kai cried. 'You said I could go.' He held on to Lorel as if to save himself from being pulled down.

'Why don't we just take them both?' Frank suggested, calming Kai down. 'You stay here, Shelby.'

'I...' Shelby had never considered it. It was always himself and either Frank or Lorel who travelled up with one of the children. He observed Mia leaning on the porch, looking smug at the unravelling situation.

'Not sure why we've never offered before.' Frank smiled at Shelby and then towards Mia.

'I mean, are you sure?' Shelby disliked the idea. They knew most of the locals in Lornsten, but with the arrival of new stock, it always brought in strangers who sometimes stirred up trouble.

'Of course. Sure as the sun rising.' Frank gave another smile. 'Seems as though Mia's been up to her tricks.' He turned to climb onto the cart.

'Mia.' Shelby turned to face her. She lost the smirk and now stared elsewhere. 'We'll talk about this when you get back. Now get on the cart.'

The thought of her being there to keep an eye on her brother comforted him. In the busy streets, where they heckled to buy and sell, looking after a volatile child like Kai would be tricky for Frank and Lorel.

'Sure.' Mia gave a meek smile.

Shelby felt anxious looking at all of them now sitting on the cart, his eyes flicking between them.

'Are you sure this is alright?' he asked. He watched the older couple with Kai in between.

'Of course, the more eyes on this little rascal, the better.' Frank grinned at Kai who returned the look. 'We taking some eggs up then? I've bottled some milk this morning to take up.'

'Sure, along with a few logs, too,' Shelby said, now switching his mind over to loading the cart.

Mia helped load the goods and sat beside the food in the back. Shelby no longer needed to remind her of how much care their extra produce needed.

'Thanks for this.' Shelby masked his stress with a smile and watched the cart turn around and head back up the hill.

'Keep the chickens happy, Dad,' Kai shouted.

'See you tonight.' Mia gave a small smile.

'They'll be alright, Shelby.' Frank turned back and tapped his hunting rifle wedged by his side. 'And if the market isn't too busy, we'll be back before the sun goes down. Enjoy your peace and quiet.' Frank winked before facing forward again, the cart continuing calmly up the hill.

'Wait!' Shelby shouted, running towards them. He caught up and handed Mia a small pouch containing several copper pieces. 'Treat everyone to some extra when you have lunch.' He knew Mia appreciated the responsibility of being given the money, even if she might have organised the whole situation.

'Oh, there was no need for that.' Lorel shook her head.

'You're the ones doing all the work today it seems.' Shelby laughed and backed away from the cart. He stood and waved until they disappeared into the treeline, his feelings of uneasiness growing.

****

It had been a long time since Shelby was truly by himself, yet he still started with his usual routine. He headed for the chicken coop at the back of the house, in the shade and out of view from the coastline. Shelby figured it made sense to check up on them while passing before tidying up breakfast. He tried to keep his mind occupied, thinking of their chickens. Shelby had promised to never leave his children, but it was proving more difficult with each passing year.

The chickens clucked away, content with their pen. Shelby smiled, seeing a fresh brown egg laying under one bird, reminding him of his conversation with Kai.

Between the clucking, Shelby heard a faint hum. He left the pen and listened again. This time he could hear the sound of wood against stones accompanying the hum. Driftwood and rubbish washed ashore occasionally, but it made far less sound.

The noise carried again on the wind, wood weighing heavy and scraping against the stones on the beach. Shelby walked around to the front of the house to get a view of the coastline. He immediately stepped back to the side as his heart lurched into his throat.

In the distance, a ship like he had never seen sat in the ocean. It lacked any form of a sail. Instead, a trail of smoke rose above it, accompanied by the faint low hum. Few ships passed his shore and seeing one was never a welcome sign.

Another loud scrape and scratch of rocks sounded on the shoreline. Shelby edged around to the front of his house again to get a better view of what was making the noise. Ahead, he saw a small wooden rowing boat with several figures dragging it up the beach, away from the tide. Shelby darted back out of view again, his heart thumping hard. If he attempted to run inside his house, they would see him. Whether he got to his rifle or not, being trapped inside and outnumbered felt too risky. There was no doubt in his mind they had landed on his beach to steal and kill. He rushed back around to the chicken pen and grabbed his axe.

Moving back up the side of his house, he crouched, keeping silent. Frank and Lorel kept two rifles at their house but there was no way of getting up the hill without being seen from the coast. Shelby remained still, listening to the unwelcome visitors' footsteps.

'Come on. We can't be here long. One run to the ship and that'll be it. Enough wood and extra food to get us through the next few days,' a man's voice ordered.

'Wood? I didn't come here for wood. Food is what we agreed. Proper food,' the second voice grumbled.

'Speaking that loud, you won't catch a thing.' The other man laughed.

'Hermann,' a woman's voice cut in after they'd stopped dragging their wooden boat. 'Great job at being the lookout, you idiot.' The woman pointed towards Lorel and Frank's house positioned higher on the hill.

'I, uh, I saw it, yes, but it seems abandoned. No one's out here.' Hermann seemed unscathed by the insult.

'And if there is?' the woman replied.

'Well, then it's bad luck on them, I guess. We've orders and can't be taking risks.' He shrugged.

Six figures came into view, walking up from the beach with their hands resting upon weapons. The guy they called Hermann used a black, silver-topped cane as he walked. Shelby screwed his face up, having never seen someone so large. The others were normal size and all rough-faced and dirty, besides Hermann who wore an old grey suit with his rifle slung across his back.

The thought of Mia and Kai returning home struck a vein of fear in him. Frank and Lorel might have forgotten something. Thinking they might return and walk into a group of pirates made his mind spark from anger to panic. He eyed up the track that led to Frank and Lorel's place and then further up into the woods towards Lornsten.

He knew the group would see him if he headed up the hill, but distancing himself from them was also crucial if he planned on surviving. Shelby stood up and peeked around the corner. The pirates stopped and waited for three more of their crew to catch up.

'Look, another fucking house,' a gravelled voice sounded. 'You led us into a village or somethin'?' The bearded man who spoke stared at Hermann's rounded face.

'I know the way, and I know the maps. Just a couple of old houses is all. If there's people living here, they'd have been out by now, or perhaps even run away. But I know for a fact it's all empty, so stop your bloody whimpering.' His face filled with a satisfied smile.

The bearded man eyed him in silence before turning towards Shelby's house.

'Chickens,' the man growled. 'You 'ear that?' He glanced around at the other five members who listened to the noise. 'That means people.' He stared back at Hermann, whose smug face dried up. They all drew their weapons and stalked towards the house. Two of them held guns, with the rest wielding blades that varied from swords to knives.

Shelby started moving away from his home and up the hill, hearing the tread of footsteps follow behind. His axe remained firmly grasped in one hand. He suddenly remembered his cow, Maisy, penned up and sheltered, but within viewing distance at the top of the hill. Hunting had given him a decent aim over the years, and the rifle from a good position might be enough to scare them off before they realised he was alone. The longer he waited, the closer they got to finding all their stock.

'Look, there,' a voice sounded. 'Breakfast for four, maybe?' Shelby heard the wooden planks of the porch creak as they stepped up onto it.

He took bigger strides towards Frank and Lorel's house, hoping the angle of his path would keep him out of view now that the pirates were on the porch.

'Excuse me!' a voice behind him shouted.

Ignoring the call, Shelby carried on walking, not wanting to cause any alarm for the group.

A sudden loud shot fired past his feet ahead of him, creating a cloud of dirt. Shelby froze, not expecting such a quick reaction.

'Do we have your attention now?' called out the voice.

Shelby slowly turned, seeing the well-rounded man to the right side of his house, holding a rifle.

'Yes, you do, Hermann,' Shelby replied, nervous but ready to stand his ground.

The obese man looked baffled at the reply. Two of the other pirates appeared beside the large man.

'Nice miss, Hermann.' The bearded man laughed. 'Looks like he knows you too. Unlikely he's mistaken you for anyone else.' The man grinned.

'It was not a miss, Jason,' Hermann quipped, keeping his eyes focused on Shelby. 'Do you know me?'

Unsure on what answer might make him more likely to get shot, Shelby hesitated.

'Perhaps.' He smiled. 'What can I do for you?'

Three other members now moved towards him up the left side of his house.

'Any more of you? I see you have breakfast for four here,' the woman asked with a smile.

'There are quite a few of us around, why do you ask?' Shelby kept up his smile, still edging up towards Frank's house. His comment made some of the group glance at each other uneasily, but Jason, the rough bearded man, began to walk at a faster pace than the rest.

'More, you say?' Jason's voice grated the air. 'Well, if they don't come out, I'm afraid they'll be one less alive.'

At that moment, Shelby turned and fled up to Frank's house. The man began catching up, brandishing a large machete in one hand. With a glance, Shelby realised the others seemed unbothered by his sudden movements.

'Jason,' a few of them called, but the man appeared to ignore their calls.

Running into Frank's house, Shelby bolted the door behind him and heard Jason's footsteps slow down outside, eventually coming to a halt. It became silent. Shelby rushed into the bedroom and opened the gun cabinet. Empty space stared back at him. He dropped his head, remembering Frank tap the rifle on his cart when leaving for Lornsten. Lorel must have taken hers, too.

A loud bang struck the door.

'You gonna make this hard for me? Got me thinkin' I should waste a bullet on you,' the man rumbled.

The wooden door cracked and splintered with each hit the man gave it. Shelby searched around Frank's for a way out, his axe still in hand. As he crossed past the front door to move into the kitchen, the door broke inwards with the man tumbling across in front of him. For a split-second they looked at each other. Shelby kicked Jason to the ground as he swung his blade. The man attempted to get to his feet while taking another swing. He lunged at Shelby, pushing him into the kitchen table and knocking over a bucket of milk that made them slip.

With a hard smack, Shelby fell back on the floor, still holding his axe, and the man landed on top of him. Shelby failed to push him off. Eventually, he managed to slide to one side and shove him away.

Shelby jumped up, but Jason remained still and quiet. Blood was pooling on the floor and Shelby no longer held his axe in hand. It became obvious why it had fallen silent: the axe was wedged in Jason's skull.

'You done yet? No one else seems to be here. Gotta load of chickens, though.' The woman's voice grew louder.

Shock and fear set in. Shelby tried pulling his axe out from the man's head but gave up when he heard more footsteps approach. He looked back at the body and then out of the kitchen window. Someone was coming up to the front of the house with a rifle in hand, and now that the front door was smashed in, little would stop them from entering.

He crouched over the body and found a small handgun holstered on the man, knowing it increased his chances of survival more than any blade. Shelby aimed it at the remains of the front door.

The footsteps stopped, causing silence to fall again. Shelby turned to his left and noticed a man peering in at him from a window. In an instant, Shelby turned and fired, missing the window and piercing the wooden wall beside it, making the man run. Shelby moved into the centre of the hallway, listening, glancing at the window and door one after the other, hearing voices. Seeing movement at both the window and the door, Shelby lost his nerve at where to shoot. He stepped forward as a sudden blow of pain erupted at the back of his head, darkness filling his vision.

CHAPTER 3 - ZARA

Zara made her way along the inner ridge of the ravine. With the vent she'd dropped from being out of reach, she headed inland. A ladder beside the dam gave her a glimmer of hope, but the metal broke into pieces when she pulled at it. Instead, her focus turned to finding a way up the steep rock.

To the right, the ridge dropped into darkness. The ledge she walked along clung on to the rock face that towered forty metres above, with the safety of home waiting at the top. On the opposite side of the ravine, over the void, she saw another rocky ledge, and above that, a dangerous place awaited. She'd been taught that the ravine stopped a toxic and uninhabitable environment from spreading across to the rest of the continent.

Pains plagued her body, making her pace slow but constant. Zara tried to distract herself, thinking of Delia, the one who'd issued the job at the dam, and whether she knew what had happened. She half presumed Delia's involvement in the situation, though doubted she would ever see her again. It seemed unlikely Zara would return to Russet now she was moving inland in the opposite direction. Even if she managed to climb out of the ravine soon, with Trent dead, heading home felt best.

After walking for over an hour, Zara stopped. She lowered herself onto the ground, careful not to cause herself any more pain, and dropped Trent's bag in front of her. Zara stared at it, remembering her own bag left hanging on the vent. She closed her eyes and let out a sigh before picking up the bag and emptying the contents onto the ground. There was an oil-stained rag, screwdrivers, a claw hammer, cable cutters, some dam blueprints, a plastic lighter, a bottle of water and a bag of croutons. She pulled the electric torch out from her jacket pocket and placed it with the rest of the items. One glance over it all made Zara realise none of it belonged to her. She looked up to the sky and shut her eyes, still trying to grasp the situation. It all seemed like a dream and that soon she would wake up at home with Heather beside her.

Taking in a deep breath, Zara looked back down at Trent's things and picked up the bottle of water. She sipped it and considered washing the dried blood from her hands before deciding against it, unsure how long she might need the water to last. Zara picked up the croutons and stuffed them into her jacket pocket. Next, she picked up the old rag and tied it around the lower half of her face, covering her nose and mouth, though it did little to mask the smell of rotten egg that was growing more pungent. Zara then packed the items back into the bag and stood up, her body throbbing at the movement.

She stepped towards the edge of the ridge and peered down into the abyss, seeing no bottom to it. With both hands, she picked up a nearby rock and dropped it over the edge, but heard no sound. She continued walking.

Eventually, both sides of the ravine closed on each other and the ridge became so narrow Zara was forced to start placing one foot in front of the other. Sunlight struggled to make its way down into the tightening gap. She stepped carefully over the few loose rocks balanced on the ridge, aware of the drop to the right. The gap spanned only a few feet across, though it remained wide enough to fall down.

The ravine continued to narrow, so much so that Zara could touch the rock on both sides. The ridge beneath her had turned into a sheer drop, with barely an edge for Zara to rest a foot on. With her arms held out, she shuffled and pushed herself up and along, one foot planted on each rock face. Pain erupted down her legs as she tried to keep herself up. Zara pressed hard with her arms to lessen the weight, but it did little to stop the agony.

As she squinted upwards at the daylight, she saw the top of the ravine only a few metres above. Dragging herself up, she felt the space become narrower until she was almost completely wedged between both sides of the rock face. She pressed on, her right hand gradually getting closer to the top of the ravine. Zara shuffled and pulled herself higher, scraping her hands, clothing and bag against the rocks.

She gazed up at the left side, where the rock loomed twenty metres higher than the right. Once again, Zara found no choice in which direction to follow. She cared less and less about climbing into the uninhabitable side, now desperate for fresh air and a place to rest. She doubted trespassing into the area would make her troubles any worse.

Her hands were torn and bloody from the sharp rocks, the pain becoming a numbness. Tired of the constant tension, her grip lessened. She stopped short of the ridge and stretched out her arm, hoping to grasp the top, but it remained a hand's length out of reach. Fatigue overcame her, her body refusing to put more effort into the climb. Staring at the ground less than a metre or so above her, she remembered the claw hammer in Trent's bag and pulled it out.

With one hard swing, Zara hooked the clawed end over the ridge, allowing herself to pull upwards, pushing both feet hard against the rock. A minute or so passed before she reached the top and dragged herself over the edge and away from the ravine. She stopped and let out a small scream as the pain and exhaustion took hold.

The sun glistened on the rocky slope that rose away from the ravine. Behind Zara stood the opposing rock face, standing over twenty metres high. She attempted to pick herself up, almost falling backwards, and dropped to the ground before she lost her balance entirely. Pain renewed itself at the movement, but after a few deep breaths, Zara started to pull herself up the slope on her hands and knees, against the slippery ground.

After several metres, the slope began to level out. Zara kept her eyes ahead and ignored the thought of someone watching her from the other side of the ravine.

Mist descended and visibility around her lessened. Shards of rock splintered from the ground, eager to injure if given a chance. Zara turned to check the opposing ridge face, but it was no longer visible through the thickening fog. She sat down and removed the rag from her face, smelling the fresher air. Zara took a deep breath and got out her bottle of water and croutons. She took a sip and munched a handful, trying to weigh up her choices. To climb the opposing rock face felt the most obvious thing to do, though it required her to move back down the slope, jump the narrow ravine, and somehow climb the hard damp rock, which in her current state was too much to attempt.

Savouring the salty croutons, Zara looked around in the mist and realised some of the shards were the remains of tree trunks. She made her way over to one, hoping to find bits for a fire, but instead discovered it was wet and rotten. *Probably just as well.* The warmth of a fire might have been comforting but the smoke could easily have attracted unwanted attention. Giving up on the idea, Zara continued to follow the slope up and keep alongside the ravine.

****

Old branches and burnt trees crunched under Zara's boots. The mist dispersed, allowing her to see the dried, sparse forest around her. The ground beneath rose in line with the opposing ridge and only the gap of the ravine separated the two sides, increasing in width, impossible to cross.

On the opposite side was a forest, full of leaves and greenery, that tempted her to jump – until the thought that someone was watching her crept back into her mind. There was nowhere on her side of the ravine to hide, so she forced her body into a run.

She crouched behind the stump of a tree to catch her breath and looked back towards the forest on the other side. Zara kept her distance. If she attracted any of the Legion, they would be impossible to outrun. She figured as long as she followed the ravine, it might eventually end – but she'd have to do so from a distance.

Zara moved off to find more cover, temporarily leaving the ravine behind, but kept focus on the direction she was walking in. She spent the next hour passing through an old decaying woodland with a few ruinous buildings dotted throughout.

The sun started to set and the temperature cooled while Zara trudged on. Her feet felt heavy and her body was exhausted.

The ground abruptly stepped up, tripping her over. She lay motionless, a new wave of pain engulfing her. Gathering herself up, she stifled her moans and struggled back to her feet. She stared at the kerbstone and cursed it before a smooth yellow line grabbed her attention. She followed the lines along until they revealed themselves to be part of an old road. The end that led towards the ravine crumbled and disappeared into the ground, but in the opposite direction, it pushed on through a group of old buildings in the distance. Zara gazed at the shapes. The appeal of shelter, warmth and a softer place to rest pulled at her. If what she knew of this place rang true, no one lived in the area.

Listening for any sort of noise, Zara started her approach. No wind, or any rustle of leaves disturbed the silence. The humid air began to cool against her throat now the temperature was dropping.

The first building she approached had a blackened front to it. The door rested on the floor, between two windowless frames. Zara struggled to see inside now the sun had set. She decided to look elsewhere, wanting more protection from the environment.

The building on the other side of the road stood taller than the first, with three floors instead of one. It appeared to have most of its windows. The door stood open and the interior looked surprisingly clean, considering the state of the place opposite.

Inside, Zara found a set of stairs and a doorway. Through it, she made out a small lounge and kitchen that reminded her of the places back in the city. She closed the front door and moved upstairs, deciding that if she was to sleep anywhere, it would be further from the entrance. She climbed the stairs and took a deep breath with each step, pain still striking through her.

Night had settled in, making it difficult for Zara to see as she reached the first floor, but she denied herself the use of a torch until she felt safe. To the right, a door remained closed and intact. Zara fumbled around for the handle and opened it. She took another breath and stepped inside, relieved to find the windows unbroken. The place looked secure, was off of the ground, and felt warm compared to the cooling air outside. Zara gently closed the door, catching the shine of a lock that she used to secure and bolt it shut. She walked further in and kicked something metal on the floor, making herself jump. A few empty tins rolled along until they stopped at a stack of books. On the kitchen counter were more books and empty tins that made her wonder how old they might have been.

Zara moved towards a window but saw nothing but darkness. Through one doorway, she found a bedroom with a bare mattress on the bed and a thin blanket thrown across the top. In place of a pillow, there lay a small square cushion, but nothing proper like she used at home. Still, it felt soft enough to sleep on. Zara put Trent's bag down beside the bed and lay on top of the blanket, attempting to wrap herself up in her jacket. Exhaustion took over, making her eyes close for a moment. Over an entire day had passed since she had last slept.

CHAPTER 4 – SHELBY

Adjusting his focus, Shelby recognised the night sky through a small circular window. He sat in darkness with light coming from a little gap in the door ahead of him. Shelby moved, causing a sharp pain to spread across the back of his head. He jolted at the discomfort and attempted to bring his hands up and calm the ache but found them cuffed to something beside him. The smell of milk became apparent, accompanying the stickiness of his shirt and jeans against his skin. He struggled to remember what had happened, finding nothing around him familiar. A low deep hum vibrated the floor he sat on, the image of a metal ship flickering into his thoughts. Shelby saw waves out of the window below the sky.

It felt as if the floor dropped. He must be on the ship, away from his children. He stared at the handcuffs, attempting to pull them off over his wrists and making a loud rattle against the metal they were attached to.

The door creaked and swung open, and a large bald man stepped inside. Shelby stopped moving. The huge silhouette came to a halt. The man's heavy breathing cut into the silence. The light flashed on, making Shelby squint at the sudden brightness. Hermann, the large man from the beach, stood resting on his cane and glaring at him. His round face sank into his shoulders and dripped with sweat.

'I'll ask the question again,' he said flatly. 'Do you know me?'

Shelby stared at him and then around the room; pipes covered the walls. He focused back on Hermann, whose stare bored into his skull.

The man's voice grew rigid. 'Answer me.'

He brandished his cane, playing with its handle a little before taking a step towards Shelby. Patterns of gold wrapped around the balled silver top, with a thin line of silver moving down the black shaft.

'No, I don't,' Shelby replied, unsure of what answer the man wanted.

'Then how do you know me by name?' Hermann leant towards him using his cane, the smell of sweat becoming apparent. 'I certainly do not recognise you.'

'Hermann…' Shelby looked down, trying to focus on the events. Feeling the sway of the ship, he went to stand, before the pipe his cuffs were chained to pulled him back down onto the floor.

'You aren't going anywhere.' Hermann smirked.

'Where am I?' Shelby asked, concentrating his attention back on home and his children. 'I need t—'

Hermann step onto his leg. Pain shot over him.

'I will ask you one last time,' the man said through gritted teeth. 'How do you know me?'

'I don't. I don't know you. I ov—'

Hermann stamped down onto his ankle, forcing Shelby to scream in agony.

'I swear I've never seen you... I overheard your name on the beach when you were talking. I swear. I don't know you. I swear it.'

The man stepped back, releasing his weight from the ankle. Shelby let out several groans, unable to rub the discomfort on his leg.

'Well, if that's true, you're a fool for pretending.' The man's sweaty face twisted. 'Such a lie can get you killed.'

Shelby moved up against the wall to create a small distance between himself and Hermann; his ankle throbbed with pain. The man reached behind himself to grab something, revealing the overhang of his belly beneath his untucked shirt and suit jacket.

'Now we have that out of the way,' Hermann resumed, in a breathy but casual tone, 'let us move on to more pressing issues.' He unsheathed a blade and held it up. 'This belonged to a friend of mine before you killed him.'

Hermann chucked the machete on the floor in front of Shelby. He recognised it immediately. It had belonged to Jason, the bearded man who had tried to kill him.

'An accident.' Shelby shook his head.

'Serving the wrong drink is an accident. Someone knocking into me can be an accident. But driving an axe through someone's skull? That is no accident, I assure you.' Hermann's eyes narrowed, his voice sharpening. 'Don't take me for a moron.'

'He would have killed me. I hardly had a choice.' Shelby stared back at Hermann, holding his gaze.

'Well, I'm sure you can guess that I would have much preferred it if you had died.' Hermann sighed. 'Jason was an arsehole, yes, but also a good hunter.' He patted his large belly. 'So, you were living with others?'

Shelby held his stare, unsure if the man knew of his children and neighbours.

'Don't worry,' Hermann said. 'We could only find you. Though on our way back, perhaps we might stop off again.' He grinned, looking up at the ceiling. 'We did leave a rather fat cow behind, come to think of it. Would feed the crew for a good few days on our way back, don't you think?'

'Why haven't you killed me?' Shelby snapped, the talk of home boiling his blood.

'Oh, that's obvious, isn't it? You killed a man of mine. So, that would mean…' Hermann waved his hand in front of him, but Shelby refused to answer. Hermann dropped his head and lost his smile. 'It would mean I am one crew member down. Naturally, I was in need of a replacement, and by sheer luck we found you.' He smiled. 'You aren't as good a tracker I'm betting, but it seems like you've got a better knack for killing than Jason did, considering he died at your hands. You should be honoured with this arrangement.'

'What makes you think I'll replace him for you?' Shelby asked, tight-lipped.

'Don't think you are in a position to bargain. If you don't play by my rules, then perhaps you won't be of any use to me.' Hermann lowered his brow and looked at the blade on the floor between them. 'Remember where you are. Far, far from home and surrounded by a crew who would love to cut your throat if given half the chance.'

Silence filled the room before Hermann lifted his head and lightened his tone.

'Luckily for you, though, I'm here. A protector of sorts, I suppose. If you do play by my rules, we'll be dropping you back off at home once we've carried out our little mission. Fair enough, I'd say.'

Hermann bent over, barely managing to pick up the blade in front of him. Shelby watched the man inspect the edge before sheathing it.

'You know, where I'm from murderers are usually sentenced to death, so consider yourself lucky. Especially since you're living in Jason's quarters.' Hermann moved towards the door, the cane tapping between his steps. 'Got a name?'

Dwelling on the information, Shelby fought the idea of staying on the ship for any more time than was needed.

Hermann gritted his teeth. 'I said, name?'

'Shelby,' he replied, focusing back on Hermann.

'Good.' The man's tone lightened again. 'Well, you know mine. I'll have dinner brought up to you along with a change of clothes. You look and smell revolting, but I'm sure having one of your delicious chickens should cheer you up.' A smile appeared on his face before the door slammed behind him.

Shelby shook his head, refusing to believe the words. He shouted, 'Hermann!'

Muffled noises broke the silence through the door and after a few seconds, it reopened.

'What?' Hermann peered inside.

'How long have I been here?' asked Shelby, unsure on the day.

'Around ten hours. You stayed unconscious for quite some time. Started to think you were going to die on us,' Hermann said cheerily, and closed the door without waiting for Shelby to reply.

Shelby felt lost; his mind fixed on home and what his children might be doing or thinking. He remembered Frank and Lorel's broken door, the house perhaps still with the body of Jason on the floor. He hated the thought of them returning to such a grim scene, with the chickens stolen and himself gone. Realising Hermann and his crew were not there long enough to know of their existence gave him slight relief.

He wanted to make his family aware that he was still alive. Shelby moved towards the small circular window to get a better view of outside, but besides the ocean, he could make out little else in the darkness.

Shelby sighed and leant back against the wall, careful not to hit his head.

I'm sorry. I'll get back soon. He took a deep breath, attempting to loosen the tightness in his throat.

CHAPTER 5 – LUTHER

The alarm on Luther's bedside cabinet woke him instantly. He hit the top of it, gaining back the silence, and rolled over towards the woman sleeping beside him to give her a kiss. She turned before he had the chance, taking the duvet with her. Biting his lip, he glared at the figure concealed beneath his covers and felt his temper rise. Luther knew she was new to the job, but loathed disrespect. He deliberated, deciding that a better course of action might be talking to the girl's superior first. If he hurt the newest girl, it would only serve to annoy her boss.

With a sigh, he stood up out of bed and picked up his silk emerald dressing gown. Luther put it on, covering his slim, pale frame. He stretched, strolling over to one of the windows, the vague outline of the city coming into view as he pulled back the curtains. Dawn approached, and already the workers were flooding into the streets below. Luther looked up towards the horizon where two large mountains loomed, catching the first glimpses of sunlight.

He walked to the opposite side of the room and flicked on the electric kettle. Leaning against his desk, he looked around the grand old room with its high ceiling, large glass windows and four-poster bed. The posts were polished wood, carved into spirals, the pillows were filled with feathers and the sheets were cotton. He owed it all to his position in the city.

Luther picked up his black notebook; the worn subtle shape of a cog caught the sun on its front. He started to read through some of his notes made the previous evening. *Oil.* If he found the necessary things, it would all be his.

A knock sounded at his door as the kettle flicked off.

'Come in,' he answered casually, still reading his notes.

The door opened. He returned the stare given to him by Ruben, his assistant, who stood in the doorway.

'Eager, aren't you?' Luther observed the lack of effort in the man's untidy white hair and judged he must have just woken.

'Sorry to bother you so early, but there has been some rather troubling news,' Ruben said.

'Project Carbon?' Luther replied, peering down at his notebook.

'No, sir. It's to do with Russet Dam.'

Confused at hearing the place name, Luther glanced up again to meet Ruben's eyes and gestured for him to carry on.

'Well, Trittle. The Eastern Legion, more specifically. They've killed someone trespassing at the dam,' Ruben said clearly.

'Killed?' Luther paused. 'And what has this got to do with us?' He started losing interest in the story, not seeing the relevance of it to Carbon City.

'There was a person messing around with the systems inside the dam. They seem to think we might have something to do with it, considering that the guy they killed was apparently wearing engineering overalls from our engineering guild.'

'Wearing uniforms from our city doesn't make him one of ours,' Luther replied, looking back down at his notebook. 'Who else knows of this?'

'Everyone else on the committee. Jetson seemed panicked about it and sent word to everyone,' Ruben responded.

'Jetson.' Luther rolled his eyes. The man lacked any art of subtlety. 'Just what we needed. No doubt Carol will have a snarky remark to make.' Luther took a deep breath. 'Call a meeting with the others for an hour's time. Better to sort it out now, don't you suppose?'

'Yes, sir, a meeting is being organised as we speak.' Ruben backed out, quick to close the door.

Luther soured at the words. *Of course Jetson's already called a meeting.* He began to feel the issue might be more of his concern, especially if everyone knew about it. Appearing unaware or incapable of handling a security situation might cast doubt among the committee. Even though Russet Dam stood halfway across the country, those who patrolled it still posed a threat.

'Tea?' A female voice spoke from the under the covers, breaking Luther out of his trance.

'Making it,' he replied, glancing at the figure through the mirror above his desk. He poured the water into a teapot.

'The sun's hardly up,' the woman groaned. 'You always awake this early?'

'Yes. It takes a lot to protect this city. You should appreciate me far more than you appear to.' Luther smiled.

'What's that on your back?' she asked.

With one shrug, Luther covered his neck properly with the gown and continued pouring the tea into two black and gold ceramic teacups.

The woman stretched in the silence, revealing the side of her body from under the duvet before wrapping herself back up. She poked her head out from the top of the covers. 'You know, perhaps you should be the one appreciating me. Can't the man in charge do what he wants? Another hour in bed?' she teased.

Anger struck him upon hearing the remark; the thought of scolding her now brewed in his mind. Luther stared at the drink in front of him. *Too bold.* He sharply inhaled and closed his eyes, reminding himself once again that she was new to the job and to talk to her superior first. He picked up the tea and walked back over to the bed, questioning whether anyone had briefed her on who she was dealing with.

'Well, I could stay in bed.' Luther smiled, observing the tea in his hands. He looked up at the young lady through the steam; she now sat upright in his bed. Luther passed a cup to her. 'Sadly, I'm not alone at the top. You ever met that bitch Carol?' His mouth twisted. 'She is in charge of the mining section. Then you have Jetson, who deals with foreign relations and sometimes trading. He's better than Carol but lacks being discreet in almost every way. Not a trait you want for foreign relations, really. They've always got something to complain about.' Luther stared out of the window.

'Well, can't say I've met any of them yet, and not sure I'd want to now,' the girl replied playfully, sipping the tea.

'Just as well. Most of them seem to make something out of nothing. All petty stuff, really. Still, the twelve of us have our roles to fulfil.' Luther set down his tea and moved to his large wooden wardrobe.

He chose his usual attire of a beige suit jacket and trousers, alongside a white shirt; a look few people could afford, making him love it all the more. His shoes were worn but shiny, matching his brown hair that he brushed into a side parting.

Standing in front of the mirror, Luther sipped the rest of his tea while sorting out his gun holster, staring at the girl's reflection in his bed.

'I won't be back until the evening. I expect you'll be gone?' Luther asked, pulling out the drawer from under his desk to reveal a black handgun. The sunlight caught the gold metal that decorated the top part of it. He holstered it and put his jacket on, concealing the weapon under his left arm. He moved towards the door and opened it.

'Yep. Work calls and I don't tend to cling to new clients that easily.' She sipped her tea again.

Twitching, Luther closed the door hard behind himself, not bothering to reply. She had lost her final chance.

****

Luther lived in the capitol building, Carbon Assembly, where every committee member lived. Eager to get some breakfast before the meeting started, he paced directly to the meeting room.

The hallway was covered with ornate decorations that ran up the walls and onto the high ceilings. Luther knew the building was a relic from the old world and of gothic design, according to their city's antiquity expert.

Passing the large staircase that led to the main entrance, he felt reassured by the quietness, seeing only his guards stationed throughout. He heard murmuring upon reaching the meeting room doors and opened them.

'Morning.' A mixture of voices hit him upon entering the room. He closed his eyes for a moment to avoid rolling them.

'Morning,' Luther replied. 'Any chance of grabbing something to eat?' he queried, looking around for someone to react.

'On its way,' Ruben replied, glancing in through the door behind him. Luther nodded, relieved at the knowledge, and found his usual spot at the round table.

After Ruben left, a tall man with shallow blue eyes and bleached blond hair walked in. *Jetson.*

'Let's begin already,' Jetson announced, making his way to his seat. Luther thought it was unlike him to speed things along, but he was thankful for it now he had dealt with the issue of his hunger.

'I gather everyone here has heard, but just to recap, we received a message this morning via the central station that one of our engineers was apparently killed for trespassing at Russet Dam. The body was requested, but apparently the Legion patrol near Russet have already disposed of it. So far, we have whittled it down to the possibility of seven people. Three of them are from Eastern District, one being a train engineer and the other two being general maintenance. Two more are from Southern District, another general maintenance and an electrical specialist. The last two, one from Central, the other from the mining town of Drove, are also general maintenance. Over the next day or so we should hopefully account for these people and conclude that this so-called engineer who was killed was in fact of no relation to us. For now, Trittle, or should I say the Eastern Legion, is assuming our involvement, so if we could all look to our own districts and ensure everyone is accounted for.' Jetson paused. 'Questions?'

Keeping quiet, Luther began to think over the situation. Ruben had worded it far better.

'What's the reason for killing and not questioning this person allegedly dressed in one of our workers' uniforms?' Carol asked bluntly. 'You can't get much from a dead body.'

'According to them, the person, a man to be more precise, managed to get part of the dam running. This alerted a patrol of theirs and once they'd cornered him, he attacked them, thus forcing them to act, which ultimately led to his death. Also, for those who may not know, Trittle and us here at Carbon City still have an arrangement in place that keeps the dam off-limits,' Jetson said firmly.

'Did they really have to kill him?' one of the committee members blurted out. 'This person they killed would have been far better alive, like Carol says. Not executed. Couldn't they—'

'I understand the frustration. If the person was a local of Russet or this city, it won't be long before someone asks for their whereabouts, which should give us the answers that both we and those at Trittle are looking for,' Jetson replied.

Luther knew of the unsavoury arrangement between his city and Trittle over Russet Dam, which had been agreed upon a few years before he climbed to his position... Not wanting Russet to grow in power, Carbon City had formed an alliance with the Eastern Legion of Trittle to enforce the closure of the dam – the Eastern Legion having their own reasons for wanting to control the infrastructure on the fringes of the Forbidden Zone.

'And what if this dead person is from our city?' Luther asked, finding more interest in the body than any old agreement.

'Then… well, they were acting alone, and the patrol had every right to kill them. We don't want to go sticking up for some rogue now or we'll cause unwanted tensions, which with the railway now in place and fully functioning, is not what we need,' Jetson replied, a slight tremble catching his voice.

'So, what's the big deal then? If we're saying it has nothing to do with us either way, why the concern?' Carol snarked. 'Hauled us out of bed for no reason, it seems.'

'Because, Carol,' Jetson dragged his words, 'it will still unsettle the waters between them and us. I would rather the Eastern Legion didn't keep a closer eye on us.' Jetson shot a glance at Luther. 'So, I'd like our relations with them to carry on smoothly.'

'But we are essentially the capital, might I remind you. We can do as we please,' Carol sneered. 'No reason to be afraid of some jumped-up mercenaries.'

'Those jumped-up mercenaries are our biggest ally and threat, so watch your words,' Jetson replied. 'And yes, we like to claim our city to be the capital, but most others are yet to be convinced. It's even more of a reason to wipe our hands of this little mess.' He stood up.

'Surely someone could have just stolen engineering uniforms?' Carol raised an eyebrow, looking towards Luther. 'Not like those grimy lot in Russet are particularly fond of us, all things considered… Perhaps they were deliberately trying to stir things up between us and the Eastern Legion?'

'That's a lot of effort for little reason, don't you think?' Jetson replied. Silence remained between them before he continued. '…But it could be what happened. Luther, check over your security footage to see if any, and how many, uniforms may have been stolen. As far as we know, Russet knows their place and wouldn't dare cross us or those in Trittle, but if we find they've been stirring the pot, perhaps they need reminding who is in charge here… Anyway, those who have people yet to be accounted for, get it done.' Jetson gestured for people to leave.

Ruben entered, carrying a tray of poached eggs and toast. Luther forgot about the issue of the day and watched his food arrive as everyone but Carol left.

'Stolen goods? Imagine that. A security breach right under your nose. You'd be in for it then, wouldn't you?' Carol stood alone in the room with him. Luther blanked her, fixing his eyes on the food now in front of him.

'At least I don't have any missing people to account for.' He smiled, attempting to cut through her arrogance. 'Items are often easier to find than people are, and I've heard reports on some vanishing ores… coal, copper and the sort. You wouldn't know anything about these missing goods, would you?' Luther mocked, digging into his breakfast and recalling the guards who had reported the stolen ore.

Carol's smug look changed to one of disgust and prompted her to leave without another word.

'Old hag.' He let out a small laugh to himself and took a mouthful of food. 'Ruben?'

At once, Ruben appeared from the hall and entered the meeting room.

'What do you think?' Luther spoke, focusing on his food.

'Doubtful, but still possible. Check footage at each city entrance?' Ruben replied.

'Really?' Luther shook his head. 'Swamplands, mountains and lakes aren't likely to have an issue with us, or Russet Dam. I reckon only the eastern side will. It's the most direct route, with or without the railway... and facing most of those who do take issue with us... Then we'll check at the engineering headquarters and see what footage the guild might have.'

'And Central?' Ruben asked.

'Central Station, yes. Quickest way east, towards the dam.' Luther nodded, resting his cutlery on the plate. 'If we've any thieves out that way, it's guaranteed they used it. I'll be out in five.'

Ruben bowed his head and left.

Luther pulled out his notebook and wrote down the day's plan, realising it might take all day to simply collect the footage.

'Ruben,' he called out.

Within a few seconds, the man appeared at the door again.

'Leave the horses and bring around the car.' Luther scribbled into his notebook, knowing the quicker he resolved the issue, the sooner he could focus back on his other project. 'Don't want to waste all of my day collecting footage.'

'Of course.' Ruben disappeared back out of sight.

With a snap, Luther closed his book and stood up. He knew the committee's oil reserve was running low, but being head of security meant few members questioned his use of a vehicle.

CHAPTER 6 – ZARA

A loud thump made Zara sit up with a jolt. She kept still for a moment, unsure if she'd dreamt the noise. Out of the window ahead, Zara watched the sky lighten. She sat listening to the silence, realising she must have fallen asleep for several hours.

Breathing a sigh of relief at the lack of thumping, Zara stood up and walked through into the lounge, stretching out the aches still plaguing her body. On the floor were the empty food tins that she'd knocked over during the night, and beside them stood a small gas stove in the middle of the room. Zara stared at it, grasping at what she might have walked into.

A bang sounded on the door, making her flinch. She turned back to the bed and noticed the scruffy blankets and tins of water on the bedside cabinet. Zara picked up Trent's bag and started to panic.

'Really?' Someone sighed. 'I've only just fitted that lock, so open up.' The voice sounded calm. 'Don't make me break my own door down.'

Zara opened the bag and rummaged for the hammer, stepping towards the door with it in hand. Attacking and fleeing felt like her best choice at surviving.

'Look,' the voice started, 'I'm only going to kill you if you give me reason to, and having me break my door down is, well... let's just say I've killed for less than that.'

Approaching the door, Zara unlocked it and took a step back.

'Could you be a darling and open it, too? Kinda got my hands full.' It sounded like a woman.

With one hand, Zara carefully pulled the door open. Facing her stood a short elderly woman pointing the end of a large handgun into her face.

'Can't say I expected that,' the woman said, lowering her gun slightly.

'I didn't know anyone was here. I swear.' Zara raised her hands, feeling herself shake.

'Well, no one *was* here, so you got that right, but I was just out shopping, see?' The woman gestured to three bags on the floor. 'Now, put that thing away so I can put on somethin' to eat.'

She eyed the hammer still in Zara's hand. 'Long as you ain't trying something funny with me, I won't kill you.' Her voice sounded sweet against her thick accent. 'Can't say I'm too prepared for visitors these days, though.' She shook her head, picking up a bag. 'Be a dear and help me in with the rest of the bags, would ya?' The woman walked past her and lit a lantern hanging on the wall. 'This place don't let much light in,' she mumbled.

Unsure whether the woman was still speaking to her, Zara eyed the stairs through the doorway. She looked back at the old lady, who currently faced away. Zara's gaze flickered to the stairs again and then to the bags on the floor. She moved forward, glancing once more at the woman, noting the gun resting in one hand. Deciding not to tempt her, she put her hammer away and picked up the two remaining bags. She returned into the room, prompting the woman to speak again.

'Young girl like you, what business you got around here then?' She turned and stared at Zara, at the blood-stained clothing and torn skin. 'You a killer?' She brought up her gun, pointing it at Zara. 'Not seen anyone covered in that much blood for a while. So, be honest with me and spit it out. I wanna know who I'm dealing with here.' The woman glared at her and waited for a reply. Zara had forgotten the state she was in.

'I'd answer that question quickly if I were you.' Her tone had turned cold.

'I, uh, no, I'm not,' Zara stuttered, attempting to explain herself faster than her mouth allowed. 'Not a murderer. The blood... My friend.' Something started catching in her throat as she recalled what had happened at the dam with Trent.

'Your friend here?' The woman's brow sharpened. She raised her gun and stepped away to check the other rooms.

'No, no, he... he's dead. Yesterday, or... I'm not sure, maybe the day before.' Zara looked down at her stained clothes again and at her hands.

The woman returned after checking the other rooms, her gun still raised. Zara wasn't sure whether the old woman believed her or had even listened to her words.

After a minute of silence, the woman lowered her gun a little.

'Seems like messy business.' She glanced over Zara. 'Can't say I hear much of friends around here, though. People keep out of each other's way.' She went over to her bags and started to dig through them. 'Well, that's if there was enough of us to actually run into anymore.' She pulled out two tins and sat down on the floor in front of the small gas stove.

'Mind closing the door?' she asked, now focused on opening the first tin.

Zara moved towards the door and closed it a little harder than she intended, dwelling on what the old lady had said.

'Others? On this side?' Zara asked before realising she had just bolted herself inside the room with the stranger.

'Yeah...' The woman gave Zara a suspicious look before she relaxed her face. 'You from that other side then? Makes sense, I guess, seeing as you don't look like you know what you're doing.' Her concerned tone turned into a cackle.

'I was told I'd die if I ever set foot here,' Zara said, regretting the words immediately.

'Well, you ain't dead yet, are you?' The woman smiled. 'Though that's not to say it can't be dangerous at times. You got a mask in that bag of yours?' She pointed to Trent's bag.

'I... a mask?' Zara replied, confused.

'Yeah, like a gas mask?' The woman raised an eyebrow and shook her head.

'Uh, I... no. No, I don't,' Zara answered.

'Well, no wonder your people across the line say you'd die. Can't be walking about without a mask now. Every time the wind blows in' – she pointed – 'that direction, it brings with it a yellow haze. Breathe that in and you're pretty much dead unless you got a friend to fix a mask on ya. Gives quite the thrill sometimes, though don't get too much of that anymore. Friends nor thrills.' Her smile dropped, seeing Zara's face. 'Sore subject,' she uttered. The woman moved to take the tin from the stove with a glove and switched off the gas.

'Here.' She passed the tin and a spoon to Zara. 'Now, sit and enjoy it.'

'Thank you,' Zara replied, not sure what filled the tin. She sat opposite the woman on the floor, with the door behind her.

'I found quite the stash a few months back, so food don't mean much to me for the very second. Ask me that a year ago though, and I'd have probably robbed or killed you on sight.' Her eyes widened. 'Hunger does frightful things, I got to admit.' She shook her head.

Quiet fell between them before the old lady started talking again. Zara guessed it must have been a while since she'd last spoken with someone.

'So, now you're eating my food and…' She passed a tin of water over to Zara. 'And also drinking my water, what brings you here?' She smiled, staring as she patiently waited for an answer. Zara took a mouthful of beans, realising how hungry she felt. She decided the old lady must have lived on this side if her concerns only involved finding food.

'I was at the dam, down by—'

66

'Oh, no need to explain where that is. I know it. Dangerous place. Those Legion soldiers an' all. Let me guess, ran into them and your friend got himself killed,' she said with absolute certainty.

'No, I was... well, we were trying to get part of it started up again, or to see if it was possible at least,' Zara replied.

The woman raised an eyebrow but kept quiet.

'Someone in Russet, a town, was paying us to get part of the dam running. They had us come in from the city. It was good money. Trent, he must, or I must have done something wrong because someone found us. He made me hide while he tried talking to them, but... they killed him. Killed him without saying a word.' Zara felt the strain in her throat again. 'I made it out and, well... here I am. I'm just trying to get home. It wasn't supposed to be like this at all.' She closed her eyes, stopping any tears from falling.

It fell silent again before the woman started to talk a little more slowly than she had previously.

'Sorry, what did you say your name was? I'm not sure I even asked. I'm Eve.' She smiled.

'I'm Zara.' Zara returned the smile. 'Thank you.' She nodded at the tin of beans in her hand.

'Not a problem.' The woman switched the gas back on and put on another tin. 'Well, Zara, now I understand why you are here, though this being the first place you found don't go too well for reassuring me that I picked a good spot.' Eve chuckled. 'Perhaps I'd better move again. Always hate it. Especially alone. Oh, the amount of back and forth, my word. That's if I even bother this time.' She shook her head. 'I'll sleep on it, I think. Been up most of the night. Prefer to shop that way.' She flashed a grin. 'Everything is on offer, you know, around here. Don't have to spend a penny or trade, ha,' she cackled, and checked the tin above the stove before getting up off the floor. 'Now let me find you a mask. I have a few somewhere, though each uses a different kinda filter. And filters, well, I know I don't have any spare.' She headed out of the lounge.

Zara finished off the tin of beans and listened to the rummaging before Eve eventually walked in with a mask in hand.

'Here, have this.' Eve offered the gas mask out in front of her. 'The filters on this one aren't too common sadly, but the ones already on it should serve you long enough.' She showed Zara where they went. 'Double the time if you have filters on both sides, but I tend to feel like it wastes them so you can always unclip the other one.' Eve handed her the mask. 'Besides the two on it, that's all I got. They ain't new either but probably got a few hours left I'd reckon.' She smiled. 'Haze don't make it this far usually anyway, and if it does, it won't stick around long. Just don't lose it and you'll be alright.'

Zara took the mask, finding her gaze fixed to the face staring back at her. The greyed plastic looked old and worn, with two circular filters clipped to each cheek and a vent in the middle. The eye holes were almost triangular and scratched, reminding Zara of the patrols back near the dam.

'Same reason the Eastern Legion wear them, too?' Zara asked, placing the mask face down, attempting to avoid thinking about Trent or the Legion.

'I assume so.' Eve shrugged, sitting down opposite her.

'Have you always lived like this, in the Forbidden Zone?' asked Zara, curious at the answer.

In the light of dawn, Zara saw Eve clearly. Her skin was dark, worn and wrinkled, her hair grey, short and scruffy. She looked skinny and wore waterproofs that were colourful but faded. Zara wondered how she had even survived to the age she looked.

'The Forbidden Zone? That what you calling it these days?' She laughed and gave a small sigh. 'Only thing forbidden about it is meeting those Legion folks. But yep, I don't mind it. I'm sure the way I live is just like yours, with its times of sadness and happiness.' Eve moved her eyes down to the floor. 'Things don't bother me like they used to, though. At the rate I'm going, looks like the tinned food's gonna expire before I do. I've been knockin' about for far too long.' She laughed and stood up. 'Anyway, I've been up all night. You setting off now or plan on staying a bit?' Eve turned off the stove and grabbed the tin above it.

'Well...' Zara paused, feeling desperate to leave the company of this stranger and get back home, but she lacked any real food or drink. She also knew little on how or where she might cross the ravine. So far, Eve had treated her with nothing but kindness and to leave without returning a favour felt unfair to her.

'Sure is nice to have company.' Eve's voice softened as she still held a smile.

'I think I'll stay for the moment, if that's alright?' Zara smiled back, wanting to believe keeping the old lady company might be enough to return the favour.

'Oh, that'd be great.' Eve's smile grew even larger, the wrinkles doubling in length across her face. 'Well, if you go out, keep your mask on you. Unlikely to happen but you never know. Shouldn't be anyone about either, but you get the odd patrol of Legions walkin' through every so often, so keep an eye out. Best bet for you would be to hide, seeing that you don't have the weapons or experience to defend yourself.' She raised her eyebrows and grinned. 'Good morning.' Eve turned and went into the bedroom, closing the door behind her.

Zara remained on the lounge floor and frowned. Back home, that phrase started conversations rather than concluded them. Her thoughts soon moved to meeting a patrol; she was confused at how Eve had seemed to find the prospect funny. She stared at her newly acquired mask, still faced down, and picked it up to figure out how to wear it. Spending time with the woman might at least buy her time to work out a plan.

CHAPTER 7 – LUTHER

'Good morning, Carbon City. This is Carbon Rocks, with your host, Ivan Hill welcoming you to another beautiful morning. Weather is looking dry but cloudy for the first part of the day, and from what I see, looks like it'll keep that way until at least mid-afternoon...' The radio blared from the front while Ruben drove on.

Luther watched buildings and people pass by from the back of his car. He often thought the city looked remarkably grey at first light, compared against the neon signs that lit up during the night. Luther knew the glowing lights shone for miles, continuously luring people into the city. This growing population had begun to annoy him; some people did not understand or appreciate the importance and stature of a moving vehicle.

He knew Carbon City itself owned quite a few vehicles, all sitting in the western scrapyard, but the lack of petrol meant they were of little use. Only Luther and other committee members possessed the rights to use them until Jetson figured out a friendly relationship between themselves and the desert city of Sol. Though seeing the relationship remain stale, Luther had started planning alternative methods of dealing with the issue.

He turned from the window to Ruben, sitting in front. Luther pushed his hand down onto the soft cream seat. He enjoyed the stark contrast of the light interior against the black square exterior, knowing few others were able to enjoy it.

'Ruben,' he snapped, irritated by the voice still droning out from the front. Ruben switched the radio off in reply and continued driving cautiously down the street. Luther sighed, seeing people who were slow to move out of the car's way, his thoughts resting on the silence. 'He says the same shit every day.'

'He does. We can read the sky well enough without him. The bloke just happens to sit on top of a mountain.' Ruben shook his head. 'Apparently gives him the right to get paid for it, too.'

'I know. It's a mindless job, one I'd rather have someone else doing – even if that someone's voice is a little grating. The man never comes down from that place.' Luther glanced towards the mountain between the buildings.

'If you say so, sir,' Ruben answered. Luther twitched at the reply, agitated by his lack of fight.

Silence filled the rest of the journey, allowing his thoughts to focus on Project Carbon. Oil from the oilfields in Sol. The only major resource the city lacked. If Jetson held his tongue, Luther believed the issue would soon be fixed.

The great wall came into view. It stretched from the mountains to the north down to the lake in the south. The car pulled up beside the only city entrance and exit in the east, besides the railway, which ran through further north. Luther ensured the wall remained braced and fortified where needed, the weaker parts being made from scrap and wire. He gazed up at its huge stone face and stepped out of the car.

The section at the main gate, down towards the lake, was made of stone. The wall spanned far higher and wider here, with two towers standing either side of the road that ran through it. Luther had queried the city's antiquity expert on it, but he knew little about it except that it had been part of a castle.

'Can't wait to centralise this whole security system.' Luther frowned, turning back to Ruben. 'I'll be back in five.' He shut the door and walked towards the guardhouse several metres from the main gates.

'Morning,' Luther shouted to the three guards standing by the gates. Their uniforms were a mixture of beige armour pads and grey clothing, some with helmets; the standard uniform he had created so the public better recognised the city guards. Besides the armoured pads, his budget did not allow for much more protection. Apart from maintaining and upgrading the city walls, the rest of his funding often went on weaponry for his men.

Not bothering to knock, Luther entered the small building and kept quiet. Knowing how gruelling some shifts were for his men, he decided to not disturb those who might be resting inside. Luther entered the surveillance room, relieved in finding no one about. On the occasions he met those beneath his position, he tried his best to bond with them and resolve any issues raised.

Upon seeing the monitor, Luther moved over to it and opened a drawer below. He had previously organised the setup of several camera systems throughout the city, with each place having their own local system, enough to store footage for at least a week before being overwritten. This current one monitored the main gates and all who passed through them. The thought of having to look through old footage crept into his mind. Luther desperately wanted to centralise the whole system and access all cameras from one single point but currently lacked the funds to do so.

Takes, what, five days to get there at the most, he thought, picking up a tape dated six days before. 'Unless...' he mumbled. 'The *Carbon Express*.' Luther picked up a second tape from four days ago. He scribbled down a note on one of the empty tape sleeves for any of the guards who might wonder why the tapes were missing. Balancing the note against the monitor, he felt smug with himself and headed back out of the building, slamming the door shut behind him. Luther waved the tapes at the guards, who all turned.

'Will bring these back tomorrow,' he shouted, receiving a nod from one of the guards. Luther got into the car and sat down. 'Central Station,' he affirmed, dropping the tapes on the seat beside him.

'Sure. Engineering guild is just before it, though, so...?' Ruben spoke gently.

'Ah yes, of course. Good. Engineering first, then the station. You know the route better than I.' Luther gave a half-hearted laugh and clenched his jaw. He took a deep breath and turned to the window as Ruben pulled away. Luther knew by now Ruben meant no disrespect and he enjoyed his assistant's awareness, but the comment still irked him.

****

They pulled up outside the engineering headquarters, the large letters 'GME' coming into view, demanding both Luther and Ruben's attention. They were painted bright red and stood above the front entrance. Luther stared from the letters to the building, which stood four levels high and looked bleak; it was a purely functional place for the General Maintenance Engineers to share and document their work. He knew that, two decades prior, the workers had helped rebuild and establish the railways and steam engines now in use.

Luther got out of the car and headed through the main entrance, focusing on the electronic sliding doors that opened on his approach. He walked over to the desk and noticed the reception area empty.

'Hello?' Luther called out, curious at the silence. 'I know it's still early, but is anyone here?' He moved down towards the hallway on his right, presuming someone should be at reception. He felt unsure if he had ever visited the place before. With it being so empty, Luther started to feel that stolen uniforms might be the case. His mind soured at the idea and what the others would make of it.

A door opened ahead of him down the corridor and a woman appeared. She saw Luther and started walking towards him.

'Can I help you with something?' She gave a smile and passed him, making Luther aware of her tall stature.

The woman kept her pace before seating herself down behind the reception desk at the front. Luther moved back across to the front of the desk and stood opposite her, his patience wearing thin at the lack of interest she showed.

'Uh, yes, actually. Do you always leave the doors open and your desk empty?' The frustration began to seep through. She barely glanced at him.

'Rarely, no. I unlock them when I arrive in the morning and lock them at night when I leave. Now, is there something I can help you with?' she replied firmly, glancing up from the paperwork on her desk and still holding a smile.

'What about just now then?' Luther asked coldly, intent on wiping the smile away.

'Just now I had to...' The smile weakened. 'I had to use the loo. What concern is this of yours?' She dropped her smile.

'My concern,' Luther looked at her name badge, 'Heather, is that there may have been some uniforms stolen from here. And being in charge of security for the entire city' – he gestured outside to where his car waited – 'I think I might have discovered just how such uniforms were stolen.'

The woman looked at the vehicle before returning her gaze to him. Observing the change of expression on her, Luther resisted the urge to grin.

'Now, if you aren't too busy...' He looked around at the empty reception. 'I need to check any camera footage you have available. Do you think you could arrange that for me?'

Her eyes darted out to the car again and back to Luther, finally checking out his suited attire. Turning to one side, he revealed the black and golds of his gun, still holstered.

'Sure,' Heather replied, rearranging her thick black hair. 'Surveillance room is on the second floor. Recordings sort themselves out.' She slid the key along the counter towards him and put her head back down into her paperwork.

'Too kind,' he replied, picking up the key. Luther held his gaze, catching the sheen of her hair sitting nicely against her smooth dark skin. 'I don't suppose you have a storeroom for uniforms, do you?'

'No, all employees keep and take care of their own,' Heather replied, giving him a quick glance from her desk.

'Lucky for you then.' He smiled and started down the corridor.

Once again, Luther struggled to recall if he had ever visited the engineering headquarters, considering what Heather had said. A few years had passed since he'd rolled out the camera initiative; he assumed the place would be using the usual tape system.

He unlocked the door of the surveillance room and entered. Ahead of him stood a desk with several monitors on the wall, though only two were on. One showed an image above the reception where Heather sat, pointing towards the main entrance. The other screen showed a camera facing at the back of the building, on a small fire door. Luther stared at the first screen, hoping to see Heather disappear again and give him even more reason to blame her for any stolen items. The woman stayed seated, and after a few moments, Luther lost interest and turned to the rest of the room.

Instead of tapes, he came upon a box with an amber light flickering on the front. Luther felt a pang of annoyance, knowing she was right. This system used computer hard drives instead of tapes.

At the desk, Luther moved the mouse, prompting a third monitor to switch on. He knew the setup might be far more efficient than tapes, but it lacked the simplicity he liked. It had been a long while since he'd used one like this and he struggled to recall how to collect the recordings from the drive. Bringing the entire system down with him went against his own policy of leaving an important place without surveillance.

He let out a long sigh and left the desk, hoping the tapes from elsewhere would prove useful. The headache of removing the system or spending the entire day watching through footage onsite was not something he intended to deal with while other options remained on the table.

After locking the door, he headed back down to the reception. His mind dwelt on how the computer setup would be of more use at Carbon Assembly or the main gates.

On approach to the front desk, Luther glimpsed Heather from behind and attempted to forget their previous conversation.

'Heather, can I have a key to either the front or back door, please?' He smiled.

'I've only got one for each, and they both belong to me,' she replied, not bothering to look up again.

'Great. If they're both yours, then I'll have the front one.' He moved closer, infuriated by her lack of regard for him. He had mistakenly presumed the girl had learnt her lesson.

Heather glared at him. 'Then I won't be able to lock—'

'I am sure you are aware, just like I am, that doors can also lock from the inside. So just lock this one here and exit out of the back.' Luther's smile widened. 'You'll hardly notice it's missing, alright?' he mocked, biting back at her attitude.

After a second of silence between them, Heather grabbed a key.

'Fine, but if there are any issues over this, you are to blame,' she snapped, dropping the key across the counter.

'Come on, now. Was there really any need for that?' Luther relaxed and picked up the key. Heather gave no reply, refocusing on her work.

'Fine by me then. I'm just here keeping you safe.' Luther leant in closer to give her a small sniff. 'Gorgeous hair, by the way. Hopefully, you'll be a little more grateful next time I see you. Let's just hope there aren't any issues with this footage.' He moved away from the reception desk and headed out of the front entrance.

'No tapes?' Ruben questioned, before Luther sat down.

'Keen, aren't you? But right. Different system here, it seems. Could do with swapping it with Carbon Assembly's setup. I'll have to pop back later if I haven't found much on the other tapes.' Luther paused. 'Or maybe I'll find someone who seems keener to do it than myself,' he taunted. 'Fancy it, Ruben?'

'I'll do it if you ask, sir.' Ruben's tone was neutral. 'I'm paid to assist you. To the station?'

'To the station,' Luther replied, feeling his irritation grow. He felt little satisfaction from Ruben's words.

****

They pulled up outside Central Station. Out of the two stations in the city, this one Luther had become familiar with, as it was used for both public and trade use. He made security around the area a top priority, knowing only too well how disruptive some people were.

Initially, Luther had considered bolstering security on both stations, but the second northern station only ran to the nearby mountains and remained forbidden from public use. He believed the miners onboard created enough of a deterrent, and if on the off chance an attack occurred, it would be Carol's responsibly to ask him for help.

He got out of the car and headed up onto the main platform used by the public. To his left lay the single railway track and the trade platform, and to his right was a small ticket office where a familiar wrinkled face met him on the other side of the glass. Luther was relieved to see the man still alive.

'Patterson. Been a while, hasn't it?' Luther laughed and shook Pat's hand through the opening in the window. The man stared at him through a large pair of glasses, squinting as he leant forwards in the old cushioned chair.

'Luther, too long indeed. Still looking slick as ever, I see. Getting all the ladies, no doubt.' He adjusted his glasses and chuckled, revealing his gummy smile. 'What'll it be then?'

'Well, I was after borrowing some tapes from the camera feeds. Got some stolen items, I believe. That okay?' He smiled back.

'Oh, sure, no problem. I still do like you say. Seven days and start again from the oldest. You want them all?' Patterson asked, leaning over to rummage in a drawer.

'No, just the fourth and sixth day, please. That should be all.' Luther watched the man keep himself seated while struggling to reach for the tapes. He'd known him since first arriving in the city, over twenty years ago, and even then he'd seemed old.

Patterson straightened back up and started to catch his breath, holding the tapes in one hand.

'Been well then, Pat?' Luther asked, trying his best to sound courteous.

'Well, you know, the usual,' he muttered. 'Getting old is no treat, I'll tell you that. Still get my buzz seeing the train every day, though.' He laughed, showing the gums of his mouth again. 'I ever tell you the story of how we got Prime, the first engine used for the *Carbon Express*? It was quite the—'

'I'm so sorry, Pat, I've really got to go.' Luther gave a nod towards the tapes still in the old man's shaky hands. 'Catch up soon, though, alright?' He liked the guy enough, but once the man got going on a story, it proved difficult to get away.

'Oh, no worries, busy man, I know it. Let me know if you need anything else.' Pat handed the two tapes over to him.

'Will do,' Luther replied. 'Take it easy now.' He turned from the ticket office and got into the car. 'Back home.' He chucked the tapes onto the others beside him.

CHAPTER 8 – SHELBY

Shelby received two meals per day, alongside some of Jason's old belongings and room. Hermann permitted him to wash his clothes and have free roam of the ship, though he learnt quickly not to venture out too much, with others on board following him and shouting insults. Having Jason's murderer join the crew, instead of having him killed, continuously flared up arguments between Hermann and the rest of the crew. Shelby began doubting the crew would let him return home, even if he made it that far.

His mind wandered to Mia, Kai, Frank and Lorel, and what they must have stumbled upon when arriving back at home. Everything would have led to the conclusion that he had died.

Ocean filled the small circular window in his room, with only sky meeting it at the horizon. No land could be seen, making Shelby agitated at the confinement to the ship.

A brief knock sounded on the door, followed by Hermann stepping inside.

'Shelby. How are we?' He smiled.

'Good. I'm good,' Shelby replied, sitting up from the bed.

'Well… Good. Ha,' Hermann snorted. 'Now, before we arrive at our destination, I'll need you to try on some of Jason's gear that you'll be needing for protection.' Hermann's reddened face nodded.

'Protection? What sort?' Shelby turned at the words, still unaware of what the mission involved. He felt Hermann might have the wrong idea about his capabilities.

'Just precautionary stuff. Trench coats, those boots beside your bed, and a mask. The mask is really what you need to figure out. We might not need it, but the fumes can be a bit…' Hermann turned his smile upside down and shook his head. 'Well… toxic, where we're going. Old machinery and the sort. All interesting stuff.' He started nodding again, a smile returning to his round face.

'I see.' Shelby tried to sound reassured by his words, uncertain of how Hermann wanted him to react.

'So, if you could follow me, I'll introduce you to Victor, who's in charge of preparing and maintaining the outfits and gear for the crew.' Hermann turned and walked out of the doorway.

Shelby stood up and followed him.

'Remember,' Hermann said between his breath and the tap of his cane, 'you killed a friend of ours, so I advise you to keep your head down until you've paid your debt. Before you know it, you'll be back home.'

'Sure.' Shelby nodded, moving past a few of the other bedrooms. He didn't need reminding.

After heading down some stairs, they entered a long and narrow room. Shelby did a double take at the sight of the figures that stood in front of him, before realising they were fake. Ahead, rows of mannequins lined both sides of the room, wearing different trench coats and gas masks. Patches of violet and grey covered the coats. At the end sat a man behind a desk who held a magnifying glass in one hand and a mask in the other. He wore a suit jacket and, to Shelby, appeared to be a lot cleaner than the rest of the crew, with his black slicked-back hair. He glanced up at Hermann and then towards Shelby.

'Victor, this is Shelby. He'll be joining us on this venture. As I'm sure you are aware, our beloved Jason is dead because of this man. So, if you could fit Jason's gear to him and run him through how to adjust and use his mask, that'd be great.' Hermann slapped Shelby across his back. 'Can't have him dying on us now, can we?' he bellowed, making his chin wobble before he turned and began walking away. 'Only a handful of days away now, if that.'

It stayed silent between Shelby and Victor, with the heavy thud of Hermann and his cane being the only interruption. Shelby waited for the footsteps to be out of earshot before speaking, eager to break the tension and direct the conversation away from Jason.

'So—'

'One… moment.' The man focused on gluing something around the mask.

Shelby averted his gaze, feeling uneasy, and looked again at the different masks, coats and materials surrounding him.

Victor put down the glue and magnifying glass before picking up a pair of small round spectacles, and stood up. The man was tall and skinny, the complete opposite of Hermann. He glanced at Shelby, appearing to judge his size, and walked over to a coat and mask.

'This' – he removed the coat from one of the mannequins – 'is yours. Already layered with a mixed lead compound on the outside for better protection.' He handed it to Shelby. 'Put it on.' Victor spoke fast, checking over the mask beside it.

Pulling his arms through the coat, Shelby noticed how thick and long it was. It reached past his knees. It appeared well-worn, containing two pockets on the front and two inside. The outside, like the other coats, had been layered with the lead compound Victor spoke of, adding both weight and an odd colour of grey with patches of purple and red.

'Well, it is a bit long, but it'll have to do. I don't have the time to cut and stitch up the bottom again. Here's your mask.' Victor handed over a diamond-shaped mask while keeping hold of a small box.

'Now this is one of the older masks we have that has this filter box connected via this tube. It sits over your nose and mouth. I've checked it all over, and if there is any issue to arise, it'll be between the seal where the tube joins into the side of your mask.' Victor pointed. 'To help you fit this comfortably, I've put a small hole in the back of the coat for the tubing to fit through, with the filter box staying on the inside of your coat pocket. The current filters should last, not that you're likely to need them.' He smiled. 'Now to fit this on, place your mouth and nose into the front of the mask, and while applying pressure, breathe out and tighten these two straps, here and here.' Victor pointed to each strap. 'This should seal the mask tightly around your face and under your chin. When you actually need to wear it, ensure the filter is in your pocket first and pull the tube through to the outside of the coat, fixing it then to the mask. Once that's secured, you can put the mask on.' Victor stared at Shelby, who then stared at the mask.

Shelby glanced at the other masks around him, too. Most had filters fixed onto the mask itself, along with eye protection. Shelby felt overwhelmed at the prospect of using this one, noticing how others looked far easier to use.

'This one... seems difficult.' He tried to sound grateful. 'Is there any other option? One with eye protection, maybe?'

Victor furrowed his brow, glaring from Shelby to the mask. 'Sadly not. There are a few newer ones going spare, but they lack filters or are broken. Your one has a radiation detector on it, unlike most of the others. If you hear it give off a high pitch every so often and the needle is in the red, my advice would be to get out of wherever you are and don't touch anything. Though, have comfort in the thought that I highly doubt we'll need any of these. Most radioactivity has dissipated since the old war. I'm yet to think of any old machinery that would give off both radiation and fumes, though Hermann loves to be vague with this mission he's been tasked. Another plus side with your mask is that you can't suffocate yourself with it if the filter is loose, unlike ones without the tubes. Anyway, did you catch the instructions?' Victor walked back over to his desk and removed his round glasses.

'I did, yes.' Shelby stared at his mask again. 'Do I need to pull the tubing through the back? I could have it coming from my filter straight up to the mask at the front,' Shelby suggested, uncertain of what it all did exactly.

'No. If you did that, you'd risk yanking it and breaking the seal, especially if you were holding a gun. My way is a little finicky, yes, but it will work.' He sat back at his desk. 'Now, did you catch all of what I said?'

'Uh, yes.' Shelby knew roughly what to do and doubted anyone would let him near a gun. He placed the mask on the floor beside the mannequin and took the coat off. Victor seemed calm enough for Shelby to ask about the mission they were on.

'Do you know what kind of machinery we're looking for?' Shelby asked.

The man studied his face again. 'I heard you murdered Jason. I don't go about poking too much into the murdering business because it's no concern of mine.' His voice sounded dull.

Shelby swallowed the words, reminded of his given title, though Victor at least avoided calling him it directly.

'Knowing Jason, though, he was probably trying to murder you.' Victor paused. 'Pretty sure he had it in for me, too, now I think about it. Still, a questionable arrangement even for Hermann to have a stranger brought on board.' Victor raised an eyebrow. 'As for machinery, I've not been told much myself other than my antiquity skills are greatly needed for this trip. The masks and all that are really just a precaution, I believe. You aren't the only one not wanting to be here, I assure you. I regretted coming the instant I stepped onto this ship. The crew are a bunch of bloody animals, all here to follow orders and collect their pay. They have no real interest in the city. Anyway, please leave, or I'll be even more behind on my work.' He gestured to the exit, giving a slight nod.

'Sure, thanks.' Shelby headed out of the room and back up the stairs, relaxed at the thought of finding machinery. The idea of being back home before a week had passed started growing on him again.

CHAPTER 9 – ZARA

Silence filled the morning. Zara tried spending the first few hours getting more sleep before finally giving up on the idea. She kept noticing her blood-stained clothes and skin in the daylight and used the tin of water Eve had left for her to wash it off. The jacket cleaned up well, but the rest of her clothes proved to be a little tougher to scrub the stains from. She could see the cuts and grazes plaguing her sore reddened hands as she dabbed off the blood.

Standing up and moving towards the front door, Zara wondered if Eve was sleeping or simply wanted space. She unlocked the door and headed down the stairs, careful not to cause herself any more pain. To occupy her time while waiting for the woman to wake, Zara decided to look at some of the surrounding buildings she had seen on arrival. The idea of leaving still circled her mind, but she needed to at least find some food of her own before making the choice. She clipped the new mask to the outside of Trent's bag, reminding herself about the dangerous yellow mist, and wondered if the mist she had walked through from the ravine was of a similar sort.

Cautiously, Zara stepped out of the building and across the street. Knowing people lived on this side made her feel more paranoid and awake than before. Even the wasteland seemed more intact than she'd initially thought.

On the opposite side of the street stood the old single-storey building Zara had passed in the night, with the two windowless holes on both sides of the doorway, the door itself broken off from its hinges on the floor.

She slowly entered the building, her feet crunching through the wooden door beneath them. Inside, colours of orange and brown popped out at her in the dim light. Between the shelves on the back wall and where she stood were half a dozen rusted and fallen aisles, with the floor covered in a mixture of ash and rubble.

Zara made her way through, avoiding the sharp metals that stuck out. Besides the colour of rust, everything else looked dull and dark, with the odd ray of light coming through the ceiling. She pressed her hands down onto a counter and, to her surprise, the surface remained solid. She lifted herself up with a groan and sat on it, staring at the wall opposite. A few shreds of paper remained pinned to the wall, faded but readable. Zara made out part of a sentence: '– any other game!' It sparked thoughts of what games it referred to and if she knew them.

Back at home, she played a whole variety of games with Heather and her friends, though her parents preferred the type they could watch down at the city hall.

The comforts of home were like a distant memory and her stomach churned at how she would explain herself when arriving back. Her parents had constantly warned her not to go, but at the time it seemed like a silly opportunity to miss. Being stuck in the city her entire life, Zara had always felt eager to explore, and the job had been especially enticing because she would be travelling with an experienced friend and also being paid.

'Trent,' she whispered. 'What now?' Zara stared at the words again on the wall and started to wonder how different things were before the old war. No one taught her much about it in the city, or even seemed to care about it.

A silhouette moved outside the shop, making Zara quickly drop from the counter.

'Wondered where you'd gotten to,' Eve cackled. 'I had half imagined you would just leave.' She entered the shop and looked at the faded poster Zara had been staring at. The door crunched under her footsteps.

'Not seen a place like this before,' Zara said softly. 'Everything seems so burnt and dusty, with hardly anything left.'

'Yeah, pretty much like all places round here. I had a glance over myself when I arrived. A few things lying about, but nothing useful. To find the real good stuff, you gotta travel further east.' Eve's voice sharpened. 'More dangerous and more frequent haze.'

Silence filled the space between them. Zara's nerves started to spike, with Eve appearing to be deep in thought. She did not intend on travelling east and felt the old lady might be more unhinged than the door she stood on.

'Get much sleep?' Zara smiled, attempting to move the conversation elsewhere.

'Some. But I never sleep like I used to,' Eve muttered. 'Anyway, it's been a while since I've had company, as I'm sure I've said before. Let's get some grub, and I'll show you some sights around here. Oh, you'll love it, I'm sure.' Eve's tone grew higher and was accompanied by a widening grin.

'Sure.' Zara held a smile and picked up Trent's bag. 'Sounds exciting.'

Eve headed out of the doorway, disappearing from Zara's view. Zara's smile dropped. She felt exhausted and not in the mood for any excitement. Taking a deep breath, she considered whether to leave, but she knew little about where else to go. After a second of mulling it over, she followed.

****

They arrived back at Eve's and lit the stove. Zara sat down on the same spot of flooring she had before.

'I got tinned spaghetti, or it's beans again,' Eve called out, looking through a bag on the kitchen counter.

'What's spaghetti?' Zara asked, having never heard the word. Eve turned around with a puzzled look. 'I've never heard of it,' Zara continued. 'I've had beans because we grow them at home, though admittedly yours tasted different.'

Eve raised an eyebrow.

'A good different,' Zara reassured her.

'Grow them? Well, that's the difference then. I live on old tinned stuff, all of it long past its date. Occasionally, you can catch the odd animal, like a rat or such, but they taste just plain awful, I'll tell you that. As for the water situation, I try to boil it before I drink any I find. Getting ill at this age will surely finish me off, though can't say that'd be all that bad.' She chuckled and placed a tin on the metal plate above the stove.

'So, grow them, how do you do that?' Eve asked curiously. 'Got the plants that grow them? Like with fruit?' She stared up at the ceiling.

'I believe so,' Zara nodded. 'Though I don't do any of that myself, so I can't really say.'

Eve lowered her brow, looking deep in thought. 'So, what do you do then if you don't grow the food you eat? I'm not sure if you told me.'

'I work. I'm an engineer,' Zara replied, not giving the answer much attention.

'What does an engineer do exactly?' Eve asked, tilting her head. 'Not often I meet one.'

'They fix things usually. I mainly fix appliances like radios, lighting and most electrical things. Machinery if it needs welding, though I only work in my section of the city.' Zara warmed thinking of it. 'I've helped redesign a few things, too, every time the need arises.'

'So, you don't have to worry much for surviving and eating then, do you?' Eve asked. 'Sounds nice.'

'Well… not to this extent,' Zara replied, unsure of what else to say. 'I get paid to do the engineering jobs, and with my payment, I buy my food, drink and clothes.'

Eve let out a whistle. 'You got your own section of a damn city, too?' She seemed baffled by the idea. 'You people sure own a lot. And yet all I got to show is the clothes I'm wearing and the bags I carry,' she cackled.

'Well, no, I don't own it, just, it's my area I work in and help maintain or make better.' Zara began to think Eve might have the wrong idea. Her family, without question, lived on the poorer side of the city.

'Fixing other people's things?' Eve seemed to ponder the thought. 'Doesn't sound like a simple life. Fixing and buying and working. Food and water is the only thing I need worry about, and that's pretty much it.' Her voice toughened. 'Everything is free, too, all day and all night, one hundred per cent off. None of that buying or trading nonsense for me.'

'You do have a point.' Zara let out a small laugh, feeling uneasy at the woman's tone.

Eve took the first tin off the stove and placed a second one on. Once it had heated, she asked, 'Spaghetti or beans? I cooked one of each.' She held the spaghetti tin out in front of her with a glove, allowing Zara to peer into it.

'Are they worms?' Zara twisted her face after glancing inside the tin.

'Worms? Worms would probably be healthier. No, spaghetti is, uh…' Eve paused. 'Not meat.' She squinted at the tin, which from where Zara sat looked utterly faded.

Looking inside, Eve assured her again it was not meat and passed her a spoon, forcing Zara to take the tin with the sleeve of her jacket.

'Might be a tad difficult to eat with that, so just eat straight from the tin if you want.' Eve sipped the tomato sauce out of hers and took a mouthful of beans before putting the tin back onto the stove. 'Only got one spoon anyway.'

They both sat in silence until they'd finished their meal.

'Mm, good, thank you,' Zara said, chewing her last mouthful. 'Same flavour as the beans, just harder to eat.' She wondered who even bothered with creating such a variety between the two when they tasted identical.

'Let's get to it then.' Eve stood up. 'Not usually one for walking about in broad daylight, but since there's two of us, anyone or anything we bump into shouldn't be a worry.' She lifted her three empty bags and slung them over her shoulder. 'Oh, and here.' Eve reached into her pocket. 'For you. It might not do the same damage like your engineering thingy, but it's a tad easier to hide.' She held out a small switchblade and flicked the blade out. Zara flinched at the sudden movement, feeling unsure about taking it. A thin piece of bare metal ran along the sharp edge of the black blade.

'Don't look so worried, girl. Chances are you won't be needing it. Still, it's better than nothing.' Eve clipped the blade back in and offered it again. Zara took it from Eve's grasp and turned it over, flicking the blade out herself.

'Do you come across people often? Do they attack you?' Zara blurted out, her heartbeat rising at the thought of using it. She would have been happy staying at the flat instead of risking the chance.

'Ha, well, not often. But chances are when you do, they'll be desperate and hungry. They won't know you, care for you, or even think twice about killing you. Anyway, besides you, I ain't seen anyone in months,' Eve answered, not seeming bothered by the prospect.

Zara shifted a little, unsettled at the idea. 'Why didn't you kill me?' she asked, unsure whether she wanted to hear the reply.

'What?' Eve stopped moving towards the door and turned back.

'Why d-didn't you kill me?' Zara stuttered.

'For a start, you opened the door when I asked. And secondly, you didn't steal from me, neither last night nor this morning when I slept. Good to have some girl company, though, I'll tell you that.' Eve's smile dropped. 'However, don't go thinking I won't kill you if you put me in that position. I might be old, but I ain't stupid.' She glared at Zara before relaxing and heading out of the door. 'But you seem the good type so I wouldn't worry.' She let out a laugh.

Zara let her go down a few stairs before she began to follow. Her heart thumped heavy against her chest. She wasn't sure if Eve was making a threat. She tightened her hands around the switchblade before placing it in her jacket pocket. With a firm pull, she closed the door and began to descend the stairs after her. Even though she was now out of the flat, Zara struggled to shake the feeling of being trapped with the woman.

Stepping out into the road, she followed Eve to the right, heading off in the opposite direction Zara had arrived from. They took the main road east until reaching a mound of earth. Cracked tarmac followed it around in a circle, splitting off into several directions.

'See the sign?' Eve pointed. 'Now if we get separated, just follow that name, Wartling, and it'll take you back to my place.'

The rusted sign was barely readable, though Zara made out the word and gave a nod. It felt like getting separated might work in her favour as she was growing more uncertain about this trip, and about Eve herself. Though the events that would lead to such an outcome might have been unwise to wish for.

Her stomach dropped as she realised Eve still hadn't told her where they were going. She moved up to walk alongside her.

'Where are we heading again?' Zara asked, as calmly as her voice allowed.

'Ah, now just you wait till we get there. I'm bettin' you'll love it.' Eve grinned. 'I sure did.' She rummaged around in one of her bags and started to mutter something about water. They moved straight across the mound of dirt and followed a sign leading towards a town centre.

As they continued walking, buildings on both sides of the road became more frequent, though most stood in ruin, much like the nature surrounding them. Rubble became a regular occurrence, eventually covering the road so much that they could hardly pass through. Old shells of buses and cars littered the road among other wrecks, rusted reddish-brown, that sat between the greys, blacks and other faded colours. Nature left it all untouched, with no plants or wildlife growing over anything.

Zara kept quiet for most of the journey, nervous about what lay ahead. The thought that she might see others crept into her mind now that the buildings grew larger. Eve never mentioned why the east grew dangerous. Zara hoped it was more to do with the yellow haze rather than people. The only small comfort came from seeing a few ruinous buildings that shared similarly styled fronts and windows to the ones back home. In the city, they were filled with shops, homes and services. Streets often bustled with people, both new and local; the town around her here felt disturbingly eerie.

'How do you know we aren't being watched?' Zara asked, glancing around at the high buildings.

'I don't,' Eve replied abruptly. 'But no one is likely to be here, for the same reason we weren't here – we think others already are. Funny how that works, ain't it? More chance of bumpin' into someone back at my place cos of it,' Eve cackled, gazing around at the buildings. 'Places like this go to waste. Some of these are fine bits of brick to hold up in.'

'We have similar at home, filled with more people than they should probably take,' Zara replied, unsure whether Eve had ever seen a large number of people. She dreaded to think what might happen in such a situation out here.

'It's just up ahead.' Eve's voice tightened with a flicker.

'Can you tell me what it is?' Zara strained, desperate to settle the anxiety in her stomach. She trembled again and placed one hand back into her pocket for the blade.

'All this way and you still want me ruinin' it. I don't think so. Wait and see,' Eve snapped before settling her face back into a smile. 'Found this place a few months ago. I come back to it every so often. Full of things I've not seen elsewhere. Maybe you've seen some of it, maybe you haven't. Don't know what it's like across the line.' She raised her eyebrows. 'You fancy people might have one in every home, and I'll feel a damn fool if that's the case.'

The words calmed Zara's nerves a little, though she still had no idea what to expect. At least it sounded like an object of some sort, one that she might be familiar with.

'We're here,' Eve announced, stopping in front of a wide entrance.

Around them on the ground were large corroded letters. Eve stepped over them, heading for a door. Zara stared up at the building, noticing the lack of windows and two giant letters hanging above the entrance that spelt 'IN'. The only difference between it and the other buildings was the broad overhang of the roof that the letters hung on. Zara knew of an 'inn', but they were not something to get excited about and were often full of people.

Her stomach twisted at the thought of meeting someone inside. Eve held the door open for her and smiled. Zara smiled back and entered reluctantly, her hand still gripping the blade in her pocket seeing the darkness she faced.

The roof was intact, starving the inside of any source of light. Zara began rummaging for the torch in Trent's bag and switched it on. The place opened into a large foyer area with posters lining each side of the wall.

'Well, look at you with that fancy thing,' Eve called out, eyeing the torch. 'And here I am with my cruddy little stick.' She gave a distasteful glance at the small glowing cylinder she'd pulled out from her pocket. 'You mind if I have a look? Not used one before.' Her tongue seemed to poke out of her mouth as she rushed over.

Though Zara would have rather kept the torch, Eve's eagerness made her give it up. She received the small glowing cylinder in return. Zara noticed two wide buttons in the middle of the light stick underneath where she gripped. The harder she squeezed, the brighter the yellow glow became, though compared against the torch, it did little to light up anything directly. She had seen nothing like it.

'So… what is this…?' Zara stared at the faded posters fixed to the wall. The yellow glow was scarcely bright enough for her to see one poster at a time.

'Call it a cinema.' Eve pointed the torch to a sign on the wall that said the word in big letters. 'Guessing it's what the sign outside said, too.'

'A cinema?' It was her first time hearing the word. 'What's it for?' She crossed the room and studied another line of posters. One caught her eye called *The Dark Arts* that showed three people wearing black, standing in front of a luminous city. Around them were swirls of yellow wisps.

'Films like the ones on the wall.' Eve smiled. 'They've got most of them, so take your pick.'

'What?' Zara stared at Eve and then to the poster.

'These posters, they are for films. You know, moving photos?' Eve said again. 'Oh, do they not have them back home then?' she mocked with a wide smile.

'No, well, not like that. We have some that show us our city and our shows. On something called a tele. At least, that's what I think,' Zara replied, a little unsure about how accurate she was being. She only knew one person who owned a working television, and they were far wealthier than her family.

'Oh, I see. Well, this place is not showing our lives, I don't think. It shows things like people back before the war and all that. Think it's of their lives or maybe stories? Like stories we tell, you know?' Eve widened her eyes. 'What they do in some, like this one, baffles me.' Eve pointed to *The Dark Arts* poster on the wall. 'They used to have abilities.' Eve's voice turned to a whisper as if the poster might hear.

Zara slowly realised why Eve kept this place a secret, though she was still struggling to understand what it did. However, the excitement of viewing moving photos surpassed any regret of missing out on the opportunity, considering she might never get the chance again.

'Doesn't it need electricity to run?' Zara asked, thinking about how the ones back home worked.

'I don't know much about electric, but I just turn a few switches, run the circle film through and before I know it, the thing starts playing, usually,' Eve replied.

'I see.' Zara forgot Eve might not have known about electricity. 'Can we watch one then?' She stared at *The Dark Arts* poster again, now in wonder at the wisps surrounding the three figures. 'This one?'

'I was going to suggest the same one.' Eve grinned. 'Follow me. I decided to hide the films I found on the off chance someone comes here, though doesn't look like anyone has. These things don't really have a real use. More of a treat, considering I'm pretty set for food and water for a good few weeks. Now be a darling would you and put that piece of metal through the door handles. I ain't expecting anyone, but just in case someone does try to get in, we'll hear them first.' She smiled and flashed the torch at a metal rod by the entrance.

Zara wedged the metal between the door handles and looked back out at the street. Her excitement waned at the reminder of where she stood.

'What you waiting for? Come on.' Eve shone the torch at her face. 'It's a long one, I'll warn ya.'

Further into the darkness Zara followed, eventually entering a small hall that opened into a room full of seats, all facing in one direction.

'Now, pick a spot in the middle or front, and I'll go set it up. Won't take a moment.' Eve wandered off, leaving Zara alone in the room with the glowing cylinder in hand for company. The place looked surprisingly clean, though the roof had fallen in on one corner and let a small amount of light through, making the outlines of the chairs visible.

Humming came from behind her, making her turn. After several seconds, a stream of light shot across the room, filling up the wall at the front and making it come alive. Zara's eyes stuck to it, and she was startled at the sight of cities that were far different from her own. Thousands of cars, people and food flooded the streets.

Before Zara knew it, Eve was sitting beside her. The picture was huge, crisp, and moving in a way she had never seen. Zara felt the relentless flicker of the screen before her, denying her a chance to think or ask questions. She sat quietly next to Eve, wide-eyed and full of wonder.

CHAPTER 10 – LUTHER

Luther continued working through the taped footage in his office. So far, he had found nothing of use and the afternoon trickled painfully on. His time began to feel wasted. Luther hated any work involving repetition, the tapes now grinding against his mood. He considered forcing Ruben into the task, though the man had been quick at avoiding his wrath lately. Luther admired him for it, knowing he kept to a straight and narrow path to get the job done. To make him sit through the footage might undermine and set back his current work ethic; something counterproductive to what Luther wanted from the man.

He looked at the television a few metres in front of him, noticing his guards relaxing at the main gate. Nothing major ever happened there, but slouching and paying little attention to the job looked unprofessional, which in turn made him and Carbon City look unprofessional. Even with the city's reputation firmly in place, he still needed his soldiers to be strong and alert.

With the training, armour and weapons Luther provided, few scavengers and outlaws attacked the city anymore. The stable security he provided helped the place establish its mines and accelerate growth in population, allowing it to become the largest settlement for miles. The only other nearby settlement that threatened him and constantly entered his mind was the town of Trittle, ruled by the Eastern Legion. Even though they appeared friendly for trading, they were heavily militarised and dealt with force along territories they considered their own. Luther knew they possessed better technology and weaponry compared to his own regiments, and this made him eager to discover some for himself.

Besides Trittle, little else bothered Luther regarding threats. Oil stayed on his mind. It was a resource that would help solidify the city's position, but those in Sol, a desert city in the north, refused to make any deals.

Rubbing his eyes, Luther focused back on the screen at the slouched guards, feeling tempted to make them watch their own footage.

'Ruben,' Luther called out, expecting an immediate response. Turning towards the doorway behind him, he shouted the name again. Still, no one replied. He twisted his face and turned back to the bright screen. Luther sat back and stretched, annoyed at how exhausting watching a tele became.

A few minutes passed before he heard footsteps in the corridor, walking fast in his direction.

'Luther.' Ruben appeared at the door.

'Care to explain where you were?' Luther queried, turning to face him.

'Yes, actually,' Ruben replied. 'The meeting this morning asked for those in charge of their districts to account for all engineers. There are two missing, or more accurately, on holiday. An electrical engineer from Southern District and a train engineer from Eastern District.'

'No one from Carol's district then?' Luther tilted his head, intrigued by the news. He valued anything to grind Carol's gears, distracting him from the blunt attitude.

'Afraid not, sir,' Ruben replied.

'So, are these missing holidaymakers in the city? If not, then murdered perhaps?' Luther turned to focus on the tape.

'They're currently following up on it, which is why I'm here. The committee, or should I say Jetson, wants you, being head of security, to investigate the homes of these two missing people and see if we can get anything from them.' Ruben paused. 'I can watch over the rest of these tapes for you.'

'What?' Luther turned to him, not quite believing the offer. Ruben had been cooperative lately but never outright volunteered for a job.

'I can take over if you wish. You've been here for hours. Go off to where it's worth you being. Jetson's in the meeting room.' Ruben sounded miserable.

'Well, then.' Luther stood up and grabbed his jacket. 'Have fun,' he jested.

Ruben seemed to ignore his comment, slumping himself down in the seat and facing the screen. Luther closed the door behind him. The thought of Ruben volunteering began to play on his mind. Perhaps the man wanted to avoid being forced into the job, knowing it might lead to the same outcome. Luther shook his head, replacing the notion with the fresh idea of interrogation that now felt possible with the new information Ruben had brought to him.

****

He entered the meeting room, which, to his surprise, only had Jetson sitting in it.

'Luther. Just who I was waiting for. You missed everyone. Busy with the tapes, so I hear.' He gave a sly grin. 'Anyway, I've got the relevant files for you here.' Jetson slid the folders across the polished wooden tabletop. Luther, who was still standing at the other end, stopped the files from dropping off the edge.

'I know, a shame. Miss anything good?' He pulled a file out and scanned over it. 'Huh, this one doesn't even live in the city.' Luther's excitement lessened. He hated leaving the city and having to deal with the uncivilised folk who lived outside in what he considered the wasteland.

'Don't start with that one. He's old. Wife is long dead and, as far as we know, he has no relatives. Bit of a dead end – unless you want to inspect his living accommodation in Crossover. Not too far on the train, thankfully, though the stench is a little disturbing.' He flared his nostrils. 'Anyway, start with the other one. It will be much more up your street.' Jetson grinned again at him while pulling out the second file.

'Interrogating parents about their children?' Luther looked up at Jetson. 'Sounds pretty sick to me.'

Jetson raised his brow, seeming unconvinced at the statement. 'Well, hopefully you'll get something from them.' He massaged his forehead.

'I'll get whatever they know,' Luther replied, the excitement stirring within him again. The dull day was turning into an exciting one.

'I'm getting an awful feeling the old guy might be our dead friend.' Jetson sighed. 'And he was one of our bloody train engineers, the moron.' He shook his head. 'This could set us years of work back with our relationship with Trittle.'

'Don't be so sure,' Luther replied unfazed. 'We might not need their relations if things go particularly well with our project.'

Jetson eyed him before looking back at the doorway. 'That remains to be seen. For now, let us hope this dead man is just a thief.' His words were heavy.

Luther gave a casual glance behind him at the doors and then to Jetson. 'Well, I'd best get started on this.' He slipped the files back into the folder. 'These old people aren't going to interrogate themselves now, are they? Who knows, the missing personnel could both be in Crossover having a nice holiday in that shit-infested town.' Luther shrugged. 'You'd be surprised at what some people are happy with.'

He marched out of the room, leaving Jetson still seated.

****

Luther opened the door to his bedroom and searched the space for the girl from the morning. He hoped to share the pleasure for the evening ahead, but to his irritation she had gone. An opportunity like this was becoming a rarity now, with most of his guards keeping civilians in the street obedient. The city acted far better for it, but it proved to be tedious for him.

Luther decided to make a drink before heading out, and flicked on the kettle. Thoughts of the impending interrogation flooded his mind. He was still deciding on how to play it. He stared in the mirror. The beige suit he wore seemed a little too friendly for such an occasion, so he decided to change into his dark red suit instead.

To accompany the new outfit, an armoured vest sat over his black shirt. Luther knew it always proved to be intimidating. He reached under his desk and unlocked a small safe, pulling out several bullets and two pairs of handcuffs. On the desk, Luther took out the file of the missing girl who lived with her parents. He poured out the boiling water and let the tea brew, continuing to read over the file, finding that the father, Aiden Black, worked in the mines. *Carol's district.* He gave a smile at the possibilities it might bring, knowing the man must hate the woman.

CHAPTER 11 – ZARA

Evening had arrived by the time they left the cinema. The film stuck in Zara's mind, as she'd seen nothing of the sort before. The people in it were not like her or anyone she knew. All of them dressed differently and owned items that looked and behaved strangely. Some people even appeared to have unnatural abilities.

Did they all die in the old war?

She glanced down at herself, struggling to believe that the film had taken place within the same world, being far from her own reality.

From what she saw in the film, the old world looked entirely different. Thousands of people and vehicles flooded the streets, covering the ground beneath them, and the sheer amount of food on-screen went by unnoticed by the people. Her own city's resources paled in comparison to the quantity in the film.

'I think if I had that much food around me, I'd be as round as a ball and as big as a mountain.' Zara laughed, walking around a large chunk of concrete in the road.

'Oh, I'd be just the same. Perhaps that's how the war started. People getting too big and exploding,' Eve replied, wide-eyed and coming to a halt.

Staring back towards her, Zara stopped to muse over her words. 'You know what, you might be on to something,' she said seriously, until breaking into a laugh with Eve.

They simmered down to silence and Eve let out a sigh, continuing on around another large piece of concrete, with Zara now following.

'Would have been nice to live back then, wouldn't it? Not like this bland, boring nonsense they left behind for us,' Eve spat, hitting her hand against some rubble before waving towards the empty street. 'Would much like one of those hot dogs right now.' She licked her lips and grinned. The tone in her voice struck Zara with panic, having half forgotten where she was.

'Not a fan of eating dog. I think I'd go for some of that pink stuff. Looked like a fluffy pink cloud.' Zara forced a smile, concentrating back on the film. 'Perhaps that's how they made them.' She eagerly faced upwards for any clouds, but a dirty grey sludge filled the sky. Zara attempted to keep her nerves at bay as the pit of her stomach dropped.

'Yeah, suppose not with that sorta cloud. Not too often you can see the clear sky here either. Worst of both, now I think about it. No pink fluffy cloud, no clear sparkly sky.' Eve looked down at a leaf blowing alongside them.

'No work here, though,' Zara replied, suppressing the dread she felt as the leaf passed her. 'I have to work almost every day back at home.'

Eve stopped walking, but Zara continued on, attempting to drown out any of the fear trying to fill her mind.

'Seems simple living here. You get every day off.' Zara laughed, stopping almost at once at the lack of reaction from Eve. 'Right?' Zara asked, concerned at the silence. She stared back at Eve a few paces behind, who no longer smiled.

'The wind's pickin' up. No good can come of that.' Eve raised her eyebrows, turning to look behind her for a moment. 'Let's get going.' She turned back and started walking again.

Zara glanced towards where Eve had been looking, unable to see anything.

'Got your mask ready, I hope.' Eve gestured towards Zara's bag.

'Yep.' Zara pulled the mask up clipped to the side of the bag, uncertain whether the tattered thing worked. 'Hopefully we won't be needing them, though, right?' she blurted out, revealing a little more nerve than she planned.

'Hopefully not. It ain't all that bad, darlin'. Worst bit is just seeing when it arrives, especially in the dark. Just got to keep our eyes peeled is all.' Eve gave a small smile and gazed up. 'Bit of rain tends to help, I find.' She stared at the dirty grey smear in the sky.

'Should we put our masks on now?' Zara asked, wanting to minimise the risk with the fading sunlight. 'We won't be able to see it in the dark, will we?'

'No need for it,' Eve replied. 'We can see it with that fancy torch of yours. Just flash it around every so often for that yellow.' She chuckled. 'And quit your worrying. I certainly feel safe with you here now. Using my little yellow glower ain't no match for it.'

****

Eve insisted they picked up the pace. Zara wanted to stop but was embarrassed at asking for a break. Her body still ached and throbbed with pain. How Eve managed to survive alone with nothing but ruins surrounding her made Zara question her own abilities. The woman appeared to be in far better shape than Zara was and looked forty years older.

They reached the old roundabout and Zara flicked her torch on to eye the other roads that met them and find the right way. Ahead she recognised the old green signpost they'd passed on the way out.

'Almost back now,' Eve husked, struggling to catch her breath, but still showing no signs of slowing. Zara's feet ached, the urge to remove her boots becoming more desperate with each step.

'We'd best get more water, though,' Eve said in a harsh whisper. 'Pretty sure we ain't got too much left.'

The mention of water made Zara realise how dry her mouth had become. She pulled out her bottle and took a sip, refusing to acknowledge the rumble in her stomach. She felt both trapped by and a burden to the old lady. The thought of wasting water earlier in the day to wash off blood made her feel a twinge of guilt.

They headed off the road and passed through the remains of a dead forest, full of bare and broken trees; the loud crunches of wood sounded beneath their feet.

'Just over there, past the house.' Eve pointed out in front. Zara made out the silhouette of a small house through an opening in the trees that sat in the middle of an empty field.

Both of them moved out of the forest. Zara noticed a large vehicle that sat abandoned to one side of the field. The tyres looked large and on the front sat a long bar of metal with sharp, twisted blades, reminding her of the drills at home. Beneath it on the ground stood a few strands of long pale grass.

'Drinking from it for a few weeks now. Got lucky for sure. These things ain't exactly common,' Eve whispered.

As they approached the house, Eve pulled out her gun and stopped.

'I usually check the house before moving on to the well. A nice home like this with its own water in the middle of nowhere makes it a sure place for people to lodge,' Eve said with certainty, giving Zara a look that made her uneasy. 'Get your blade out and stay quiet.'

Tension started to rise in Zara's mind as she thought through what might happen next. She attempted to focus on the ground in front of her but her mind fixed on how they had just walked so casually across an open field.

If anyone were in the house, they surely would have seen or heard us.

Raising her gun, Eve peered through the window and shook her head in dismissal, though Zara doubted she could have checked the house so swiftly in the fading light. They kept still for a few minutes, listening for any noise, but only silence met their ears. Eve approached the front entrance where the door had broken off. She stepped inside with Zara following close behind, gripping her blade in one hand.

Dark empty space met them around each corner, with Eve's occasional whisper accompanying it.

'Empty,' she whispered again, now heading back out of the entrance. Zara thought it might have been a little early to announce such a thing before checking the actual well, making her question how Eve had stayed alive for so long when she behaved so recklessly.

Outside, Zara followed her around the side of the building and to what the woman called a well. From what she could make out, there was no hole or bucket but instead a corroded metal tap with a long curved handle fixed onto the top.

'Not seen one like that before,' Zara remarked.

'Really?' Eve sounded surprised. 'What kind of wells you got then?' She pulled out an old petrol container from her bag, the volume of her voice growing.

'The ones we have at home have a hole, bucket and a small wall around the water to stop you from falling in. They look much better than this…' She paused and stared at it. '…This tap. Taps aren't usually for wells.'

'Not impressed, huh?' Eve's voice tightened. 'This well seems more functional than your fancy one. Can't fall into a hole for a start. Now, you're a strong young lady. Push down on the top a few times for me?' Eve pointed at the handle.

Unsure if she had struck a nerve, Zara stepped in front of the tap without question.

'Sure.' Zara put one hand on the top and attempted to push down before stopping to drop Trent's bag. She grasped the handle with both hands, pushing hard. It eventually moved down with a creak.

Eve cackled and gave a grin. 'Bit stiff, ain't it? Now let go of it and do that a few more times.'

'No kidding.' Zara started to sweat as she kept pushing down the lever and letting it rise back up. After a minute, water began to pump out of the tap, giving Zara a flash of relief. The sound of it pouring into the container gave her a thirst, too.

'Well, this is definitely harder work than the wells back home, but it seems to work much quicker at least.' She let out a small laugh, thinking of home. 'You'd like our taps better, though. A simple twist gives you instant water.'

'Really? Well, I bet people queue up all day for it then.' Eve shook her head and pouted.

'Not at all. For us that own a place in the city, we get our own taps in our houses. You've probably seen them before,' Zara replied, more hastily than she would have liked.

'Eh, so basically like the old ruined buildings? Each place got their own, not that they work here, of course.' Eve frowned. 'Still, this water is better than most, so don't be complaining.'

Unsure whether she had complained, Zara kept quiet and gave no reply. She watched Eve move the full container of water out of the way and put a smaller bottle underneath the spout. After filling it up, Zara took a sip from her own bottle before topping it up, too.

They headed back towards Eve's place, silence keeping between them in the dark of night. Zara offered to carry the large container of water, which she soon regretted after feeling the weight when Eve passed it over.

'Again,' Eve mumbled, approaching the buildings ahead of them.

Without speaking, Zara turned to look behind her and switched her torch on. 'Clear,' she whispered, twisting back around and turning the torch off. Zara had done the routine twice since leaving the well, checking to make sure the yellow haze had not descended upon them in the pitch black.

'Good,' Eve replied.

A few minutes passed before Zara recognised Eve's building ahead.

'Shame you can't move that well closer,' Zara said between breaths, hoping Eve would take the joke.

Eve chuckled. 'I know, I know. Cheeky one, ain't ya. Still, least there is one.'

With both arms, Zara gripped the water container and headed up the stairs first, her torch balanced between a few of her fingers. She reached the top and turned back for Eve, who she heard still climbing up the other flight below. Her hands were full when she approached the door, and she was unsure whether she should wait for Eve to open it.

After hesitating for a few seconds, Zara put the container down and went to open the door herself, but upon touching the handle, the door swung inwards, already open. She eyed the gap between the frame and the door, struggling to remember if she had closed it on the way out.

'I could have sworn...' She stopped talking, noticing Eve gesturing to be quiet. The woman edged up the stairs with her gun drawn. Zara stepped back from the door and reached into her pocket for the switchblade. She heard nothing.

Aiming the gun towards the door, Eve turned to Zara and whispered, 'Sure you closed it?'

Zara nodded, mouthing a yes in reply.

Eve pushed it open with the front of her gun. Neither of them saw anything in the darkness as Eve stepped in, the floorboards creaking.

Suddenly, a hand covered Zara's mouth from behind her. She immediately tried to pull away and scream, but a long cold blade pressed up against her throat, making her freeze. The smell of the hand so close to her nose made her want to retch.

'Water,' a man's voice sounded, dry and desperate. 'Where is it? I heard you talkin' 'bout it!'

Eve twisted around and lowered her gun.

'What water? We barely got enough to survive ourselves!' she growled back at him.

'Don't play stupid with me, old lady, or I'll cut her throat.' He nodded to the gun beside her. 'I'm betting you ain't got no bullets neither for that.' He pressed the blade harder against Zara's skin, creating a warmth that trickled down her neck.

Eve stayed silent and changed her expression to a look of reluctance. 'Fine, you got me. Take our water.' She gestured to the container on the floor between them.

'You hard of hearing? Or stupid? Where you gettin' it from?' the man wheezed, adjusting the blade against Zara's neck. She stared at Eve, who appeared calm, while trying to reach for her pocket.

'Alright, alright. We got a well. But there ain't no way you'll be finding it at this time of night. Now, I'd be willing to take you there myself on the condition you lower that blade of yours.' She gave a small smile and softened her voice.

The man remained still, gritting what teeth he had left. Eve started talking again.

'You look exhausted. Agree to this, and you can even have some water right now. No harm in sharing, is there?' She holstered her gun and picked up the container full of water.

Eve unscrewed the top and poured some into a tin, the water's splash echoing into the metal container. The man gazed at the tin, licking his dried lips. She brought it closer to him, and he stared at the smooth, shiny surface.

'Please, put the blade down. It won't do any of us good. I wouldn't be playing no tricks over my daughter here, alright?' Eve smiled, offering the tin up to him.

The water glistened in what light it picked up, making the man lower his blade and loosen his grip on Zara, who moved her mouth away from his hand and took a gasp of fresh air.

He was skinny, his gaunt face full of beard, and the skin on him was patchy and worn. Taking the tin from Eve, he still gripped the blade with his other hand close to Zara, who began moving to one side of him. The man tipped the tin straight back, swigging down the water and taking his eyes off them.

A flash filled the room, followed by a deafening bang, as a bullet pierced through the man's neck. Zara jumped to one side. Water and blood started to spurt out of the man's neck as he choked and dropped the tin, attempting to breathe and stop the blood from pouring out. He fell to the floor and, after several seconds, stopped moving.

Blood began to pool around the body. Zara moved her hands up to her own neck where the knife had cut her and winced. The thought of Trent entered her mind, making her cover her mouth. Zara faced Eve, who stood watching the blood drip down the stairs, her gun still in hand.

'Why?' Zara asked. 'He only wanted water.'

'You don't live out here, darlin'. Everyone for themselves.' Eve sounded irritated. 'He had a knife to you anyway, so why you gotta stick up for some arsehole like that?' She moved to the body and started to search over it for anything of value, but besides the food he had stolen from her place, he possessed only a blade.

'For you.' Eve turned and placed the large blade into Zara's hands. 'It'll be more useful than the small blade I gave ya.'

Zara faltered, still shocked at what had happened. She looked down at the rusted blade in her hands. The weapon had almost killed her. The blade was several inches long, and the gripped handle was made of rubber.

'Everyone for themselves, yet you didn't kill me.' Zara felt her words turn bitter.

'Well, you didn't have a knife, and you ain't no man neither. Sure, there are women who can be worse, but more often than not it's men. You've not seen them out here. They're savages.' She spat on the body and turned through into her flat.

Anger lingered in Zara for only a second more before it plunged into panic. 'Couldn't there be more of them?' Zara called through the doorway to Eve.

'Oh, there's always more. But with this guy, I'd bet there ain't. Would have seen them by now. The times I come across people, they're often alone... and well, those that are in groups aren't as shifty as this one was.' She eyed the body slumped outside her door. 'Anyway, that gunfire might draw some unwanted attention. I say we quickly grab something to eat and move on.' Eve started to pull out some food from one of her bags. 'Two people in almost a single day.' Her voice grated against the air. 'Looks like my luck's at an end. We've overstayed our welcome here.'

We? Zara stared at the woman preparing the food, her thoughts turning back to Trent and then to Heather and her parents in the city. She slipped the long blade under her belt and moved the water container inside, locking the door behind her. Zara's mind began to fix on the ravine and how she might tell Eve she needed to leave and get across it. Now more than ever, she wanted to go home.

CHAPTER 12 – LUTHER

The city continued to buzz into the night with talk of a new factory being built in Northern District. Most were eager for an excuse to celebrate and drink, which often caused headaches for both Luther and his men.

Luther sat in the back of his car while Ruben slowly forced it through the crowded street. He had organised for two guards to meet him at the house to ensure numbers were on his side if they kicked up a fuss.

As they drove further into the district, the crowd began to lessen. They entered a suburb, where few people remained on the streets. The houses were built high and huddled into long lines, each one connected to the other. To Luther's relief, the place they were looking for stood at the end of a street. He resented having to see and deal with any more lower-class people than necessary. Luther peered at the house in question as it came into full view. The luminous advertisement board made him squint. Though a marvel to behold, the idea of it being fixed onto the side of his own place made him frown.

'Sickening how people live like this,' Luther commented. 'I'd have it down if it was near me,' he muttered as Ruben pulled over in front of the house. 'Still, for them it's far better than being out of the city.'

Ruben turned off the ignition and gave no reply. Luther got out of the car and faced Ruben as he got out himself.

'Stay.' Luther pointed back inside the car and turned to the two guards who waited on the pavement. He nodded at them, prompting them to move through the scruffy front garden.

They stopped at the front door, illuminated by the harsh glow of the billboard around the corner. A slight buzz that came from it began to grind against Luther's mood. He knocked on the door and stepped back.

'Not exactly warm out this evening, is it?' he mumbled to his guards and crossed his arms.

The door opened, making Luther adjust his stance. Opposite them stood a short bald man wearing coal-covered overalls, who gave the impression that he had been asleep.

'Yes?' The bloke looked at Luther and then to the guards, making him close the door slightly.

'Aiden Black?' Luther smiled.

'Uh, yes. Yes, that's me.' The man fully opened the door. 'And who might you be, if I may ask?' He peered at the car parked outside the front before returning his eyes to Luther.

'My name's Luther.' He paused, wanting to avoid shaking the man's hand. 'I'm head of security in our city. In charge of keeping you and everyone else safe.' Luther widened his smile. 'I've got a few questions, if I may come in?'

He watched Aiden glance at the guards beside him and then at their guns. One guard had her handgun out and the other had a rifle over his back.

'Don't be alarmed by them, they come with me everywhere for my protection.' He looked at them both and chuckled. 'Never thought I'd need them, you know, but given the important position I'm in, better safe than sorry.' Luther sighed and shook his head. 'Especially with all these new people coming in.'

'Certainly, of course.' Aiden stepped back and leant against the wall, gesturing for Luther and the guards to come in. 'Through to the right, at the back,' he croaked, clearing his throat.

'Thank you.' Luther walked through with the two guards, entering into the small dreary lounge where a woman appeared from the kitchen ahead of him.

'Michelle, I presume?' He nodded towards her, taking his mind off of the discoloured walls.

'Yes,' she replied, shooting a glance at Aiden, who appeared behind Luther and his guards. 'Would you like a drink?'

The quick expression between the two of them did not go unnoticed. Luther often recognised it when people started to get on edge. He began to dislike the woman.

'Yes, all three of us would love a drink. Hard day at work in Central District as usual.' Luther smiled. 'What's on offer?'

'Well, we have water, some juice and...' Michelle paused. 'And also, tea.'

Luther's face lit up.

'Tea all round, please.' He took a step towards her. 'If that's alright with you, of course?' Luther knew the costly price of tea and the expenses when making it.

Michelle hesitated before going back into the kitchen to prepare the tea. Luther followed her, turning back to Aiden as they entered the kitchen, too.

'You're a hard worker, I see,' said Luther. 'The mines, I assume?'

Aiden gave no reply, looking down at his overalls and hands.

The lack of talk made Luther aware of the unease between him and the couple. He kept his eyes on Aiden.

'Would you like a seat?' Michelle pulled out a chair at the small dining table that sat in the middle of the kitchen. Luther took the seat, still holding his gaze on Aiden, who eventually returned a look, with a glass of water in hand. Luther smiled.

'Yeah, well, the rail has made all the difference,' Aiden eventually replied, setting his glass down. 'But I can't help wonder what this is about. Why are you here?'

'We'll wait for the tea. Nothing too serious, don't you worry.' Luther started disliking him, too, and decided to test the water.

'I've just got a few questions for your daughter, Zara Black.'

The couple shared a glance.

'She… uh, she isn't here, I'm afraid,' Aiden spoke up.

'Oh, is she not?' Luther sounded surprised. 'When will she be back?' He counted on the man being an honest worker.

'Not for a—'

'She's out in the centre, I think... with her friends,' Michelle interrupted, letting out an anxious laugh. 'What were the questions? We'll make sure she gets them.' Michelle set three teacups down on the table and poured out the tea.

'I see.' Luther acted disappointed, controlling a jolt of excitement that shot through him at the challenge. 'Do you see much of Carol then?' They both seemed puzzled by the question. 'She's in charge of the mining operations,' Luther pressed on, watching the steam rise from the cups. 'You have any milk?'

'Oh, her.' Aiden turned his head, watching Michelle bring over a small jug of milk to set on the table. 'She's hardly there herself. But keeps the place running, I guess.'

'I fucking hate her. She does my head in at every meeting I see her. Guessing she hasn't done a day's hard work in her life, dressing up skimpy like she does. A bit much for her age.'

'Well, she's management, so different roles to us miners,' Aiden replied warily. 'So, you were saying something about our daughter?'

Luther's attempt at bonding with Aiden had only seemed to make him more wary. He picked up the jug and splashed some milk into each teacup, enjoying the silence. Luther guessed Carol would be a tough subject for the man to navigate. For all Aiden knew, he might be disciplined for insulting a superior. He liked him for that at least.

'Ah yes, well, I fear perhaps that the questions I have don't really matter if she is still here...' He paused. 'In the city.' Luther looked at them both and stood up from his seat. 'Never mind, sorry to have bothered you.'

Michelle and Aiden eyed each other again before Aiden spoke.

'I was going to say earlier.' He gave a sideways glance to his wife, who put a hand on him. 'Zara is actually out of the city. Booked a little holiday with her friend. All done officially, of course, with the time off from work. You can check at her guild.'

It fell silent. Luther enjoyed watching others squirm under pressure.

'I know. Terrible what women do to some men.' Luther stared at Michelle.

'But... I only thought,' she stuttered, 'she might be in trouble.'

'She is one for getting herself into odd situations.' Aiden gave a nervous smile.

'When did she leave exactly?' Luther dropped his smile, still standing by the table.

'Uh, about five days ago, I think,' Aiden answered.

'You say she was with a—'

'What were the questions for her?' Michelle's voice trembled. 'You said you needed to speak to her.'

'These are my questions.' Luther glared back at her, his hands firmly on the table. 'Now, who did she leave with? A friend, you say?'

'But that makes no sense, these questions are—' Michelle started to tear up, allowing Luther to continue.

'I knew she was out of the city. My questions are aimed at you. It was brought to my attention yesterday that a body was found outside the city, wearing clothing that belongs to our engineering guild.' His words rang out sharp.

Michelle burst into tears. Aiden tried to comfort her, while Luther's lips curled.

'She left with a work friend,' Aiden said, failing to hold back his tears.

'Do they have a name?' Luther leant forward.

'Trent. His name's Trent. An old fool who poisoned our daughter's mind with ideas of leaving the city. We never wanted her to go. We all told her it was foolish.' Aiden covered his face with a hand.

'We all?' Luther tilted his head.

'Yes. Both of us and Heather,' Aiden replied. 'She ignored us all.'

'Heather? The receptionist at the engineering headquarters?' Luther queried.

'Yes,' he responded. 'She's her partner.'

Luther turned his head and stopped himself from smiling. Heather had irritated him a great deal.

'I see. I'll stop by tomorrow and let Heather know the details of what's happening, too. Again though, myself and the committee are unsure on who the body belongs to, but when I find out, I'll have you notified.' Luther gave them both a gentle smile. 'Now, back to my questions. Did they mention where they were going?'

'All I know is they took the train out of here, probably to Crossover where her friend Trent lives. Besides that...' Aiden

fought back another burst of tears. 'I don't know anything else...
Heather might know more.'

It fell silent again. Luther stared at both of them and began
to speak.

'Now, as much as I hate to bring it up at such a hard time,
it still stands that your wife attempted to hide such information
from me.' Luther glared at her. 'It is a disgusting thing to lie to the
authorities whose sole purpose is to protect you,' he spat, twisting
his face and pulling out a pair of handcuffs. He turned to Aiden.
'Though it seems that you, Aiden, were willing to trust me, and
without her, we might have been able to speed this whole thing
along.' Luther turned from him back to his wife. 'But you, Michelle,
it looks like you have an issue with trusting the authorities. And that
issue has wasted my time in this investigation.' He saw both pairs of
eyes focusing on the cuffs. Luther had forgotten just how thrilling
all this could be.

Straightening, he slowly moved behind the seat where
Michelle sat and pressed up against her chair to rest a hand on her
shoulder.

'You know, I could arrest you for that behaviour. Your
husband, too, for that matter, and it'd be all your fault.' He moved
off from her and walked behind Aiden. 'Thankfully, though, I rather
like your husband. Hardworking. The main money earner.
Probably would be honest all the time, too, if it weren't for you.'
Luther gave Michelle a dirty look, catching a glance from her.
'Perhaps...' Luther grinned. 'Perhaps I ought to take you back with
me. Or maybe even teach you manners right here.' He looked over
her. 'Though you are getting on a bit.'

She looked down at the table, avoiding eye contact with him. Aiden glimpsed the guards standing in the lounge and focused back on his glass of water that sat on the table. One of the guards still held her handgun.

'Eye contact tends to be a thing, you know, Michelle, when people are talking to you. Perhaps you don't get out the house much,' Luther sneered and put the cuffs away. 'Might pop in tomorrow for some more tea and questions, so I expect better service next time. I feel so sorry for you, Aiden. It's good to know you've got my back, though.' Luther patted his shoulder, making him flinch. 'If I hear any more news, I will be sure to update you.' He walked towards the front door. Aiden's face still stared at the glass in front of him while the guards left the lounge and followed Luther back outside.

Luther grinned, knowing he had stirred up trouble between the couple. His mind dwelt on the three cups of tea that remained untouched on the table. Luther had no intention of coming back. He turned to the two guards.

'Dock your extra hours on the books, and I'll make sure you're paid well for them.' Luther got into the back of his car and pulled out his notebook. Learning about Heather would prove to be of some fun.

CHAPTER 13 – SHELBY

Shelby spent his time away from the crew, rarely venturing out of his room. The safety Hermann promised felt weak when he thought back to what had happened with Jason – he had ignored the shouts from his crew. It stood to reason that the rest of the crew, if given the chance, would do the same.

The mission remained a mystery to Shelby. He presumed Hermann hid the details from him due to him being an outsider, but after overhearing conversations around the ship, it appeared that no one knew the destination. Scavenging kept being brought up and that made sense enough to Shelby considering how he'd met them.

According to Hermann, their destination remained only a day away, and with it, the arrival back to land. Shelby lay on the bed, dwelling on Mia and Kai. Once off the ship, he stood a better chance of escaping.

On the floor above, shouting broke out, disturbing his trail of thought. He gazed at the ceiling. Several arguments had broken out since he'd been onboard, some regarding himself. The voices were drowned out by several heavy footsteps that then carried the shouting away. Silence followed, before the argument found its way back into the room. Shelby stood up and listened, fearful the fight might be about him.

'... can't be serious? I never signed up for this,' a man's voice rumbled through his thick accent. 'That stuff outside ain't natural.'

'You will do what is required. You are a mercenary, are you not?' Hermann met the reply coolly.

'Aye, I am, but going past the Eastern Belt was not part of the deal. You know the stories.' His anger lessened, but kept its weight.

Though Shelby took little interest in maps, he still knew of the Eastern Belt: the last edge of land before the earth had cracked open and fallen away.

'Really? You can't tell me you believe that shit. I'm disappointed, I truly am. Though I'm not sure if I mentioned the extra pay that you'll be receiving for this,' Hermann said with disinterest, creating a short and sudden silence.

'It'll have to be double pay, not some extra clap on the back. Otherwise, I'll not be leaving this rust bucket of a ship,' the man snarled.

'Oh, good, because your pay will be triple your usual rate, so plenty to keep your mouths shut I gather?' It fell silent again. 'Glad we finally got there. Now, if you'll excuse me, I need to thin out the creases with a few other members, too.' Hermann's heavy footsteps moved away, leaving the voices to grumble among themselves.

Shelby sat on the bed, failing to recall any of the maps he had previously seen. He had little interest in places outside of Lornsten. Hearing the commotion made him question what had caused it and, if it had distracted and disrupted the crew, he was keen to take another glance at the top deck.

With the opportunity, Shelby left his room, hoping the crew would be too absorbed in themselves and their money to show him any attention. He made his way up the stairs, passing two of the members, who ignored him, before the door that led onto the deck swung open.

'You're in for a real treat,' a bloke scorned upon seeing him and carried on through the doorway, passing him. Shelby returned a half-blank stare, uncertain of what he meant.

Out on the deck ahead, Shelby realised most of the crew were there, still discussing the topic with Hermann. His heart jumped at the growing number of them, but to his relief, they took no interest in him moving across the deck. He kept to one side and noticed a handful of small rowing boats sitting down the sides of the ship. Shelby glanced around. Then he understood what had caused the dispute, seeing most of the members looking at it.

In the distance, dark shards of rock splintered out of the water between small scatters of land. The shapes sent a shiver down Shelby's spine. He'd never seen something so sharp and unnatural before.

'Quite something, isn't it?' Hermann approached. 'Ever been out this way?'

'No.' Shelby still stared at the rocks. 'I've never left home. This is far east of where I live, I'm guessing?'

'North-east,' he replied, pulling out a small hand-drawn map. 'We are roughly here.' He pointed. 'And we picked you up there. Quite the trip, eh?' Hermann laughed.

The few bits of land sparked Shelby's attention, with the chance of escaping becoming real.

'Can I?' Shelby held his hand out for the map, unsure if Hermann would allow him to look closer.

'Oh, sure. Don't suppose you're one for geography, are you? More of a small-time farmer, right?' Hermann grinned, handing the map over.

'Pretty much.' Shelby let out a small chuckle, cautious about how he should react.

He felt Hermann watching him. Shelby began to realise the distance between his home and the ship as he scanned the map in his hand.

Several shouts came from within the ship, making him turn and exchange glances with Hermann, who still stood beside him.

'Keep that one. I've got a wad of them inside. Now, if you'll excuse me.' Hermann raised his sweaty brow and headed towards the noise, his cane alerting the crew of his approach.

Shelby returned his gaze to the sea then looked over the map again. The eastern side of the continent drawn on the map appeared fractured, much like the shards of rocks out at sea. To the west, the land became whole again, and at the other end, he read the name of Lornsten.

He looked up from the map again, searching the horizon for the mainland between the rocky shards. The more he stared at the shards, the more unnatural they looked. Shelby knew the common knowledge that the old world had destroyed itself in a war, but anything more than that remained of little interest to him in his daily life.

'Well, no one bothered to tell me where we were heading. Wankers. The lot of them.' Victor appeared beside him, his voice shaken. 'Now I fully understand the need for all the outfits and gear.' He leant against the railing on the side of the ship. 'We shouldn't be doing this.'

'Doesn't look like a wholesome or friendly place.' Shelby folded the map up and leant against the railing with him.

Victor turned to face him, bewildered at his comment.

'You have heard of this place, right?' His voice tightened.

'Not really,' Shelby replied.

'This place is past the Eastern Belt.' He studied Shelby's face.

'Past it?' Shelby had never given it much thought. 'Assumed there was nothing there, which looks about right from here.'

'What?' Victor shook his head. 'Oh, there's land alright, I assure you. It's called the Forbidden Zone, and it's off-limits for being a toxic and dangerous wasteland.' His words had sharpened.

'What makes it so forbidden?' Shelby asked, returning a blank stare, having never heard of the place.

Victor's eyes widened beneath his glasses. 'What's forbidden?' He frowned. 'The place is unnatural and full of a lingering toxic haze. It's said to eat you from the inside out, if you breathe it in. You'll learn about it all soon enough, I'm sure, now it's open knowledge to everyone on the ship. Most stories tend to be embellished a bit no doubt, so who knows what we'll find out when we anchor.' He turned to the sea. 'And that's without the Legion.'

The information played on Shelby's mind. He had never been one for tall stories or chatter, so decided not to pursue his curiosity further.

'Never taken much interest in travelling or knowing other people's business.' Shelby smiled. 'I find it's less complicated that way. Just have my family and me to worry about, and that's it.' Unease took hold of him, unsure if mentioning family was a smart idea.

'I'm guessing that keeping to yourself where you've been living is an easy task. Where I'm from, it's far harder to keep it that way. Before you know it, you've been dragged into something... like this.' Victor looked around at the deck. 'Anyway, I need to crack on. Got to ensure the radiation gauges, masks and coats are fully repaired and usable now, seeing that the possibility of using them has just been guaranteed. Feel free to pop down to my office if you fancy helping.' He flashed a smile and headed inside.

Now alone, Shelby focused on Victor's words. He unfolded the map and glanced at it again, looking at the settlements listed on it and then to the north-east where 'The Forbidden Zone' had been labelled across a huge chunk of land whose eastern coastline was fractured and broken. It was joined to the rest of the continent only by the mountain range to the north, the Eastern Belt – a huge ravine – separating the lower reaches of the area from the rest of the land mass.

On the west side of the continent, he spotted Lornsten again on the coastline. He faced back out to sea, seeing the disfigured terrain gradually move by. Shelby felt a long way from home.

CHAPTER 14 – ZARA

They spent the night walking in silence as they trekked through the darkness. Eve had packed what she could into the three bags hunched over herself, with a one-wheeled case in her hand. Zara offered to help carry something, but Eve dismissed this and got her to bring extra water instead.

Thoughts of home lingered in Zara's mind, desperation beginning to take hold. Though she might have owed her life to the woman, relying on Eve made her nervous. They had scarcely spoken since she had killed the man. The death had set Zara in a constant state of paranoia about meeting others while she was with Eve, and what the old woman might do to them. Regardless of Eve's reaction, Zara needed to discuss the concept of her leaving.

'Eve?' she asked softly.

'Yeah?' Eve turned in the darkness and gave a strained smile under the weight of her bags.

'I... I need to get home.' Zara's throat tightened with a tremble.

'Oh, I know you do,' Eve replied bluntly. 'You don't belong here.'

The words made Zara uncomfortable. A brief and erratic image of Eve trying to kill her flashed in her head.

'You're too good for this place, Zara. You'll get yourself killed far too easily. Need more of a backbone,' Eve spat.

'I, uh…' Zara frowned, unsure whether to be thankful at the comment, though she was happy Eve seemed to agree she shouldn't stay. 'So where are we going? Some other place that you've been to before? A safe place?'

Eve laughed. 'Where you need to go ain't no safe place. Funny to think about it, though… to get to your perfect little safe place, you gotta go through a dangerous place first.' Eve seemed disgusted. 'Why that just ain't right, is it? Damn Legion. Anyway, I'm taking you to a bridge. Leads to the other side, so I hear.' Eve smiled. 'Though I've not actually been up to it myself, just heard of it. Another day or two of walking, I'd say.' Eve shifted the bags on her back. 'Here, would you mind?' She held one out. 'Change of heart. I best use you while I can,' she cackled.

****

The sun began to rise, bringing daylight into the surrounding dead forest they stopped in. Zara noticed a mist accompanied dawn, which Eve assured her was regular mist. They sat on the floor beside a row of old tree trunks that marked a clear edge to the forest.

'Perfect weather for a stop, that's for sure,' Eve said calmly, preparing something to eat. 'Low visibility is always a welcome thing, day or night.'

'So how often is it you run into people?' Zara looked around warily through the mist, still fearful.

'Could have sworn we had this conversation,' Eve groaned. 'Used to be maybe once every month this close to the line, but was becoming less frequent till you showed up. I hadn't seen anyone for quite some time, and now within the space of two days, I've bumped into two people. Feels like I'm back in town again with all the people knockin' around.' Eve shook her head. Zara stared at the ground, her mind slipping back to Trent.

'These people. My people. We aren't like you, Zara,' Eve said, raising her voice. 'There ain't no guilt in my actions. It was either him killing you, and then me killing him, or just me killing him before he got the chance to kill you. There ain't no way I was gonna have your death playing on my mind, which is why you need to get out. The sooner, the better,' she croaked, her eyes glistening.

Unsure of what to say, Zara kept quiet. Knowing Eve wanted her gone as much as she herself wanted to be gone gave her relief. The man's death gnawed at her mind, and Eve's choice of killing him still felt unjustified considering he only wanted water.

'We'll walk till we find a good place to stop,' Eve said after finishing her meal. 'Heading up this way in broad daylight ain't the smartest of ideas. Sure, there shouldn't be any people knockin' about, but where we are now, there are more reasons to hide in the daylight than to be out in the open with it.'

Zara kept silent and decided not to ask any further questions.

****

The mist cleared after they had been walking for another hour, and as it receded Zara and Eve heard a gentle clanging noise through the trees. They altered their direction to investigate where the noise was coming from.

A road cut through the forest. The noise had grown to a loud but still gentle clink. Next to the road stood a line of old houses, facing them. Zara spotted something small and shiny swaying on one of the porches, still making the noise.

'Looks good to me.' Eve sounded relieved. 'We'll stay here for a bit.'

'That one seems alright.' Zara pointed to the most intact house at the end, shielded by a hill. Although she presumed Eve had spotted it, she wanted to be of some use to her.

'Nope, not that one,' Eve replied.

The abrupt shutdown made Zara drop her head, shaking it in disbelief.

'It's good, but that's the exact reason we shouldn't go for it.' Eve smiled weakly. 'Have a guess at which one someone else is likely to stay in?' Eve scrunched her face. 'See. Best we go for the one in the middle with the noisy metal thing. That one there looks stable enough and still has two floors.'

Nodding in agreement, Zara felt more useless than ever.

Both of them sat between the trees and waited, ensuring no one else was around. Everything remained still and quiet, apart from the chime moving in the breeze.

'It's a windchime,' Zara spoke softly, 'the thing making the noise.'

'Never heard of it.' Eve shook her head and stood up, leaving her bags on the ground. 'Stay here with my bags while I give it a going over.' Eve pulled out her gun and crossed over the road, entering into the end house.

Several minutes passed, making Zara anxious at the lack of signs from her. Eventually, the woman appeared at the other end of the houses, waving her across.

'Seems safe,' Eve said in a hushed tone. Zara crossed the road, passing a couple of bags to her. 'Least, it doesn't look like anyone's been here for a good while.' Eve smiled. 'Cut that down, would ya? If we heard it, someone else might.'

Zara collected up the rest of the bags and put them by the front door on the porch. She pulled out her small switchblade and stared at the windchime gently swinging in the wind. Zara wondered how long it might have been there for. She reached up and cut it down in one piece. The metal had rusted, and the glass had turned to a tint of green. Crouching for a moment, Zara placed it down on the floor, careful not to make a noise.

She picked the bags back up and headed straight upstairs to the room Eve had chosen. They wedged some old furniture in front of the doorway so they'd be able to hear if any intruders attempted to get in.

'Well, time to get some shut-eye,' Eve mumbled, spreading out some old blankets on the floor. Zara lay down on one, a little distance away from Eve.

The room looked out from the front of the house, a single window letting light pour over the wooden floor.

'Tap me on the shoulder if you need me,' Eve said, turning away from her.

****

A few hours passed before Zara woke. She bolted upright after remembering where she was sleeping. Eve sat on a chair facing the window. Zara stood up and stretched, trying to stay quiet, unsure if Eve was awake. Her stomach rumbled.

'Probably is about that time, I suppose,' Eve muttered. 'Glad you got some rest.'

'Did you?' Zara asked, feeling she'd overslept.

'Don't worry about me, I've had plenty. Never like it used to be, though.' Eve sighed. 'Don't think I was always like this, you know. Killing ain't nice, I know it. But out here... out here it's needed.' She let out another sigh. 'Least that's what I tell myself.'

It went silent between them.

'I... I understand.' Zara tried her best to sound convinced before Eve interrupted.

'That's the thing. You don't. You come from a good place by the sounds of it. Got plenty of food, water, and don't have to decide whether to flee or kill the next person you meet.' She sounded bitter. 'You've not had to live it day after day. It's a way of life, my way of life. Trust a stranger like that man and you'll be as good as dead the minute you turn away from him. It ain't worth the chance.'

Another length of silence settled between them. Zara began to feel shameful about her own life back home.

'You know, you could always come back with me. You'd have plenty of everything and meet people who are often friendly,' Zara said, unsure of the reaction. Bringing her home would be difficult, but it was an offer she wanted to make. Thankfully for Zara, Eve seemed lost in thought.

A few more minutes of silence passed before Eve replied.

'I've missed my chance on that one.' Her voice fell low and heavy. 'I made my choice a long time ago.'

'Whatever choice you made, you don't have to stick by it. Why would you stay?' Zara asked. 'My home could be yours just as much.'

'Why go? Ain't no place for me on your side, I just know it. And you know it, too. Reckon I'd fit in with everyone, do ya? I think not. Only person worth trusting is yourself,' Eve bit back. 'This is my home. Always has been, always will be.' She let out a long sigh. 'Now, we best get something to eat and then head off.' She got up and started searching through one of her bags.

Zara knew it was true. Eve would likely cause more trouble than anything else. She moved to one of the bags and started to help her prepare a meal.

CHAPTER 15 – LUTHER

He hit the alarm on his bedside cabinet, causing the woman beside him to murmur. Sitting up out of bed, he took little notice of her, fixing his mind on the day ahead.

Luther flicked through his notebook before suiting up for the day, deciding to wear his armour and cuffs again with the usual beige suit. After the entertainment he'd enjoyed last night, Luther began to feel like he had forgotten about something. The excitement still lingered around him, though it would soon disappear with the day ahead.

'Tea?' he called out, walking over to his desk to switch the kettle on.

Another stir came from the covers, but he received no answer.

'Whore!' Luther shouted.

The woman jumped up, pulling the covers off to face him.

'Sorry,' he said casually. 'I was asking if you'd like tea?'

She narrowed her eyes at him. 'Such a gentleman, aren't you, Luther? Yes, tea, please.' Her eyes rolled before she lay back down.

Smiling, Luther turned around and started brewing the tea. He had always liked Bonnie. The woman knew her business.

'With that new girl you have, you should be grateful I requested you.' Luther glanced at her in the mirror and waited for an angered reply.

Bonnie behaved with the right amount of feistiness in her, which he had grown to love over the years, but more importantly, she respected him.

'Oh, please. I don't think I'll ever get rid of you. I'm your old favourite toy,' Bonnie teased.

He let out an audible sigh. She was certainly older and always knew how to please him, though he would never let her know it.

'You might be my favourite, but you're still replaceable,' Luther replied with a grin, finishing making her tea. He decided not to bring up the behaviour of Bonnie's newest girl, wanting to keep the mood light.

'Fuck you.' She sat up in bed and stared at him with a slight curl to her lip.

He picked up the small black and gold teacup and passed it over to her.

'Anyway, I'm off to make sure this city stays secure and safe so you're able to keep doing what you do best.' He leant over and kissed her.

'Oh, my hero,' Bonnie replied, kissing him back.

Luther turned and headed for the door.

'There's a little extra silver for you on the table.' He winked, closing the door behind him.

Down the hall, he found Ruben sitting in front of the television screen where he had left him the day before, the tapes still playing.

'You going to tell me you've been up all night?' Luther asked, surprised to find Ruben already up and working. The man had seemed far from keen on watching over the tapes the previous day.

'Don't worry, I've had a kip. Woke up about an hour ago. Good news is I've found our two engineers leaving. The station camera caught them. Patterson seems to know the bloke, judging by their expressions. Headed out six days ago, or seven now, I suppose. Want me to show you?' Ruben stood, picking up a tape.

'Yeah, go on. Would be handy to get the faces of these two.' Luther sat down on the arm of the chair beside the seat Ruben had just vacated. On a typical day he would have sat in the chair Ruben had been sitting in, but considering his own mood and that Ruben had found the two missing workers, he decided not to annoy the man for now.

Ruben swapped the tapes in the player and sat back down, rewinding the footage with the remote control.

'Around about here, I think… There. The older chap and a young girl.'

'Matches the loose description we have of our holidaymakers then, along with the stuff I discovered from her parents last night.' Luther got out his notebook.

'Scared them to death or charmed your way through them?' Ruben asked, keeping his eyes on the tele.

Luther let out an unexpected laugh. 'Both, actually. Charmed the man, scared the woman.'

'Usually goes the other way around.' Ruben raised a brow and smiled, catching Luther off guard again.

Adjusting his eyes, Luther looked around the room and stared at Ruben, who fixed his gaze back on the tele. Luther reasoned his bold words must have been down to his lack of sleep.

'It does, but the mother was being a total bitch. Avoiding the truth for some petty personal reason. Apparently, this headache of a daughter they have causes them problems anyway. Who would have guessed? Still, choosing their daughter over the security of the city is disrespectful. The father had his senses, though they both seemed ungrateful. Perhaps I came off a little too strong.' Luther laughed.

'Can't say I've ever noticed you do that,' Ruben replied. 'Anyway, there's a meeting this morning in an hour.'

Luther twitched. Ruben rarely made jokes, but at the current rate, it was starting to sound disrespectful. Luther swallowed the comment, intent on keeping his mood light for the day.

'Eh, I'll give it a miss. All they'll do is kill my mood.' Luther stood up. 'To the station?' His mind moved to Patterson, the ticket officer. If the man knew the missing couple, he might have information on them.

'Sure.' Ruben ejected the tape from the player and put it on the stack of others. 'Want to return these?'

'Not sure I can be bothered.' Luther gave a brief look at them, not wanting to waste time in his cheery mood.

'Leave it to me.' Ruben picked them up and left the room. 'See you out front.'

The man's newfound keenness for work and wit seeped scepticism into Luther's mind, even if it meant less work for himself. He switched off the television and headed for the main entrance. Luther stepped down the grand staircase, careful not to make too much noise on the marble. Four guards stood inside the entrance, smiling at his approach.

'Morning, sir,' one of the guards said, with the others nodding.

'Morning,' Luther replied, sharing a smile with the man.

The guards opened up the two large doors ahead of him, allowing him to exit outside. Stone steps led further down to the road, a handful of guards stationed outside the building. On appearance, Luther had made the front look open, trustworthy and safe for the public, with minimal security on display. He felt it helped give the illusion that any member of the public could walk in. In reality, the procedure he had put in place only allowed committee members through the front entrance, with all other workers, such as Ruben, having to use smaller side doors where searches were in place.

****

The car pulled up outside Central Station. Luther picked up the correct tapes and got out, leaving Ruben in the front. Patterson sat in his small ticket office beside the platform.

'Pat, my man, I've got one tape back for you. Sorry if it's throwing you out of routine. I've kept one just for the time being but will return it soon.' Luther smiled, placing the tape onto the counter.

'Luther.' Patterson looked up and revealed his gummy smile. 'Was they of any help?'

'Oh, yes, yes, they helped very much, thank you. I actually needed to ask you a question or two about something else.' Luther paused for a second, before realising Pat might take the opportunity to start on another one of his stories.

'You see, maintenance has been on at me for ensuring the tracks are kept clean, and well...' Luther stopped at the visible confusion now spreading across Pat's face.

'Why they got you doing this? You're security.' Pat adjusted his glasses.

'Ah yes, well...' Luther leaned in closer and spoke almost in a whisper. 'We've got some information that might prove to be a security threat concerning the track. I can't say much more. I need to find someone with more experience than me on the matter.' Luther dropped his smile, causing Pat to imitate him. 'You know anyone?'

'Course I do.' His eyes lit up. He replied in a hushed tone, 'I know just the man, very knowledgeable indeed. Almost old as me, too, though, yes, he is much more knowledgeable than myself here.' Pat slowly twisted his chair around and pulled out some files from a drawer, making Luther's patience fade.

Luther was tempted to simply ask for the details he needed directly. But the footage found on the tapes showed Pat behaving in a friendly way with at least one of the missing workers, so he wanted to avoid the old man getting too emotional by telling him his friends were dead. Pat would be of no use after that, and at his age, the news might kill him. Luther thought caution might be the best approach first.

'Want me to fetch him for you?' Pat turned back and placed a book down on the counter, flicking through the pages. 'He should be in the train yard.'

'Oh, yes, that would be great,' Luther replied, his mood dropping at the words, knowing Pat must be thinking of someone else. 'I'm not wasting too much of your time, am I?' He now wished he had requested the file on the Trent character upfront. He felt time had started to waste.

Pat struggled up from his chair and came out of the office, leaving his door open behind him.

'Usually over here, if he's about.' Pat smiled, eventually moving past Luther.

Luther eyed the open door of the office. At the rate the old man was walking, Luther would be in and out of there before he could turn around, though he expected Trent's work file would be of little use considering Jetson had already given him the most complete one.

Pat had stopped moving. 'You alright?' Luther called.

'Bugger,' Pat mumbled, turning back around. 'I just remembered, he ain't here. Not been in for a week, maybe.'

'Ah.' Luther gave a sincere look. *Good.* 'When will he be back?'

'Hmm, not sure. Last time I saw him he was heading to Crossover – where he lives – with a young girl. A bit too young, if you ask me. Can't say I thought he was like that, though.' He paused. 'Friends maybe. Anyway, I think they were heading off somewhere after that. She was excited to see the coast, I remember that. All excited and such. Don't think she really understands how dangerous it is out there. It's definitely not for me. Anyway, none of my business, I guess.' Pat gradually headed back to his office. 'Want one of the younger chaps to help you out? Some of them ain't too bad, you know.'

'No, thank you, I'll wait for your friend.' Luther walked back with him. 'Did he say where he was going? What's his name?'

'Hmm.' Pat entered his office and sat back down. The old man looked grave. 'Trent's his name. Now, I do know it, where he was heading, but I reckon he wanted to keep it on the quiet side, you see. Asked me not to tell no one, but I know that you being security an' all, he wouldn't mind it. That place on the coast, the one with the colourful lights.'

'Russet?' Luther knew the place strung small coloured lights about their town.

'That'll be the one. Gone there, you see, could be a little honeymoon for him and the girl. Wanted to keep it quiet. See, he was lonely after his wife and all that,' Pat whispered. 'Probably be back in a couple weeks, I reckon. So afraid getting the security thing done here won't be possible for you.' He pulled a worried face. 'I can get you another one of our engineers for the track? They're good at it, you know.'

'It can wait, Pat, don't worry yourself. I'll monitor the situation for now, but if you could notify me when he returns, that would be great. What's his surname?'

'Uh, just Trent. Nothin' else to his name. Not many train engineers to get confused over I'd say anyway,' Patterson replied.

'Ah, fair point. Well, it was good seeing you again, Patterson.' Luther turned away.

'Well, alright, sorry I wasn't much help.' Patterson picked up the files and went to twist in his chair.

'Oh, actually...' Luther stopped walking. 'What did the girl look like?'

The footage Ruben had found on tape was blurry but matched the rough descriptions on Jetson's files. Zara had stood further from the camera than Trent in his overalls.

'The young girl?' Pat sounded curious.

'Yes, the young one.'

'Well, she was quite pale, had short dark hair and was young, of course.' He cleared his throat. 'Young man like yourself might be better suited to her perhaps, much more than Trent. She was wearing a leather jacket, which isn't standard work uniform, though it was their holiday, I guess. Come to think of it, Trent shoulda really wore something else. Changed back home maybe.' He paused. 'Can't say much else. You know, I've always liked the girls with shorter hair. Gets in the way less, you—'

'I see.' Luther nodded. 'Yes, I quite agree. Notify me when she gets back, too, would you? Been a while since I've had a proper date.' Luther gave a wink. 'Anyway, got to run.' He turned away and pulled out his notebook again, the faded circular pattern on the front catching in the sunlight.

'Ah, alright, will do. Lucky girl, I'd say, if she ain't with Trent.' Pat mumbled on. 'The whole thing just isn't right, I tell you, far too much of a difference for anything serious.'

Luther's high mood started to sink as he turned the conversation over in his mind. He had forgotten that Trent had lived in Crossover, and it now seemed inevitable that his investigation would lead there. His skin crawled at the idea of leaving the city for the wasteland outside. Luther toyed with forcing Ruben to go in his place.

Sitting back in the car, he sighed. 'Well, it looks as if I'll be heading out to Crossover.'

'Want to drop the tapes off or head back?' Ruben replied.

'Take me back to headquarters. Need to talk with Jetson, considering I missed the meeting this morning.' Luther felt irritable, unsure what good would come from the head of security taking off to a farming town.

'Sure, I'll drop you back first and then return the rest of the tapes after, sir,' Ruben said.

****

On arriving back at Carbon Assembly, Luther summoned Jetson into the meeting room, the prospect of visiting Crossover lingering in his mind. Jetson entered a minute later, closing the doors behind him.

'Missed the meeting this morning.' His mouth was tight, and accompanied by a reddish glow in his face. 'So, what have you managed to find with your newfound time? Are these missing holidaymakers to do with this... mess of a situation?' Jetson stood at the opposite end of the table from where Luther sat.

'Learnt quite a lot actually, so keep your head on.' Luther retained his composure. 'The two missing holidaymakers left the city for Russet together, seven days ago. I've obtained security footage from Central Station that shows them leaving.' Luther paused, seeing Jetson's face relax.

'Good. That is good.' He nodded.

'Good?' Luther raised a brow at him taking it so well. 'I thought we were hoping it was a thief with a stolen uniform?'

Jetson's eyes widened before he buried his head in his hands.

'Fuck. No, that isn't good. But, I mean, shit. We have proof they're acting alone, though, right?' Jetson trembled.

'I suppose... if Trittle decides to buy it. Though, let's not forget there are two of them, and only the guy, if it is this guy, was found and killed,' Luther replied, still staring at him. 'Anyway, according to my sources, they got off at Crossover, where this possible dead guy lived, which was also stated in those files you gave me this morning.' Luther leaned back in his chair.

'At least that works out.' Jetson lifted his head. 'This morning's meeting was about actively displaying our presence more, and with this news, it feels like the right move. We don't want Trittle and their Legion thinking we are weak. I assume you'll be travelling to Crossover? Two regiments with you, I reckon?' Jetson sat down on one of the chairs. 'An act of confidence if you head out, yes. This relationship we have with them needs to last, Luther, especially considering our project.'

Luther wanted to cut in, but the man continued.

'How did the interrogation go?' Jetson gave a sly smile, but Luther returned only a blank face, knowing he had deliberately changed the subject.

'It went well. Charm and threats go hand in hand. Pitted them against each other. I told them their daughter might be dead, which soon got them behaving.' Luther kept his tone professional. 'Now, Crossover.'

'Yes, how long will it take to group up two regiments' worth of our regulars?' Jetson spoke quickly.

There was little reason for Luther to refuse going out to Crossover, and Jetson knew it. To do otherwise might make him appear like less of a man, not something he intended Jetson to think. He bit his lip.

'I'll notify them today, but it'll probably take until this evening or tomorrow morning if I'm to do it without taking any of the city guards.'

'Sounds good. Don't really want to be taking them for the moment, do we?' Jetson's eyes widened and he gave a small laugh.

'Everything alright?' Luther noticed his nerves. 'Seems you got the better deal here with me having to handle Crossover and its stench.'

'Oh, well yes, I know. It's just that the talk of this body is getting around town now, and we're yet to make a public statement on the issue.'

'Fuck what the public think. Seriously? We own the newspaper. Just print some shit story about it.' Luther could hardly believe what he was hearing.

'Yes, but what Trittle thinks does matter.' Jetson sighed. 'We don't have the sort of soldiers they do, Luther, or armour or weaponry, we both know that.'

'For now. Within a month, things might have changed.' Luther wanted to believe his words. 'Just label our missing people as traitors. We have their possible names now and what they look like. It'll keep everyone happy and break any silly notion we're involved with the dead body at the dam.' Luther felt the plan would shut him up. 'Print it on the front page, perhaps.'

Jetson eyed him. 'You know, that isn't actually a bad idea.'

'Saying I don't have good ideas often?' Luther folded his arms.

'No, I'm just saying' – Jetson's voice hardened – 'that sometimes your ideas are a little unsavoury, that's all.'

'I think only about the greatness of this city, not the people in it.' Luther stood up. 'I'll let you know how I get on at Crossover. Just keep calm, alright?'

'Easy for you to say,' Jetson snapped. Luther twitched at the reply. The whole ordeal seemed to have produced a headache for more than himself.

'Give it time.' Luther stood up and moved passed Jetson, patting him on the shoulder. He headed to his office where he expected to find Ruben, but found him gone. Luther searched outside the front entrance to see if his car remained parked, but to his irritation, that was missing, too. *Odd.*

He pulled out his notebook and flicked through it, finding he still needed to check the cameras at the engineering headquarters. Luther lifted his head and looked down the street. Few people filled the roads and pavements, with most still at work, much to his relief. A short walk would give him time to reflect on his plans for Crossover and what to tell Heather, who would be waiting for him.

CHAPTER 16 – SHELBY

Another day passed before the ship finally anchored. Between the breaks in the mist, Shelby kept seeing the coastline, deformed, with no trees or greenery in sight. It differed vastly from the coastal area back at home. Even the water looked unnatural, masking its depth in darkness, without a hint of blue or green. He doubted any fish survived in the murky waters.

Shelby stood on the top deck with the rest of the crew, wearing his trench coat and keeping his mask and filter in one of the inside pockets. Everyone wore their lead-lined coats, with some wearing their masks already. Victor had announced that the surrounding mist was normal, but gave up trying to convince people when some of the crew began to give him grief.

Hermann appeared on the deck, leaning against his cane. 'Alright, men and women. Now, I know some of you aren't happy about where we are. It's not ideal, sure, but you also know why we had to keep the location a secret. You were all selected because of your skills with tracking, killing and treasure hunting. Your home needs you, and for that, we are paying you very handsomely.' Hermann beamed. 'But we all have to remember that *we were never here*. None of us have ever been here, and most of us don't even know where here is, even if someone were to mention it to you. Got it?'

The crew murmured in agreement.

'Now, because we have been entrusted with this vitally important project, your superior has allowed me to take these' – Hermann gestured to two men behind him – 'rather nice weapons from our home armouries.'

The two men rolled out some material on the floor, revealing an array of guns that were wrapped in it. An excited buzz came from the crew as they gawked over the weapons.

'To be clear, we do not want our presence to be known. If you see someone, either stay out of sight or kill them. Too much gunfire, however, may travel to unwanted ears. If those bastard Legions find out we've been here, you can be sure they'll rip us a new one. If they do happen upon us, we'll have to kill them all without witnesses, hence these guns. Understood?'

The crew all replied in agreement as they approached the weapons laid across the floor.

'Now, now, no fighting over them, we're on the same team,' Hermann mocked, seeing a few of the members try to grab the same gun. 'Anyway, I expect we shall be finding more when we're back on land, so there's no need for everyone to have a gun. Just be sure to spread them out evenly.'

'Uh, so...' a voice stuttered from the crowd.

'So, what are we looking for?' another voice cut in.

'Good question. This is where Victor comes in.' Hermann turned to Victor, who was standing beside Shelby.

Both of them looked at Hermann, a few paces from the crowd.

'Victor here isn't just for fixing our gear. Oh, no. Some of you may already know that he is an expert in old-age antiques and other various items. Sure, he isn't like the rest of you.' Hermann grinned. 'But he is of great value because he will find what we're looking for.' Hermann moved over towards Victor and placed an arm on his shoulder. 'Better get geared up soon. You're the VIP of this trip.'

'We agreed back in the city I'd stay on board the—'

'Last time we stopped' – Hermann glanced at Shelby – 'you were quite keen to get off, Victor. A sudden change of heart, have we now?'

The crew let off a laugh, some still busy taking weapons.

'There isn't a mask left for me,' Victor bit back.

'Oh, don't worry, I shall be staying here with the ship captain, so you'll be able to take either his or mine, though I'm betting his one will fit better,' Hermann bellowed and patted his belly, making the crew laugh again. Victor looked in shock.

'We'll look after his lanky arse!' a woman shouted.

'No doubt you will.' Hermann nodded. 'Anyway, I don't think there will be many, if any, people around here.' He pulled out a large map and pinned it up against one of the doors. 'We are located here, roughly, and you all need to make your way up to this abandoned city here.' He placed one of his thick fingers on the map. 'There should be an old military base, which Victor will be able to recognise. Bring back all the weapons you can and keep an eye out for any unusual ones, too – the sort we might only dream of.' He raised his sweaty brow. 'Think big. That's what we want.' Hermann signalled to get the boats ready for lowering into the water. 'Be sure to take one of these backpacks here. Each is packed with some provisions for your journey, along with a map and space for your own loot.'

Shelby tried soaking it all in, getting to grips with the number of guns around him. He needed to get home. The crew lowered three of the boats down into the water. On deck, he counted over twenty people making up the entire group – an assortment of men and women, all rough and hardy looking. Their clothes were a mixture of crude armour and clothing, mostly overlaid with the lead-lined coats Victor had given out.

'Into the boat now, lad,' a man with a heavy accent boomed. 'I'm in charge now since Hermann isn't moving his fat arse off this ship. The name's Roy.' The man with a thick ginger beard that matched his short rugged hair stuck his hand out.

'I'm Shelby.' Shelby shook the proffered hand after a second of hesitation. He recognised the voice as the bloke who had argued with Hermann the previous day.

'Aye, I know that. Seems you're here because you owe us a favour. Well, the quicker we get this job done, the quicker you'll be heading back home.' Roy glanced towards Hermann, who now stood on the other side of the deck, observing a boat being lowered into the water. 'Victor, you're in this one with me, come on.'

Now wearing one of the lead-lined coats, Victor made his way over and kept silent.

'Don't be sulking now. You're a grown man. Nothing scary out there besides a bit of yellow shite.' Roy stared at the second boat being lowered down with some of the crew onboard. 'You don't have to be wearing your masks now, fucking idiots. It's just mist,' he shouted, shaking his head. 'You're wasting your filters.'

'I didn't sign up for this,' Victor brooded.

'Neither did he.' Roy nodded at Shelby. 'Don't hear him complaining, though, do you? I didn't sign up for this place specifically either, and neither did the rest of the crew. So, shut it.' Roy got into the boat with Victor and some others, choosing to sit beside Shelby. The boat gently lowered into the calm dark waters surrounding the ship.

The mist followed close behind the boats as they rowed towards land, making them lose sight of the ship. After ten minutes, they reached the coastline and pulled the boats ashore. The land looked oddly smooth compared to the shards of broken rock and rubble surrounding them.

The dark surface beneath Shelby's feet reminded him of Lornsten and felt familiar. *A road.* His eyes followed it inland and then the other way, back down under his feet where it sank into the ocean.

'That'll be our path to follow,' Roy called out, lugging the backpacks off of his boat. 'You fuckers gonna just stare, or help?' He chucked the bags towards the crew, turning to get the rest out of the boat. 'This old road should lead us right to the city we want, providing the maps are accurate.' He dragged a backpack over to Shelby. 'All got to share the load. Food, tents and the like.' Roy strapped one of the bags over his shoulder, picked up a gun from the boat and loaded it; it was a two-handed weapon with a large round barrel on one side. Rifles made of wood and metal were the only guns Shelby had used back home, and they looked far less clunky than the one Roy was holding, though Shelby guessed this one packed more of a punch.

'Right, we all ready?' Roy called out, getting a few nods and shouts of agreement in return. 'Good. The group you came with on your rowing boat is the group you'll be sticking with. Erma is in charge of one, and, uh, I forgot what lot was in the third boat. You'll sort out who's in charge, I'm sure.' Roy started walking down the road, leaving the third group to shout and squabble with each other.

The road stretched four times wider than the ones back home and the actual surface appeared smooth. Being back on land with a map rekindled Shelby's idea of escaping at the first chance.

A sudden shunt almost pushed him over.

'Come on, murderer, get a move on,' a man spat from behind. The bloke had a pointed chin and a long deep scar down the side of his face. 'We don't want to be dragging your body just yet.'

Shelby quickened his pace at once, passing most of the crew, and caught up with Victor who was walking beside Roy at the front.

'Can't say I'd like to be you right now,' Victor said, keeping his face staring straight ahead.

'Staring at the road for too long,' Shelby replied.

'Doubt it. Give them a reason and they'll use it,' Victor replied honestly. 'One with the scar was Jason's mate. Another friendly tracker who has more reason than most to want you dead.'

With the crew now behind him, an uncomfortable feeling of being watched edged into Shelby's mind.

'Jason was an accident, I swear it.' He knew Victor might be his best bet for believing him. The man appeared to have little love for the crew.

'I'm sure you had every right to do what you did, accident or not,' Victor whispered. 'If I were you, I'd try to find a gun when we get to this military base. It might be your best chance for not being...' He used his fingers for quote marks. 'Accidentally shot.' He paused. 'In the back of the head most likely.'

They stared at each other until Shelby glanced behind him. A few of the crew glared at him. Without Hermann's authority around, Shelby felt like his chances of surviving the mission had dropped significantly.

CHAPTER 17 – LUTHER

Luther entered through the main entrance of the engineering headquarters and headed straight down the corridor. He decided not to bother with Heather first, hardly glancing at her when passing. He wanted to browse through the camera footage upstairs, curious to see whether more could be discovered about the missing pair. The idea of leaving the city gnawed at him, so any new information he found might prevent or shorten the chances of him having to go.

Upon reaching the surveillance room, he unlocked the door and sat down on one of the stools in front of the computer desk. He moved the mouse, making a third monitor flicker into life, allowing him to search for the previous recordings. Luther clicked the mouse several times on the list of videos he found but the computer froze in reply.

'Really? Fucking really?' He sighed and stood up, kicking his stool away. 'Old piece of rubbish.'

He went to turn from the screen, but then a video popped up in a new screen, catching his attention. Luther grabbed the mouse and went to play the video, but he was faced with several windows popping up across the screen over each other, displaying the other recordings. Luther closed his eyes and let out a deep breath; the less time he spent with the machine, the better. He started closing the irrelevant videos, according to their date. Of the two that remained open, one showed footage from the day the pair were seen at the station, and the other displayed video from the day before that.

Immediately, Luther skipped through the footage until Heather arrived and opened the building up. He was already struggling to keep his eyes focused.

After the first hour had passed, Luther decided Heather's job must have been one of the most boring positions in the world. The only thing worse than her job was the one he currently had watching her. The live camera footage still displayed itself on another screen next to him, showing Heather sitting at the reception desk; it was identical to the recorded footage.

He shifted in his seat and stretched from the hunch he found himself in before moving the stool up against the wall behind him, allowing him to lean back. The room became stuffy, and with it, a drowsiness settled over him. Between slow blinks, he noticed Heather finally talking to someone on the recorded footage.

The figure leant over the reception desk, laughing with Heather. Luther sat up, squinting for a better view without having to stand and move closer to the desk again. The quality looked far better than the tapes. Luther recognised the tatty leather jacket and girl from the description both Pat and Jetson's file had given him.

He pulled out his notebook and scribbled down a precise description of her before closing the video and leaving the room. Luther no longer felt the need to scan through more footage. Seeing Zara Black messing around with Heather gave him confidence enough that the receptionist would prove useful.

After locking up the surveillance room, Luther headed back downstairs and stood in front of the reception desk.

'Manage to find your thief, then?' Heather snarked, not bothering to face him from where she sat.

'No,' Luther replied slowly, giving himself time to think. Her sharp attitude caught him off guard.

He glared at her, trying to shake off his drowsiness. 'Found a dead body and two missing people instead.' The comment made Heather lift her head, prompting Luther to continue. 'Or it could be only one missing person now, and one dead.' He raised a brow in confusion.

Heather moved back in her seat, reflecting his own look back at him. 'In here?'

'No, not in here. Think I'd let that happen in my city?' Luther rolled his eyes.

'Well, I… That's not something to confuse stolen clothes with, is it?' she snapped back.

'Say, you wouldn't happen to know anyone who has left the city, would you? These people I mentioned are local, but they're out of town for the moment.' Luther frowned and shook his head. 'I really don't get it.'

Heather suddenly became a little hesitant and began to mumble, staring at Luther, who reached for his notebook.

'I know some—'

'I've got a… possible identity of Zara Black for this dead body.' He saw Heather's face break.

'She…' Her eyes started to fill with tears.

'Oh, did you know her?' Luther dropped his mouth a little in shock. 'I am so sorry.' He put his notebook away and moved around to her side, behind the desk, placing a hand on her shoulder. Heather shielded her face with her hand, covering the tears that escaped.

Luther smiled to himself, seeing the woman broken, her foul attitude gone.

'I know this must be hard, but is there any information you could give me to help catch whoever did this to her?' Luther gave Heather a sincere look and waited. He swore half his job involved having patience and struggled to imagine others coping with such a position.

He watched the teardrops run over her smooth skin and down onto her chest, waiting for her to reply.

'Zara left a few days back,' Heather sniffled. 'With her friend.' Heather paused, wiping the tears away. 'You say *possibly* her?'

'I do, yes. We aren't sure for now, but reports are saying the person was wearing a tatty jacket.' Luther pulled a concerned face. 'So, do you know where she was heading at all? Or if anyone had issues with her?' He spoke softly.

'I didn't want her to go. We told her.' Tears started streaming down Heather's face again. 'Do her parents know?'

'They have been informed. I spoke to them myself and assured them I would do everything in my power to discover what's happened.' Luther smiled and rubbed her shoulder. 'Now, do you know where they were heading or why?'

'To the coast. She only wanted to see the coastline. Zara always spoke of it. Russ...' Heather fumbled with the word. 'Russet, I think? The closest and safest town from here that was on the coast.' Heather eyed his hand resting on her shoulder. 'For a job or something. Zara said she didn't know much more than that.'

'Thank you, Heather. Now, remember, we don't know for certain it's her.' He squeezed her shoulder in assurance. 'I will let you know once I find out more details on the situation.' He smiled. 'I promise.'

Heather smiled back. 'Thank you,' she muttered, finding a tissue to wipe her face. 'The other missing person, do you know who it is?'

'Some old bloke named Trent,' Luther said frankly, forgetting to soften his tone now his mind was focused on Crossover.

'Trent?!' Heather broke down into tears again.

'I am so, so sorry. A friend of yours, too?' Luther sighed. 'He works with the trains, you see. I... my words are not enough. Look, it might not be either of them, Heather. They might both be fine and this dead body, unrelated. A thief in stolen workwear.' He forced a small reassuring smile. 'Though, the body.' He paused, fighting over whether to tell her. 'The body was found near Russet.' Luther looked grim.

'He was no friend of mine,' Heather cursed. 'But he could survive out there. If he's dead, then she's as good as dead, too. Zara should have stayed here, at home where it's safe.' The woman stifled her tears.

'Look, I'm sorry. I've got to go, but I'll pop back when I have more details.' Luther smiled and turned to leave. A small part of him pitied the woman. Heather at least had the sense to stay in the city like himself, and the state of her gave him the satisfaction that she had learnt her place.

Outside the front entrance, Luther noticed his car parked up with Ruben sitting at the wheel.

'Ruben?' He peered through the window. 'How did you know?' Relief washed over Luther at not having to walk back to Carbon Assembly.

'One of the guards directed me this way, and I know you aren't one to stroll around the city for the fun of it. So let's call it a good guess, sir.'

'I couldn't be happier to see you. Just had a depressing conversation with the reception girl, but it proved to be worth it. Our two leads both headed to Russet for a job, it seems, not a holiday, and I'm certain the dead body is the older bloke from Crossover.' Luther opened his notebook. 'Only he was wearing work attire, unlike the girl.' He glanced up, realising the car remained still.

'I see. Where to now?' Ruben asked.

'Uh, back home. I've got to organise two regiments that will leave with me for Crossover tomorrow,' Luther said bitterly. 'Jetson wants me to make an appearance as a show of strength or something of the sort.'

Ruben kept quiet and nodded, pulling away into the road.

CHAPTER 18 – SHELBY

Shelby spent the night failing to sleep in the ruins of an old petrol station, along with the rest of the crew. It became cold and uncomfortable, knowing everyone else around would kill him if given half the chance. Much to his surprise, the ship now became far more appealing to him, with the safety Hermann had promised.

Roy and the other two leaders had set up a watchpoint that rotated and changed throughout the night in case of any unwanted visitors, though Shelby couldn't shrug off the idea that the sentries might have been for him. From what he had heard of the Forbidden Zone, he doubted there would be others around them.

Escaping remained on his mind, but without a weapon, the idea was suicide. Time spent around the crew without Hermann began to feel borrowed. The sooner he fled, the better.

The sun was rising when Roy woke the crew up; some were still wearing their masks. Shelby sat to one side and watched them stir while wolfing his breakfast down and then heading out of the building.

Within half an hour the group had set off from the petrol station, continuing down the same blackened road that was now filled with old wreckages and rubble. Shelby kept a constant eye on who surrounded him each time the groups split between the remains of vehicles, choosing to keep close to Roy and Victor when possible.

According to Roy, it would take another day until they reached their destination. Between the talking, Shelby knew the trackers had picked up no signs of people or Legions around them. The information made him uncomfortable and eager to run, though he still needed a weapon – something the military base would hopefully provide.

The group, approaching a large town, started to slow their pace. The road shot straight through it and underneath the ruins of a collapsed building that blocked the route. They halted in front of the rubble. Shelby scanned either side of the road between the group, noticing half the buildings were intact, some looking safe enough to escape through.

'Going over or around?' Roy shouted, turning from the front of the group. Shelby kept quiet, listening to the crew discuss the decision among themselves.

'Around,' a few voices replied.

'Can loot through some of what's here while we work our way past these buildings that still stand,' another voice said.

'Fine with me,' Roy replied. 'We'll meet on the other side of this heap, so don't be spending too long or go wandering too far because we won't come looking for you.'

The words echoed in Shelby's mind. The crew would jump at the chance of seeing him make a break for it. Not only that but the provisions Hermann had provided for each of them contained some stale bread, a small pot of jam, some dried fruits and jerky, along with a bottle or flask of water. It appeared the rations would hardly be enough for the trip, let alone enough to last him all the way home if he escaped.

'Shelby and Victor, with me.' Roy gestured for them to come over. 'I've got to keep my eye on each of you for various reasons.' He looked at Shelby first and then to Victor. 'Now let's get through this before the rest of the groups make their mind up on where they're going.' Roy turned around and headed between the remains of two small shops. Shelby kept close behind him, with Victor following.

The area ahead opened up after they had passed between the shops, revealing a sparse expanse of ground lined with buildings to form an open square. Strands of long pale grass and charred stumps of trees were scattered across the opening. It remained quiet between the three of them as they continued walking and distancing themselves from the rest of the group.

'Never seen anything so miserable,' Victor said, looking out across to a disfigured play park that stood on the other side of the field.

'Agreed. Not much to look at. Makes life working Carbon's security look cheerful,' Roy replied.

'Where are all the plants and wildlife?' Shelby asked, his curiosity getting the better of him.

'All that's dead here stays dead,' Roy replied.

'I've theorised that the yellow haze smothers pretty much everything and prevents growth. If it's toxic to us, it has to be toxic to plants and trees, too. Everything seems to suffer here because of it,' Victor said, turning to Shelby. 'I didn't think I'd ever say it, but I can't wait to be back on the ship, and I bet neither can you.'

'Aye, me too,' Roy chipped in. 'Don't think I'm wanting to be here, either. You'd have to be fucking nuts to stay here longer than needed. Hermann had the right idea to stay on that rusted can of his.' Roy stopped to step through a doorway on his right. Most of the other buildings seemed to lack one. 'Through here. Hopefully, we've passed the worst of the mess. Guessing you two aren't up for much looting?'

'I'd be up for it,' Shelby replied, glancing at them both. Weapons were on his mind. Looting might mean the others would busy themselves and allow him to find something of use.

'Doesn't seem to be much of anything around here anyway, it's all turned to dust.' Victor wiped his hand over some rubble, stepping into the remains of the building. Shelby warily entered, seeing half of the roof had collapsed in on itself.

'Any guesses?' Roy picked something up.

'That's a necklace,' Victor replied, staring at it.

'No, not what I've picked up,' Roy grumbled. 'I know a damn necklace when I see one. I mean, what this place used to be?' He saw the dusty ash on Victor's skin. 'The person who wore this is probably that dust on your hands.'

Victor quickly patted his hands together to dislodge the dust, causing Roy to laugh.

Shelby continued walking through the room, something shiny catching his eye on one of the counters. He picked up the tiny piece between a finger and thumb and held it towards the dull light that came from the cracked roof.

'Never seen glass before? Some on the ship, you know.' Roy laughed. 'I forget you aren't from—'

'Roy, that isn't glass he's holding.' Victor moved closer to Shelby. 'Pass it here for a moment.'

Unsure, Shelby passed the small piece over to him, noticing Roy stare oddly at it.

'It's glass, Victor. I thought you were the antiquity expert here,' Roy said, stepping closer.

'I *am* the antiquity expert.' Victor adjusted his glasses. 'Which is why you think it's glass. We're in a jewellers.'

'What?' Roy seemed confused. 'I know that. What's the glass then if it isn't glass?'

'It's a diamond.' Victor held it higher towards the light between his finger and thumb. 'At least, I believe it is. They used to sell these alongside other metals and stones for people to dress themselves up in. Well, those who were wealthy enough to afford it. All bought from a place like this.' Victor sounded entranced.

'Jewellers?' Shelby repeated, never having heard half the words before. He never wore anything besides what would keep him covered and warm.

'Aye, that's what he said. Though if you wear something sparkly as that, you'll be drawing eyes from anyone who passes you. Asking to be mugged or killed, I reckon,' Roy snorted. 'Worthless now, though, all this.' He kicked some rubble ahead of him.

'Not necessarily. Gold is on the rise, along with silver and copper, thanks to the mines. Sure, bartering is still and always will be a thing, but eventually...' He looked around the room. 'Eventually, rare gems like these could become much more valuable to people who find they have too much time or money.' Victor passed the diamond back to Shelby. 'And they hardly weigh a thing.'

Roy stepped closer. 'How valuable?' His eyes wandered over towards Shelby.

'More valuable than gold if you were to hang on to it long enough. Then you—'

'Shh. Hush your tone,' Roy whispered, moving next to them both. 'And you give that back to him?' Roy eyed Shelby, who still held the diamond in his hand.

'Look at the counter he got it from.' Victor nodded towards it. Among the rubble were more diamonds. 'I'm betting if we clear some of these counters there'll be a whole array of different valuables.'

'Right. Let's get to it then. This is between us three. No word to anyone else, otherwise they'll ask questions about what we got, and I don't intend to share.' Roy moved the rubble away from the counter, collecting up what he found. He stopped and turned to Victor and Shelby, who stood watching.

'I won't complain you aren't helping but could you give me a hand with this, either of you?' Roy attempted to move a wedged piece of concrete that sat in front of a smashed cabinet.

Victor seemed to ignore the request, so Shelby moved towards Roy. He grabbed the top of the concrete and helped Roy push it out of the way, making it roll and meet the floor with a thud. The metal doors on the cabinet came off easily from their rusted hinges. As they peered inside, rows of watches and a collection of necklaces and jewellery glinted back at them. Shelby moved away and started looking elsewhere in the shop, not wanting to intrude on Roy's space and loot.

'Bloody hell, Victor, you've hit the nail on the head with your reading. Maybe I ought to get into that.' He seemed dazed by the number of jewels inside. 'Even if they don't gain much worth, I could still sell them for a few pieces back home with the shine they give.'

'Don't get craftsmanship like that anymore.' Victor stepped over to Roy. 'Any watch I've seen is made with a leather strap, not metal. They really did have a lot of time back then.'

'It didn't last for them, though, did it?' Shelby gazed outside the front of the shop at the street.

'Aye, killed themselves off. Probably bored with it all. Once you peak, there's only one way to go,' Roy replied, stuffing the jewels into his bag. 'Now hurry and take what you can, the both of you, cos once I'm done, we're moving on.'

Shelby walked behind a large desk and trod on something with a crunch. A small bag rested beside his boot. He bent down to pick it up, faltering for a second after realising what had made the crunch. Bones turned to dust under his feet. Fingers still gripped the small pouch, but they crumbled when Shelby pulled it from the hand. Opening it up, he found a few more jewels, one being a large yellow shard with a pale streak through it. The other pieces looked like fragments broken from the larger piece. He stuffed it into his pocket and looked up to see the other two still rummaging through the counters.

At the front of the shop, Shelby followed the metal bars around the space where a window must have been. He followed the metal over to the door, which, to his surprise, still stood intact and open. He passed through it and went outside, hearing Victor and Roy's steps behind him.

'Loot much, then?' Roy asked, happy with his share.

'Just a small amount.' Shelby smiled back. 'What about you?'

'Aye, me and Vic found some nice watches, rings, earrings… I could go on. Plenty, mate, though I'm starting to worry we won't have space for whatever we'll be finding at this military base.' Roy laughed and then pulled a concerned face. 'Well, this looks to be the same road we were on, but I can't see anyone.' All three scanned up and down the road, moving further into the street.

'Where is everyone?' Victor asked, his relaxed attitude wearing off.

They stopped walking to listen, keeping silent in the breeze.

'Strange. You'd think our lot could be heard a mile away,' Roy commented.

'I can hear something,' Victor mumbled. 'A vehicle,' he said in a raised voice, turning to Roy.

All three of them ran back into the jewellery shop.

'Quick, give me a hand with this!' Shelby shouted, attempting to push the door closed. Victor cleared its path while Roy helped shove the door shut.

All three crouched and peered through the bars, waiting as the sound of the vehicle approached the front of the shop. Another sudden noise and screech of tyres sounded at the back of the shop.

'Fuck. Fuck, fuck, fuck.' Roy unholstered his gun and moved towards the back exit where they had entered, his face turning red.

'Both of you stay,' he whispered harshly, being the only one with a gun.

He moved up to the back exit, hearing a mumble of voices grow louder.

Another vehicle pulled up outside the front, followed by the sounds of people jumping from it. At the same moment, a figure entered the back door and walked towards where Victor and Shelby were hiding. The silhouette stopped, spotting them both. Roy lined his gun up at the man.

'Roy?' the figure called out, looking at Victor. 'Not much need for you now, is there?' He laughed.

'That a threat, is it?' Roy scowled, noticing the guy was part of his crew.

The man jumped at his sudden appearance. 'Where the hell have you been? Made us search through half the street. Playing hide-and-seek, are we?'

'Where did you find these damn vehicles?' Roy snapped, his temper erupting.

'Military base, mate. Found three good trucks that still drive. Enough to fit us all on along with some loot. Our trip just got shorter.' He grinned. 'Pretty much what Erma will say to you, but you know, she's the leader of her group, so she feels the need to repeat everything.' He shook his head. 'Need you and Victor to check it out if you're done hiding. Seems the map was off a few miles.' The bloke headed out the back again. 'We found them,' he called ahead, leaving the building.

All three of them took a deep breath before moving.

'Thought we were in for it there,' Roy laughed, a little out of breath. 'Seems like we're shouting now, too. Anyway, let's get a move on.'

Roy moved out through the back exit. Shelby allowed Victor to follow second, giving himself a moment to catch his breath.

CHAPTER 19 – LUTHER

Luther watched the *Carbon Express* steam engine come into view as Ruben drove up and stopped outside the station. The locomotive remained an impressive feat and the gold letters spelling 'Prime' along its side always caught Luther's attention. He knew the effort put into building it by the engineers; the city's wealth of coal allowed it to run throughout the day. For all the smartness of the guild's engineers, it appeared his journey to Crossover questioned one of their best. Luther still struggled to understand why anyone wanted to go east.

Two groups of soldiers were geared up and waiting for his arrival. Catching the first train before sunrise turned out to be a joint decision between himself, the drivers and train guards, as they all agreed it would be less disruptive for the public. Luther wanted to keep his men from most crowds, even though their trip was supposed to be a show of force. Any fights or quarrels might slow the process and Luther intended to stay in Crossover for the minimum amount of time.

'Don't be late this evening when picking me up,' he said coldly to Ruben while getting out of the car.

The sight of the soldiers did little to establish his confidence. He knew they had woken up a few hours before him, fetching their gear and weapons from the armoury and then walking to the station. All of them wore similar uniforms and carried rifles. Their presence scared most people away, though the majority were not of his concern. Against the Eastern Legion, his men hardly stood a chance, and the further east they travelled, the more likely their presence.

Within the group, Luther noticed the two captains who would be in charge. They were far from his best soldiers, but due to the timing of this mission, alongside Project Carbon, they were all he had to work with.

'Follow me,' Luther called out, not bothering to stop beside them. The sooner he boarded, the quicker he returned.

'This coach here is yours.' He turned back to the following crowd of soldiers. 'I assume you've all been briefed. No killing anyone. Arrests and warnings if need be, but limit yourself today. This is just a show of presence and to uphold the protection agreements made with our friends at Crossover. If we all do our part, we'll be back before sundown, I'm sure.' He gave a quick smile and continued further along the platform to the first-class carriage. He climbed into the cabin and upon finding it empty, allowed his shoulders to relax. Luther realised he'd forgotten to greet Patterson, who he'd seen sitting inside the ticket office, staring at the regiments of soldiers. He turned from the window and closed his eyes, eager for the day to be over.

Most rides remained undisturbed now the train itself used its own security enforcement. It left a bitter taste on his tongue knowing he collaborated with Trittle and their Eastern Legion on this effort, but it meant the responsibility for the train shared itself across the only three stations: Carbon City's Central Station, Crossover (the middle station) and Trittle Station (to the east). Luther had set up the arrangement three years prior and it continually proved its worth on the railway. His only lingering doubt was about the surrounding Eastern Legion, since the train linked them so closely together.

****

The train finally stopped at Crossover, causing Luther to let out a sigh. Failing to sleep on the journey had aggravated him, as his mind had cast back to his two previous visits to the town; once had been to set up the standing agreement for protection of the town, and the other was when he had first made his way into Carbon City.

A stench shot up Luther's nose as he stepped out of the train. The farming town had been growing in recent years with their exports, and the smell seemed to reflect it. Luther focused on the grass, trees and greenery that he saw in the distance. He admitted the city lacked a certain amount of wilderness about it.

The two regiments of his soldiers grouped in an orderly and professional manner on his right.

'Luther,' a voice called out.

Luther turned towards the sound.

'I got your message late last night. My name's Brock, we've met before. I'm mayor of the town.' The man put his hand up between them to shake.

Looking at his hand and then at the man, Luther started to recall why he hated the place. He shook the extended hand, skimming over the man again. The mayor was not of the same class. His worn, broken skin showed between the dungarees, sandals and flat cap he wore. Luther forced a smile, seeing the scruffy black hair poorly hidden under the hat.

'Brock, pleasure seeing you again. Been quite a few years since I was here last.' Luther noticed that most of the shops had remained the same.

'Three years, give or take.' Brock shook his head in disbelief. 'So, what business do us important men need to discuss?' He rummaged around in his front dungaree pocket.

The comment made Luther twitch. He forced a smile.

'I'm thinking more on the details of this missing person you mentioned in the letter.' Brock pulled some paper out and shook it. 'Perhaps over some breakfast, after the long trip you've just had?'

'Thank you for the offer, but this matter is of quite some urgency. It's giving me a real headache.' Luther paused. 'This place here, your place, is of the utmost importance, more so than the city. It delivers such a vital service to the surrounding areas, which is why I have personally come to investigate the matter, along with our top recruits.' Luther gestured with his head back to the soldiers who stood lined up. 'We have a missing engineer named Trent. No surname. He worked on the railway and steam locomotives. His disappearance has disturbed us, and we wish to see if he is at home

or not so we can uncover any clues as to who may have possibly...'
He leaned in. 'Kidnapped him.'

Brock's face pulled no signs of shock, and instead he opted
to chew his lip.

'Well, I know the guy. Not many pioneering locomotive
engineers live here, as you can imagine. He was always quite the
handyman. Here, come with me.' Brock started walking ahead. 'He
lives over on this side of town.'

Luther turned back and signalled to his captains to start
with their given duties of patrolling the area. Two of the guards
caught up to accompany Luther a few paces behind him.

After a few minutes of walking, they stopped in front of a
small wooden house.

'This is Trent's place. Now, I must say by my judgement I
don't believe he is missing,' Brock said, walking up to the door. 'You
see, I saw him about a week ago leaving town with a young girl. New
love interest perhaps, I don't know. Way I see it, they left south for
a little holiday, though suppose the girl might have been leading him
astray.' He unlocked the door with one of the keys in his hand.
'Master keys.' He shook them in front of Luther. 'Can't imagine
having them for an entire city, though.'

'South, you say? Walking?' Luther asked, stepping into the
cabin.

'Horseback. Nothing much down south. Well, nothing civil
for quite a while that way, not like us folks here.' He raised his
eyebrows. 'Unruly bandits and raiders, that sort of thing. Burnhelm
isn't too bad, if they like you, so... So anyway, what you looking for
here? Possible link to a kidnapping?'

Luther picked up a small photo frame of two people. 'This him?'

Brock peered at it, taking the frame in his hand and holding it a little closer. 'Uh, yep. That's him and his wife. She died years and years ago, though still a sore subject with the man. I'd suggest not to mention it to him.' He tried passing it back to Luther, who moved away to look at something else.

'Has he always lived here?' Luther asked, picking up some seashells placed along a windowsill.

'Since I've been about, sure, though his wife came from the coast. Near Burnhelm, now I think about it. Not sure about his parents, mind you. No, wait, I think they were from Russet.'

This piqued Luther's interest.

'Hell of a trip if he's going all the way to Burnhelm, not to mention a dangerous one, regardless of his age. I mean, if he was relocating, he could've gotten a good price for his house. If that was what you were thinking. Though kidnapping, eh, I don't buy it. Sure, she was pretty the girl, but he didn't look like he was being dragged—'

'Hang on, just be quiet for a second.' Luther pulled out his notebook and started to write down a few of the things spewing from Brock's mouth. The man started talking again. Luther focused on a small row of coloured bulbs. He relaxed a little, listening to Brock confirm things he already knew. It was more than likely that this Trent was the man killed in Russet, and since Trent lived outside the city, this meant the issue wasn't one for his department of internal security. He could pass the case back on to foreign relations, Jetson's department.

'How's the town?' Luther asked, interrupting Brock.

'Oh, it's good. Produce is up, the population is slowly on the rise, but as I'm sure you know we send anyone looking for better work up to the city. Still, less trouble and less pillaging and plundering by any malicious waste-landers now, since you guys helped buff the security, which we all greatly appreciate, I tell you,' Brock replied.

'Good.' Luther felt satisfied with the answer and happy to hear his involvement had secured the town further. Knowing the holidaymakers had acted on their own accord, and that the probable instigator was likely dead, a weight started to lift from him. Luther had completed all he needed to do and the incident no longer involved any internal security problems regarding stolen uniforms. The issue now became one of rogue residents, for someone else to clean up.

'Breakfast?' Luther asked, giving a pat on Brock's back.

'Why, I thought you'd never ask.' Brock seemed chuffed at the idea. 'We'll spoil these two guards of yours too.' He tapped one of them who stood by the front door.

****

Breakfast went surprisingly well with the two guards at his table. Luther realised it kept Brock busy having more people to talk to, enabling Luther to eat in peace. The meal itself tasted delicious, with two poached eggs, and a few rashers of bacon that sat beside some tomatoes and beans, all sitting on top of buttered toast. The freshness of the food almost made up for the smell of the place, with his guards appearing to think the same.

While eating, Luther focused on the missing couple again. Trent was not a true local to the city, but once the committee discovered his history as one of the pioneering engineers to build the Prime engine, there would be an uproar over why he had been allowed to leave. The whereabouts of the second person, Zara Black, remained a slight concern, but with the information gathered, the woman was likely dead.

By mid-afternoon, Luther had arrived back at the station and said goodbye to Brock. He stood on the platform waiting for the rest of his soldiers to turn up, having sent his two guards to find them. All in all, he believed it had been a smooth and successful day for him, even if it had been a little wasteful. The responsibility for these missing people was now someone else's on the committee, Luther having done all he needed.

Luther almost forgot why he dreaded coming out of the city so much, seeing the town so green, peaceful and guarded.

The *Carbon Express* approached from the east, a cloud of smoke pluming into the air above it. Luther gave a nod, seeing his men arrive onto the platform.

'A high-ranking man of the city, so I've been told.' A deep voice rumbled behind Luther, accompanied by heavy footsteps. The voice started to speak again, making Luther turn. 'It's good to see the investigation is underway.'

Luther looked up to meet the man's eyes. His face appeared like stone, hardly moving as the clear words spoke out from his mouth. The sheer size of him cast a shadow down upon Luther. A shaved head matched his stubble that sat atop his dark skin. The man's clothes appeared clean and not of the local fashion. The coat he wore was stained rich burgundy and had a symbol stitched onto the shoulder in a darker shade of red: a circle with three swirls in a triangular shape over it, each swirl enclosed by two sharp prongs either side that met back in the centre.

'Investigation?' Luther replied, unsure what this guy had heard. He recognised the Eastern Legion symbol on the shoulder pad of the man's coat.

'Yes, when delivering the previous messages to your committee, I was first assured this trespasser had nothing to do with you before his death occurred, and then after finding such blatant evidence, you still held your position.' He paused and held his gaze. 'And now I see you out here, searching for your own. So, have you found anything you'd like to tell me?'

'A rogue. Connections to Russet.' Luther replied with confidence, before falling short of what to say next.

'I see. A dead rogue now, though it has been brought to my attention that there is a second person involved?' The man kept his eyes fixed on Luther.

'Uh, yes, a girl, well, woman,' Luther replied. He decided it would be in his best interest not to lie. 'Was last seen with the man you killed.'

'His death was unfortunate.' The man kept his eyes on Luther. 'This woman may still linger at the dam then and is presumed to be another one of yours?' His face remained motionless.

Though Luther's head filled with confusion, he refused to look like a fool in the situation. 'Another rogue, not one of ours. Do as you please with her if she's found. If she returns to the city, I will notify you and arrest her.'

Nodding once, the man glanced at the soldiers and moved away. Luther stared at him until he disappeared from view, noticing the long sharp spear-like weapon that rested across his back.

The train pulled into the station, making Luther turn to his group of soldiers who stared at him with their rifles in hand.

'It's all good, I know the guy,' Luther shouted. 'Are we all here?' He received nods from the captains. 'Let's get home then.' He waved them on. 'Oh, and I'd like to speak to our captains, please. Join me in first-class so we can do some catching up.' Luther smiled and stepped aboard, followed by the two captains. He gestured to a four-seat compartment with a table. The captains sat down while Luther went to fetch some drinks. His mind was fixed on the Legion he had just encountered.

Returning with some whiskey, Luther sat opposite the waiting captains. 'How did the day go then?'

The two captains started to talk while he poured them a drink. But Luther wasn't really listening. His mind went back to the figure that had approached him. The Legion had been talking to someone from the city who knew about the events. Luther poured himself a glass of water and sat looking out of the window, attempting to listen to how the day had gone for his soldiers. There would be more than enough headaches when he arrived back in the city.

CHAPTER 20 – SHELBY

Shelby stayed by the military trucks, keeping away from most of the others who were searching the base. The only people near him were Roy and Victor, who stood talking to some other crew members about how the site was further from the city than Hermann had said. All the crew were now spread out across the area to lessen the search time for the large weapons.

The group picked and looted their way through the buildings that still stood. Shelby watched, noticing how the large pale surface spanned across the entire compound and slipped under the buildings. Down one side of the complex stood several rounded hangars with huge doorways on the front. The peculiar shape at the opposite end of the site caught his eye. It appeared to be a disturbed metal dish surrounded by rubble at the foot of a tall broken tower.

Shelby sat on the back of a truck. An open-back vehicle like this would be far better than the cart and horse he used at home. The amount of wood and produce it could contain, combined with its thick rubber wheels, made it ideal for the job. His mind wandered back to Mia and Kai. He was desperate to let them know he was alive. The urge to jump into the front of the truck struck him. He stood a better chance of getting back home with a vehicle, but before taking the chance he needed to find a weapon; attempting an escape without one guaranteed his death if the crew caught up with him.

The truck parked next to him was stacked with weapons the groups had found, though none fit the description of 'big'. Most of them looked like the ones given to the crew already, including shotguns, machine guns, rifles and handguns.

Listening to Roy and Victor talk to the other group leaders, Shelby gently dropped from his perch on the back of the truck.

'Well, what else could he mean?' Erma asked. 'Surely it'll be a gun but obviously large? I mean, large in his eyes must be huge considering the size of him.' She laughed.

The truck full of guns grew closer with each step Shelby gradually made towards it.

'To my understanding, yes, it should be along the same sort of lines. Though if I'm honest, I don't think even Hermann knows what he's looking for.' Victor sounded uncertain. 'It's one thing to keep things vague, but not to tell anyone what we're actually after makes me think we're on a wild goose chase.'

'I see your point,' Roy replied. 'Well, if it is here, then it shouldn't be hard to miss, should it? We'll go over the place a few times and perhaps make a few trips back to the ship now we've got the vehicles. Hermann can enlighten us a little more when we get back there on the first round, and we can have the others still searching.' Roy nodded.

'Alright,' Erma agreed. 'Not sure the rest of the crew will like being left here, though.'

'Aye, but they're getting paid enough so just remind them if they get fidgety,' Roy said through gritted teeth.

Shelby approached the truck and began searching over the pile of weapons, trying to see if any were similar to the rifle he used back home. He kept one eye on the others, who were still deep in conversation.

'Whatever you think seems big could be it. Just give me a shout. The old world saw things differently, so keep your mind open to anything,' Victor said.

'Certainly not got the weapon on you then, by anyone's standards, old world or new,' Erma quipped at the other group leader and grabbed his crotch.

'You mind, bitch?' He scowled, pushing her off with a slight grin. 'You'll pay for that.' He walked off towards one of the buildings.

Raising his eyebrows at her, Roy spoke. 'We'll loot and load as we go, so get these trucks filled. Sooner we do that, the sooner we leave.' The conversation concluded and the group dispersed.

Shelby had almost grabbed a weapon when he saw Victor turn and walk towards him. He grappled with the impulse to take the gun but instead leaned nonchalantly against the truck.

'Found it yet then?' Shelby asked.

'Hard to find something you've never seen before. Imagine you've been told to find a truck without knowing what one was.' Victor gave a small but irritated laugh. 'Still, at least we've got a quick route back to the ship now.'

The comment prompted Shelby to smile. He knew the basics of how to run old vehicles, but decided against telling anyone.

Victor sat down on the back of the truck beside the pile of guns, but then a woman's voice called out, 'Oi, Victor, you're gonna wanna see this.'

'There I was, thinking I could relax. Want to come and see what they've found? Wouldn't mind the company, being surrounded by this gruff lot.' Victor dropped off the truck without waiting for an answer. Shelby allowed him to continue walking, his own interest still with the weapons. He turned from Victor and found Roy staring at him. The man moved his head to indicate Shelby should follow on.

Without saying a word, Shelby started walking towards Victor. He wondered if Roy had seen him eyeing the guns. Roy appeared friendly but still remained part of the crew, most of whom wanted him dead. The three of them approached where the shout had come from.

'What is it?' Victor asked. 'Think we've found it?'

'Nah, it's something just for you, Victor. Looks bloody technical and all that. To get past this sealed hatch we burnt and smashed our way through its lock,' one man said, walking in through the front of an old hangar. 'It's down the ladder at the back here.' He pointed. 'Take a torch.'

The man passed two to Victor, who gave one to Shelby, though he had never used an electric one before.

Roy kept a few paces behind, already holding a torch.

'I hope you ain't afraid of the dark.' The man laughed, climbing down a ladder and disappearing out of sight.

Victor peered down into the darkness and turned to Roy. Roy glared at him until he climbed down the ladder. Shelby and Roy followed. When they reached the bottom, they all switched on their torches. Shelby's nerves grew at the proximity of the others beside him in the darkness; he was keen to keep alert to anything or anyone that might come towards him.

A narrow passage stretched ahead of them. The walls were made from a mixture of metal and concrete, showing few marks of damage or rust.

'Through here,' the bloke directed, walking up ahead. Shelby recognised him as the man with the scar who'd pushed into him when they started on foot from the boats.

A chunky metal door with a wheel in its centre still hung on its hinges in a large metal frame.

'Thankfully, this door was open. I don't think we'd have been able to get in otherwise,' the man said, stepping over the metal frame to enter the room.

Inside, the room opened to show dozens of desks lined up with old computers. At the front of the room sat an arrangement of controllers and dials, with multiple monitors fixed onto the wall above. Everything seemed untouched and clean.

'You weren't joking when you said technical.' Victor rushed in front of them, looking at the big screens mounted across the wall.

Shelby felt a little out of his depth, having never seen or heard of whatever they were. They didn't look like a traditional weapon and weren't that big.

'What are they?' Shelby asked cautiously.

The man with the scar flicked his eyes towards him but said nothing. Shelby stared back at him, considering the blunt, heavy torch in his hand.

'We got them back home,' Roy started. 'Used for all sorts.' He paused. 'I'd be the wrong person to talk to about all of that, though.'

'These ones would have been used to send instructions in the military for efficient communication.' Victor moved the torchlight over the controls. 'Think Hermann would be interested in taking any of it?'

'Eh, maybe. We'll mention it to him when we get back from the first run with the trucks. Reckon it's more of Luther's thing than Hermann's,' Roy replied.

'Don't they need petrol?' Shelby blurted out. The other man still eyed him before realising what had been said.

'The trucks? That's a fair point. Doubt the petrol station we passed has any in it,' Roy said.

'As a matter of fact, we found some underground oil drums.' The man looked at Roy. 'It'd be worth draining them all. Probably more valuable than whatever Hermann is after. That stuff's better than gold.'

'Oh, right, barrels and containers it is then,' Roy agreed.

'That's what some of the others are out finding. Hermann and the entire city should be more than happy with this stuff,' the bloke replied. 'And what's this about a first run? We agreed to take what we could and that would be it.' The bloke narrowed his eyes at Roy.

'Now, the group leaders agreed because we've got the trucks, we'll make good time and do two trips. You know, so Hermann's appetite is filled. That's all. You're getting a good wage, don't be forgetting.' Roy pressed his words.

'Huh, I see. Not sure I agree with that.' The guy glanced around towards Victor and Shelby.

'You can take it up with Hermann. You can come back with us on the first trip to talk it over with him, if you like,' Roy almost growled.

'Good. Because I won't be coming back, I can tell you that much.' The man flicked his eyes between the three of them and headed for the ladder.

After a moment of silence, Victor spoke. 'This stuff all looks intact. It'd be worth trying to see if it all runs before we think about dismantling it and taking it with us.' He looked at the wires, following them along the wall. 'A place like this should have...'

'Generators?' Roy finished his sentence.

'Exactly. Probably petroleum ones, if they have a load of that lying about. Know what they look like, Shelby?'

'I do.' Shelby felt the question jabbed at him. He knew he was not a well-travelled man but he did know how to use generators from his time in Lornsten.

He followed the cables with Victor. The mixture of wires started grouping up and splitting off. Roy resorted to seeing if there were any other closed doors along the edge of the room. He began mumbling to himself and, from what Shelby heard, the man thought the large space needed a toilet or it would be a stupid design.

'Here,' Roy shouted. 'Seems there might be a double door. Anyone got a metal bar or something to lever it open?'

Shelby moved over to him and saw a crease in the wall before glancing around and spotting some chairs. 'Could try a chair?'

'Good enough for me,' Roy said, failing to prise the gap open with his fingers.

Shelby folded the chair and passed it to him. Roy shoved it into the gap. 'Now you two pull on a door each while I yank them open, but careful if they snap shut.'

He started pulling the chair back at an angle. The legs bent under the pressure, with Shelby and Victor gradually managing to ease each door open.

Metal clanged, making them both jump back in fear of catching their fingers. Shelby looked down to find the chair on the floor beside Roy. The doors remained open.

'Fuck.' Roy got up from the floor. 'That came apart easier than I'd expected.' He laughed. 'Still got your fingers?'

'Just about,' Shelby replied, starting to laugh at the fright of it.

'Careful now,' Roy warned, pushing the doors further apart, making them sink into the walls either side. 'It's a lift, I reckon, with these types of doors. Means just in front might be a drop enough to kill you.'

All three approached the opening with their torches, finding Roy to be right. Ahead of the door it dropped down into darkness. Shelby kept further back, wary of his position between the two of them.

'Yeah, I'm not going down there,' Victor exclaimed. 'Before you get any daft ideas, Roy, Hermann said I'm the important person on this mission.' Victor held his head a little higher.

Roy rolled his eyes. 'Alright fine, you stay up here, Mister VIP. As for Shelby, you'll have to come with me. Two pairs of eyes are better than one, and sadly you've not got much of an excuse like this pompous twat.'

Shelby nodded. Assisting Roy seemed like his next best bet for securing his safety until the chance to escape presented itself.

'See if there are any generators around here, Victor.' Roy tapped the wall before kneeling on the ground and rummaging through his bag. 'Good job I've got some of this.' He pulled out some thick brown rope and looked for a place to tie it.

Shelby closed his eyes. He hadn't considered how they were going to make their way down the shaft, and using a rope in the darkness didn't appeal to him.

'I'd argue Shelby isn't a fan of heights by the look of his face.' Victor laughed, blinding him with the torch. 'Better you than me though, mate. I'll be sure to stay here and look after the rope. Got to make sure no one tinkers with it.'

Shelby closed his eyes again. Heights were fine, but climbing down a rope into darkness with no bottom in sight, surrounded by people who wanted to kill him, made him panic.

'Shelby, I'll go down first and you watch how I do it, alright? I'm not saying you're an idiot, I just don't want you falling on me before we reach the bottom.' Roy sounded concerned.

'Fine by me,' Shelby replied, thankful Roy would be on the rope first.

'Just keep the torch on me as best you can, and I'll give a shout up when I've reached the bottom.' Roy tied a knot in the rope and began to climb down.

As he started to descend, Shelby hoped for someone to appear on the ladder and announce they had found what Hermann wanted. Though he disliked the rest of the group, having an interruption now felt more favourable than dangling in the darkness on a rope and going deeper underground.

Roy moved further out of sight and, after a few minutes, shouted up to him.

CHAPTER 21 – LUTHER

Luther enjoyed the train journey from Crossover, listening to the two captains sitting opposite him. He spoiled them with whiskey and heard the stories they spewed out in their merry state. Though he had initially considered the trip to Crossover a waste of time, being approached by the Legion member had disrupted the entire investigation; they were never ones to take things lightly. He just needed to make sense of it.

When the *Carbon Express* arrived at Central Station, Luther wasted no time in exiting the carriage, feeling relieved to find Ruben parked up and waiting. He headed straight for the car and sat down in the back, pulling out his notebook.

'A meeting has been called for your return...' Ruben stopped talking, noticing Luther's book in hand, and pulled away from the station.

'How was Crossover?' Ruben asked a minute later.

'Waste of time mostly.' Luther felt unsure whether to tell Ruben about the Legion, while deliberating the situation. *Someone's been talking to them, but who?*

'Nothing worth the trip?' Ruben arrived at Carbon Assembly.

'Well, the dead man found is undoubtedly one of our train engineers who has a connection with Russet, though it would have been nice to see the body so we could verify it ourselves.' Luther sighed. 'And I met one of the Legion. Seems to think we've had more involvement in this dead body than I'd thought.'

'How so?' Ruben asked.

'It's complicated. I'll explain later on.' He put away the notebook, got out of the car and headed up the front steps of the building.

Upon entering the meeting room, surprise took hold of Luther, seeing everyone seated around the table. The talking simmered down as he took his place.

'How was Crossover?' Jetson asked before Luther could speak.

'A success, I'd say.' Luther paused and got out his notebook. 'With the surveillance footage I had set up, I've found our two missing engineers, who are apparently on holiday. These two on-camera also match the descriptions given to me by various sources, two of which are our central station ticket operator, and Brock Ashfield.'

'Who is Brock Ashfield?' Carol narrowed her eyes at him.

'Really?' Luther raised a brow. 'He's the mayor of Crossover.'

'Not a local then? Why should we trust him?' She sneered.

Recognising her attempt to already disrupt his work, he rolled his eyes at her. 'Are you saying all of us here are trustworthy, Carol?' He paused. 'Because we're all local?' Luther tilted his head. 'We prove our trust by our actions, and Brock has never given reason for doubt.'

Another committee member spoke up. 'Brock is in charge of Crossover. He knows the locals and does a great deal of trading with us in return for Luther's security. Our security. The reason to lie is very minimal,' the woman said sternly.

Luther looked at her. It was Ana, the member in charge of Trade and Health, who seldom spoke in meetings. He knew Jetson liked to meddle with her trading negotiations, believing himself to be better suited for them with his foreign relations. Luther gave her a nod of acknowledgement.

'Anyway,' he continued. 'From what they described, it matches the two missing people we have here. One Zara Black, and the other, Trent, one of our pioneering train engineers.'

Murmurs broke out between the committee.

'Pioneering?' one member queried.

'Yes, he was one of our top blokes, helped with the build of the Prime engine in the *Carbon Express*,' Luther replied, eager to expand on the question.

'Who's in charge of his district? They shouldn't have let him leave!' one of the other members erupted.

'He lives outside the city,' Luther explained. 'He's free to move how he likes. And, yes, it is a shame he might be lost to us.'

The same man spoke again. 'It's more than a damn shame. You can't just relearn the skills that man had, you know.'

'Look, whoever is in charge of Central District would have signed them off, but it isn't their fault,' Luther assured them. 'I've spoken to someone down at the station and they've said our other engineers have plenty of experience and knowledge. It won't make a bit of difference.'

The committee fell silent.

After a moment of deliberating, Luther began talking again. 'I was also informed these two people were heading to Russet, the previous owner of the dam before it was taken over.' The committee members glanced at each other. 'There is a solid case against us that our workers might have been on a job for another town, with one of them having a clear connection to Russet.'

Murmurs broke out between the group.

'What next then? Trittle might be souring with us,' one member uttered. 'Might think we're stirring the pot.'

'No, they won't,' Jetson began. 'I've had an artist working hard to create images of the girl seen in the footage.' He picked up a poster and showed it around the table before sliding it across to Luther. 'What do you think?'

Luther glanced over the drawing. 'Well, I can't remember what she looks like, if I'm honest, but short dark hair, yeah, that looks about right. Guessing you got them to draw more than one?'

'Obviously.' Jetson laughed. 'They're still drawing now. Offered the artist a handsome sum if she got a few hundred done in a day or so. We've started posting up the ones we already have, seeing as it'll be good to get the word out.'

'"Traitor. Reward if brought in alive to any guard station",' Luther read from the poster. 'Short and to the point, though it is likely she's not in the city.'

'Well, like you quite rightly said, it sets a precedent that we're not tolerating such behaviour and that we have no ties to this... situation,' Jetson replied.

'What of the man? Not planning on getting one drawn up for him?' Luther queried.

'You said the body was him—'

'I said it was most likely him, but I could be wrong. It was a guess, Jetson. I've not seen the body myself,' Luther snapped.

'Well, you're probably right in the matter.'

'What makes you so sure?' Luther said sharply. 'Another set of drawn posters is surely no issue?'

The room went quiet.

'Yeah, why not get them both drawn up, Jetson?' Carol spat. 'Both are traitors to the city. Regardless of whether they're alive, their friends and families should know what sort of people they were. Besides, the girl could be dead, just like the guy.'

'It would be a waste of our damn time and resources.' Jetson reddened, tightening his words.

The room fell quiet again. Luther felt Jetson was being overly stubborn about the issue and tested the water. The man never concerned himself over the sparseness of resources.

'You know, Jetson, I met someone today in Crossover. He was a member of the Eastern Legion, I'm assuming there to represent Trittle. Tall chap, shaved head, with a deep voice. He was quite blunt with me.' Luther paused and glanced around the room at the serious faces. He continued, 'You are never going to guess what he asked me.'

'You told him we have nothing to do with this whole thing, right?'

A few of the committee members muttered, shifting in their seats.

'Well, you see, that is exactly what I was going to say. However, the man seemed to know far more of the situation than I had realised.' Luther focused on Jetson. 'He knows of our missing people and asked what they should do this time if they find the second one.' He stood up and held the poster beside him, looking around the room again. Everyone seemed confused.

'Spit it out,' Carol said with impatience.

'The man said he had met with someone here.' He pressed his finger down onto the table. Luther's words turned bitter. 'From our committee.' He glared around the table. 'And whoever it was essentially endorsed killing off our train engineer. So, it appears we're facing an even bigger security threat than just a dead body on the other side of the continent. It appears we might have the real traitor in this very room, someone who has neglected to tell us the truth.' He stared around, noticing Carol face towards Jetson.

'Weren't you the one they delivered the messages to, Jetson?' Carol paused. 'I must say, you were confident in the dead body being that bloke just now, weren't you?'

Everyone stared at him.

'I deal with foreign relations, yes, Carol. It's my job.' His words boiled along with his face.

Resisting a grin at Carol's jab, Luther started to talk again. 'I endorsed the same actions against our second missing person, not because I wanted to, but to uphold the view that we in Carbon City knew of it and that we know what we're doing. Otherwise, it would have been noted by him that us at the top here, equals in the committee, do not communicate or work together at all.'

A mumbling of agreement broke out around the table at Luther's decision.

'So, as it stands, we gave instruction for the killing of this man to begin with?' Ana asked.

'Essentially. Though the guy seemed to find the death unfortunate.' Luther put a hand on his forehead. 'So, to not point the finger at someone yet, does anyone here have information for me? To help enlighten the situation?' Luther shook his head. 'Or perhaps, just perhaps, this man from Trittle is making shit up. They all seem like a nice jokey bunch over there, do they not?'

The committee groaned in disagreement. Everyone knew that the Eastern Legion were far from jokey.

'No? Well then, we have discussed all we can. I'll look personally into this matter and keep you all updated.' Luther stood up. 'Guards,' he called out. A handful of guards entered the meeting room. He turned to them. 'Please call over the radio to the outposts that we are on high alert for this evening and that no one is allowed to leave the city until eight tomorrow morning. Double the guards around the building, too. No one is allowed in or out until my word, understood?' The guards nodded and left the room.

Luther turned to the committee, who were now quietly speaking to each other. 'I will not have the person responsible for this fleeing. I take security very seriously and treason is not accepted.' He turned to Carol, softening his tone, uncertain how she might react. 'Carol, it'll set back your miners' work routine, which I apologise for in advance, but I hope you understand the urgency.'

'Not a problem,' Carol replied.

'Everyone back in here tomorrow morning at six so we can discuss this further. If you do not attend, it will only arouse suspicions, so I strongly advise against missing it.' Luther moved to the door and stood with it open, signalling people to leave.

Everyone left the room until only Jetson remained, still seated in his chair. Luther closed the doors and moved back towards the table.

'Do you think I'm stupid? Even Carol can see the guilt in your face,' Luther said harshly. 'What are you fucking doing? Keeping secrets? We're on the same side.' Luther always hated what he perceived as cowardice. It had no place in the committee.

'I deal with foreign relations and I assure you they only told me what I told—'

'I. Hate. Liars. Speak the truth,' Luther spat.

'Trittle… they let me know of activity happening within the dam and asked if we were involved. There had been talk in Russet of some Carbon City folk apparently, so I told them, like anyone would, that it was a load of rubbish and whoever it was had no relation to us.' Jetson tried maintaining eye contact with Luther. 'It's the truth.'

'Did you give the order to kill our train engineer?' Luther moved closer to him.

'Not really,' Jetson replied. 'I mean, all I said was to do as they pleased with them. Not my bloody fault it actually was an actual engineer.' Jetson shrugged. 'How else co—'

'Ever think to search through our employee lists here before giving the go-ahead? I mean, have you forgotten about our project? Hermann will be back within the week and it isn't time to be fucking about with Trittle and their Legion.' Luther's rage began to build, though he still attempted to keep his voice down. Years of work had gone into his project for oil, and to have Jetson disrupt any chance of it succeeding could not be tolerated.

'I know. But surely this will strengthen the bond we have with them? Knowing we were still serious about that area. The Forbidden Zone being patrolled correctly is a good thing. They get serious about that stuff,' Jetson replied, growing more confident.

'It has only attracted unwanted attention, you idiot. What am I to do now? I've permitted them to go poking around for the girl, too, if she is even still alive. What if they decide to look a little further into the zone and find us?'

'You should have kept quiet about your talk with Trittle. No one needed to hear it,' Jetson said in a quiet but severe tone. 'It does little to ease us all, knowing someone in the city is going behind our backs.'

'Perhaps if you hadn't gone behind my back in the first place, it wouldn't have been a problem.' Luther scowled.

'Could you not have spoken to me first before blurting it to everyone?'

'How was I to know it was you?' Luther replied. 'It was only after I announced it that the guilt was written plainly across your face. So don't you dare blame me.' He refined his tone and leant across the table.

Jetson stood his ground. 'It changes nothing, though. We're still in the same position, regardless. You've just made it worse. And don't forget about you. I know you aren't as honest as you'd like to think. Those from the oil fields are still on the lookout for you, you know.' Jetson smirked. 'So, you and I are more alike than you think.'

Luther kept his face frozen, forcing his temper to settle. Jetson's actions had undermined the strength of the committee, but an actual threat towards himself he would not endure.

'Once again, I deal with foreign affairs, so it's my job to know these things.' Jetson tilted his head forwards, his words cooled.

'I suppose so.' Luther moved closer to him around the table. 'What do you suggest, then, for this mess we are in?'

'Well, of course, because you told everyone, we'll have to find someone responsible for it,' Jetson said.

'So, perhaps pick someone random for the culprit?' Luther asked him, swallowing the jibe with a twitch.

'Yeah, a scapegoat. It could be anyone you want.' Jetson leaned back in his chair.

'I'd like that. Give the committee a whole make-believe backstory, yes.' Luther nodded to himself. 'That'd be fun.'

'See. Not so bad, is it?' Jetson gave a short smile. 'Finding someone so quickly will bring confidence back into the committee, too, I'd say.'

'That's true. You know how to work those relations, after all.' Luther forced a smile, too. 'Well, I'm tired, which isn't helping my mood. Sorry for the outburst, Jetson.'

'Good,' Jetson replied.

'I'll think of something tonight for tomorrow's meeting. Just, if anything comes your way tomorrow, Jetson, just do what I say and it'll work out fine.' Luther smiled again, opening the doors and leaving Jetson still seated.

CHAPTER 22 – SHELBY

Climbing down the lift shaft felt easier than Shelby had expected, though not knowing the distance below him kept unsettling his mind. Eventually, he reached the floor, where Roy stood waiting. Thankfully, Roy had left his gun at the top and now only carried the large blade that he kept on his belt.

Both of them shone the torches around at the walls before looking at the ground they stood on, realising the smallness of the space. Shelby noticed a handle on top of a small hatch beside him, but stayed quiet, unsure if he wanted to head further below. In the middle of the floor, thick metal cables went straight up to the top of the shaft. Roy unsheathed his blade and hit them, creating a loud echo.

'Seems sturdy enough.' Roy tugged on one. 'Probably safer than my rope.' He looked down at the floor. 'And this'll be the lift.' Roy attempted to peek down the small gap on one side. 'Appears we can't be going further.'

Shelby remained quiet, reflecting on the options. To return up meant going outside to the trucks, but also being near the crew. The option of staying below meant dealing only with Roy, and for all he knew, the hatch might lead to another way out.

'What about this?' Shelby crouched and placed his palm on the handle, giving it a pull.

'Huh, well, that is a way in, yeah. Seems in good nick, too, judging by the crazy condition of this place.' Roy crouched down beside him and poked around the handle for a hole, before giving it another yank himself. 'Don't suppose you got the key, do you?' He stood up and stretched his back.

'Afraid not,' Shelby replied, standing up beside him. 'Now what?' He sighed, relieved that the choice of going deeper appeared to be a dead end.

'Eh, what about that?' Roy pointed the torch upwards to a set of lift doors a few feet above them. 'Doubt they'll lead to the generators, but I could be wrong. We might find something good.' He grabbed the rope and climbed up to the doors, attempting to pull them open with one hand. 'Ah, shit. These are as stiff as the last ones.' Roy dropped back down to Shelby, staring from him to the doors.

'The chair?' Shelby replied, not knowing what else to suggest.

'Yep, but I ain't climbing back up for it just to come back down. And I'm guessing you aren't up for that, either. A lot of hard work for a fucking chair.'

Roy was right, though Shelby felt he had little choice, being the outsider.

'Victor!' Roy called out and waited for a response. Silence filled the shaft until Roy shouted his name again.

A few seconds passed before they heard Victor call out, 'That you, Roy?'

'Yes,' he replied, looking towards Shelby. He added at a normal volume, 'Who else would it bloody be? The idiot.' He faced upwards again and put his hands to his mouth. 'We need a chair.'

'To sit on?' Victor replied.

'No, to…' Roy went from shouting to mumbling the rest of his words. 'To sit on, what the hell do you think we need it for?' He seemed to be losing his patience.

Shelby found the whole situation amusing, unsure if Victor was messing around or being stupid.

'Throw a chair down!' Roy screamed.

'Right, got it. Throw the chair down,' Victor repeated. 'Stand back. Dropping it straight down from my end.'

'Be a stupid way to die, wouldn't it,' Roy grumbled.

'By the chair or by Victor?' Shelby replied.

'Both,' Roy replied, making both of them laugh uneasily.

A clang of metal sounded above them. Shelby and Roy jumped back, attempting to cover their heads.

They flinched at the crash of the metal chair hitting the lift. A deafening ring echoed on impact, prompting both of them to cover their ears.

'Didn't expect that.' Roy scrunched his face.

'Got it?' Victor called.

'Yes,' Roy screeched. 'Now fuck off.'

'A thank you would have been nice,' Victor replied.

Roy glanced at Shelby in disbelief, considering the man could have killed them. He picked up the deformed chair and attempted to fold it back up. Shelby climbed the rope and gripped onto the small ledge below the lift doors, pulling himself onto it and up against them. He struggled to balance on the ledge, it being only a foot wide. Roy stretched up and jumped, passing the chair to Shelby, who wedged it in the gap between the doors and began pushing it with his feet to one side. The doors opened slowly.

'That'll do,' Roy said, starting to climb the rope.

Shelby dropped the chair down onto the lift and moved through the gap to open the doors further, flicking his torch to see in front of him. Ahead spanned a clean, narrow corridor with a thin layer of dust covering the place. Roy jumped in from behind him, watching where he pointed the torch.

'There's gotta be stairs down to the lift,' Roy murmured, eyeing the doorways. 'Eh, maybe,' he spoke up. 'We'll check this floor first. I'll take the left.' He turned into a doorway, splitting off from Shelby.

Happy with the arrangement, Shelby moved through the entrance to his right and found a small room with old computers and screens like the ones in the control room. It barely interested him, but he knew Victor might be keen on seeing them. He searched the room and lit up one of the walls, revealing a map pinned up onto it. Shelby stared at it, struggling to recognise the location, before he noticed a smaller map beside it, appearing to show the layout of the military base. He unpinned it from the wall and folded it into his pocket.

Leaving the room, he headed further down the corridor. The more distance he gained from Roy, the better chance he stood of finding another way out.

The hallway opened into a small living area with a few settees that looked untouched. Next to them hung a large screen placed upon the wall. To the left, Shelby scanned over a kitchen area looking capable of feeding large groups.

'Shelby!' Roy called out from behind him.

'You found the generators?' Shelby asked, moving ahead.

'Nope, but something better,' Roy replied. 'Come here.'

Stopping for a moment, Shelby decided to turn back. To ditch Roy when he remained unarmed and uncertain of another way out would be a mistake. He moved back through the corridor and walked into the room where Roy's voice had come from. Shelby's torch lit up the items opposite him. There were shelves upon shelves of stored food and drink, more than he had ever seen in a single place.

'More valuable than gold and jewels to me,' Shelby said, dazed at the sight.

'In some places, perhaps. I gotta admit, I've not seen anything like this. All this… variety.' Roy picked up some spice pots. 'Good job we got our bags. Can't ever have enough food, and if we got leftovers, it'd trade well. Bet no one's ever heard of' – he opened a box and peered inside – 'salt and vinegar crisps before.' Roy chucked a packet to Shelby and then opened one himself.

Opening up the packet, Shelby stared at the yellow pieces before picking one out. Roy sniffed his before taking a bite.

'Damn, that makes your mouth water.' His eyes widened before he crunched the crisp. 'Bit hard and got a chew to them, but they taste good to me.' He stuffed more into his mouth, browsing the selection.

One bite caused Shelby's mouth to water, too. He had never tasted something so strong and wondered what crisps were exactly. The only word he recognised from the packet was 'salt'.

Shelby rolled the packet up and put it into his backpack before browsing the shelves with Roy. The extra food stoked his thoughts of escape. It would give him far better odds of survival. He still needed a gun before attempting it, though.

CHAPTER 23 – ZARA

Another night of walking. Eve insisted that travelling at night provided more safety, though Zara wondered if she meant for themselves or for others they might come across.

Zara ached for something soft under her feet instead of the hard road they followed. The boots she wore were not made for constant walking; her skin was beginning to blister.

'How much further?' she asked, almost exhausted.

'Another few hours and we'll be in sight of the bridge, I reckon,' Eve replied between half a breath. 'If it's there.'

'If it's there?' Zara replied, now worried the walking might be for nothing.

'Yeah, if it's there. I ain't been myself,' Eve snapped.

Panic started to seep into Zara's mind. With the woman's tendency to kill instead of chat to others, she wondered how Eve had heard of the place if she'd never been there.

'How do you know about it then?' Zara questioned.

'Rumours and such,' Eve said bluntly.

Unsure whether to press the subject further, Zara kept quiet for a moment. Eve began to talk again.

'Town called Grimsfoot. Don't know and don't care if it's still there. Place full of people like me. Scavengers. Murderers. Rife with lies and the such. The bridge was one such rumour for some looking to escape. I guess we'll see if it exists soon enough.' Eve's tone was hostile.

'A town?' Zara abruptly asked.

Eve pointed left into a forest and they began to leave the hardened tarmac behind them. Zara's boots pressed into the soft damp ground. The leaves and foliage of the forest shaded them from the sun that had begun to rise. Zara spotted only a handful of dead trees among the growth.

'Is, was. Only town I knew of anyway.' Eve's voice became brittle as the surrounding land softened. 'Can't imagine it lasted long. Probably killed themselves, if the Legion never done the job. Too loud and too many.' She let out a quiet sigh. 'A mistake.'

'The town?' Zara asked, but Eve ignored her. Quiet fell between them while they continued through the forest.

'So, got any plans after the bridge then?' Zara smiled, attempting to lighten the mood. Eve's face remained unresponsive at the words, prompting Zara to continue. 'You know, back to the cinema? Or...' She hesitated at the lack of reply. '... Or something?'

'Don't think I've ever been one for plans, though I doubt I'll be heading back to any of these places. I'll just keep moving like I do, though I ain't got much left in me anyway.' Eve focused on the ground. 'Least I can do now is get you back a little of the way home.'

A thin, brief smile appeared on her lined face. 'Hopefully something I'm able to do right.'

They stopped by the brow of a small hill to have a drink. Green foliage covered the wet muddy ground around them.

'Thank you, Eve. You know, you could always—'

'Get down,' Eve whispered harshly, pulling Zara down beside her.

Zara dropped the bottle of water in her hand and fell to the ground, grabbing a handful of mud in the process. She wiped it down herself and tried to pull the sleeves of her jacket up, feeling stressed at dropping her bottle in the darkness.

She noticed Eve's outline crawling up to the brow of the hill. Zara sat, annoyed at the sudden change in things and the disappearance of her bottle. After a few seconds, she crawled up to Eve and lay beside her, looking down the hill. Ahead of them, several lights illuminated a small wood-and-rope bridge that swayed over darkness.

'The ravine and the bridge,' Zara whispered, seeing dim yellow lights move around it.

'Not just. Seems like it's their bridge. Not sure it's a good move.' Eve sounded agitated. 'We should head away from this place.'

'What? Why?'

'Legions. A whole lot of 'em. Each yellow light could be one of their helmets,' Eve replied briskly.

'What's your point?' Zara felt confused at her words. The presence of the Eastern Legion hardly surprised her, and she had presumed Eve had thought the same.

'They might only be here at night. Perhaps I can cross in daylight?' Zara continued, the thought of home pushing at the forefront of her mind. She could be back with her parents and Heather before the week ended.

'Might be true, but how you supposed to hide in plain daylight from them? You get spotted and they'll kill you, no questions,' Eve warned.

'Did them being here not cross your mind?' Zara asked, a little too boldly.

'Look, girl, I knew there would be some, but from here I can count at least a dozen of those little lights they have on their helmets, meaning this lot down here's no small patrol.' Eve tightened her voice. 'Being sneaky ain't no option.'

'But, what if… what if I said I was from there?' Zara whispered. 'If they know I'm from the city, they might—'

'I thought you said they killed your friend,' Eve cut in. 'You call me a savage, but them lot, they ain't just gonna let you pass on through. It's their bridge. And who says they aren't looking for you? Chances are if they lay eyes on ya, you're as good as dead,' Eve fumed.

Zara knew Eve was right. She was clutching at straws. A few days ago she wouldn't have even contemplated trying to talk her way past the Legion. She let out a sigh. 'Well, what now then?'

Both of them watched the bridge in silence. The clearing in front of it was dotted with a handful of cut tree trunks that gave little cover.

Eve cleared her throat. 'Now hear me out, because if you want to get across, it'll have to happen,' Eve said severely. 'If we could try to lure one of them near us without the others realising, I could kill 'em and you can put on their clothes. Then I'll make a distraction. While they busy themselves with me, you could stand a good chance of crossing the bridge. How does that sound?' Eve asked. 'Unless you got something else that'll work?'

Feeling uneasy, Zara faltered at the thought. 'I'm not—'

'I'll do all the killing. It'll be quick. An eye for an eye. They killed your friend, we kill one…' Eve turned to their left.

Zara looked to where Eve faced and spotted the yellow glow of two Legions approaching their position.

'Two of them.' Eve pointed. 'One each. Zara, can you do that?' She checked the ammo in her gun and holstered it. Eve then took out a switchblade similar to the one she had given Zara. 'Get a blade out.'

One hand felt the knife in her pocket, but Zara decided to pick the larger one from her belt.

'Eve…' Zara attempted to talk but nerves trapped her voice in the back of her throat. Her hands trembled around the blade and she was unsure how successful her attempt might be. Eve acknowledged the weapon in her hand and nodded.

'Remember, quietly.' Eve moved to a crouch and peered over the hill. The two guards were now within earshot. Eve pointed to her neck and then at her blade, gesturing to slice their throats. She hurried to another tree several metres away but still in sight of Zara, who continued to lie on the ground. The sky had lightened enough to give a visible but difficult view of what surrounded them.

The two Legions stood between her and Eve, both wearing their masked helmets and each holding a weapon. Zara kept still as they passed the trees beside her and continued on, passing Eve, who gestured for Zara to take the one on the left. Zara felt sick and her legs were weak. A different plan was no longer an option.

Zara slowly moved to a crouched position. The patrol halted. She froze. The faint yellow glow of their masks seemed to be angled at the ground. She saw Eve move closer to the one on the right, stopping only a metre away. Mud squelched beneath her feet as she stepped towards the pair in the silence of the forest. Zara kept her eyes fixed on the left figure, hoping to catch up before they started moving again.

Suddenly, she slipped. She grabbed a branch to stop her fall, glimpsing her water bottle by her feet. The branch made a loud crack and broke off from the tree, causing her to lose her balance and drop her blade before hitting the ground with a thud. Both the Legions twisted around, their guns raised, one moving closer to investigate the noise in the dim light.

Zara froze, unsure if they could see her half-hidden under the fallen branches. Behind the sole approaching Legion, she witnessed the other one struggling against Eve, who exposed and cut their throat. Blood poured down the man's front as he choked and fell to the floor. The second Legion turned at the sound, seeing Eve with her knife out. Zara hesitated before she jumped up and grabbed their arms from behind. She locked them between her own and pulled them around their back to stop the Legion shooting.

Dropping the gun, the figure tried to break free from Zara's grip. Finally, the Legion kicked her leg, knocking them both to the ground.

After a few seconds, the wriggling slowed to a halt. Zara closed her eyes, still straining to keep her grip tight.

'Keep them like that,' Eve whispered, standing up from one knee. Zara opened her eyes to see Eve wiping her blade. 'Try not to cover the clothing in blood. The other one certainly won't be of any use now.' Eve shook her head.

Realising she had already slit the Legion's throat, Zara let go of the body, causing it to fall limp.

'Oh, now come on,' Eve said with irritation, pushing the body back on its side. 'Can't go in with a uniform soaked in blood. I know it's your usual fashion, but that ain't how these folk roll. They'll know something is up before you even reach the bridge.' Eve removed the masked helmet from the body, revealing a young woman's face beneath it.

'Well, ain't that handy. Her uniform is likely to be a much better fit.' She glanced towards Zara, whose stomach wrenched with guilt. 'She would have killed us just the same so don't be letting her face fool you.' Eve raised her brow and chucked the helmet down beside Zara. She scowled. 'Don't go playin' that game with me, now. Women can be just as nasty as men.'

'I know,' Zara replied, finding her blade on the floor and slipping it back through her belt. Her fear turned to rage for a second at the two people now dead because of her. Zara felt she should be thankful, considering Eve had done so much to help her.

'I'm just not used to it, that's all,' she said solemnly.

'Sorry,' Eve responded. 'I forget sometimes. It's why you need to get home. Now, let's see if it fits ya and then I'll hide the bodies. Won't be long before they realise two of their people are missing.'

CHAPTER 24 – LUTHER

Luther woke earlier than usual. He'd set an alarm for an hour before the meeting. He wanted to review the plan he'd developed during the night and arrive first into the meeting room. To his own surprise, he'd slept well and so decided to make use of the extra time and have a shave and bath so he'd feel fresh and ready to endure the day's events.

Sitting by the desk, Luther sipped his tea and picked up his small notebook, brushing his hand across the indents of the faded cog that marked the front. He closed his eyes, recalling the burning sensation of smoke down his throat.

A light knock at the door disturbed the thought.

'Come in,' Luther said softly, his mind still half-occupied.

'Breakfast.' Ruben entered with a tray. 'Guessing you might want a bite before heading in.' He placed it beside Luther on the desk.

'Thank you.' Luther flicked through his notebook and took another sip of tea.

'All still good to go ahead?' Ruben asked, moving back towards the doorway. 'From what we discussed last night?'

Placing his notebook down, Luther pulled his breakfast closer and eyed the toast and eggs on his plate. He faced Ruben, who awaited an answer.

'All good, yes, Ruben,' he replied with a nod and took a mouthful of food.

'I'll start making the arrangements.' Ruben closed the door on the way out.

****

One by one, the committee members entered the meeting room. Luther sat in his usual spot. A few groans sounded by some who appeared to have just woken up. He remained unsure about how everyone would take the next few minutes, double-checking his gun and handcuffs. Once all the committee members were seated, he got to his feet. Jetson eyed him with a calm and collected look, much to Luther's liking.

'Glad to see you all here.' He paused. 'Lessens any suspicion surrounding some of you.' Luther found a mixture of faces, some half asleep and others looking a little more nervous. 'As we learnt last night, there is someone within this committee who has been acting out on their own and unsettling the waters with Trittle and their Legion. I discovered this by having one of the Legion commanders talk to me as if we were all somehow aware of this communication.' Luther shook his head. 'I spent the whole of last night trying to find out more... and, thankfully, I did. I have discovered the person who is responsible for this mess.' He paused before sharpening his tone. 'And yes, yes, they're sitting right here.' Luther stared around at each member.

'Dear Jetson. Please would you stand up,' Luther said, gesturing towards him.

The man stared back in disbelief, his calm and collected appearance vanishing within the instant. He remained seated before Luther gave a subtle nod and smile to assure him. Jetson stood up from his chair and kept his eyes focused on Luther.

'I knew it, Carol knew it, and I think deep down we all knew it. Your guilt was written all over that face of yours yesterday and it's starting to show through yet again. So then, was it you, dear friend?' Luther started to make his way calmly over to him.

Jetson hesitated, keeping his eyes fixed on Luther, who gave him another subtle nod.

'Yes... it was.' Jetson tightened his jaw, holding his gaze.

'Ah, so I thought. Now we have the confession, I ask you all, what do we do to people who act against our city?' Luther looked around the room. 'Is this not treason?'

'He should be locked up,' a man said.

'We're here to protect and help this city and the people, and this man has brought us closer to conflict,' a woman shouted.

'People, please,' one member pleaded. 'He did just admit to the crime, so surely this honesty should be shown mercy?'

'Mercy?' Luther said, making the others fall quiet. 'Why, I cornered him last night and he was keen to blame someone else in this room for his actions. This man is a coward and a liar, and it will not be tolerated.' Luther's face twisted.

Still standing at the table, Jetson's face reddened.

'I was trying to do what was best for—'

'Guards, arrest him,' Luther directed.

Three guards entered at once and cuffed Jetson.

The man glared at him before one guard shoved a cloth in his mouth and put a bag over his head. Several of the members shifted in their seats.

'And not discuss it with the rest of us?' Luther continued. 'That isn't how a committee works. It is not single-handedly your city to rule. We are all equal in votes. Now, be quiet while we discuss your terms.' Luther faced the rest of the committee around the table. 'So, I'll ask you again, what do we do with him?' Luther needed the choice to be a group effort, even if he had already decided the outcome.

'I'd kill him, depending on whether his actions bring about a war,' Carol said. 'We should have little tolerance for such behaviour.'

'Kill him?!' A few gasps came from some of the others, shifting again in their seats.

Ana started to talk. 'We'll be as bad as Trittle and the rest of the wasteland if we murder people in such a manner. He hasn't brought war upon us, nor has he committed murder himself. He's just caused some... complications? I say lock him up.' Ana turned to Luther. 'So, considering you're head of security, what's your view on the matter?'

'Ana.' Luther smiled. 'Well, I side with both of the two suggestions. Killing him seems a little extreme considering he didn't kill the engineer found in Russet himself... But prison, well, that seems far too lenient. I propose we lock him up, and if war should come out of these events, then we can consider the option of sentencing him to death. Though before you complain, war does seem unlikely, don't you think?' There were a few murmurs before Luther continued. 'He'll just be serving some time, most likely. Best of both choices, really. Are we all in agreement?'

Each committee member nodded, some more easily than others.

'I will personally escort him to his cell. I think we'll all agree that the public should not know about this, along with Trittle and their Legion. We need to look strong and stable to the world, not a group who fight among themselves like the savages elsewhere. For the time being, I will take on his affairs in foreign relations, now that my face is familiar to Trittle. I will encroach less on your trading, Ana, unlike Jetson. In time, we will find a suitable replacement for his position, so if any of you have suggestions, we'll start putting together a list.' Luther moved towards the doorway once the guards had removed Jetson from the room. 'You're all free to carry on as usual. Security measures will be lifted, too.'

'What about this other engineer, the girl?' one of the committee members asked.

'I'll deal with that headache later on today. We have some cleaning up to do.' Luther raised his brow.

'What about Jetson? You said he confessed last night? I want to know what he said,' another member asked.

'Ah, well, he was warned by the Legion we had someone from the city poking around at the dam. He presumed they weren't from here, not bothering to check with us, and allowed them to kill the trespasser. The whole thing is his bloody fault and could have been avoided. It *would* have been avoided if he had brought it to the table before considering such violent actions. We would have checked our districts, found we had people missing and avoided the whole mess.'

Murmuring broke out between the committee members.

'Make what you will of it.' Luther backed out of the room, following the guards. 'We can discuss it further soon.'

Luther, with the guards and Jetson, headed out of the back entrance of the building and got into a different car to his usual choice. One guard got in the back with Jetson and Luther sat in the front beside Ruben, who was driving.

CHAPTER 25 – SHELBY

Shelby accompanied Roy on the stairwell, descending further underground. He noticed the stairwell only went down, and that the floor they had climbed to seemed to be the highest floor linked to the control room above via the lift.

Besides discovering the first storage room, full of food and drink, he had found little else. Everything looked clean except for a thin layer of dust. They found beds and bathrooms untouched, like the kitchen and storage room on the floor above. Shelby had never seen a place still intact from the old world.

'Seems a waste no one ever used this place,' Shelby said, continuing on down a corridor to glance into the next room.

'Perhaps they didn't get the chance to climb down before their little war started.' Roy peered into another bedroom. 'Still, they've left it nice and clean for us now.' He hit the bed, throwing dust up into the air. 'Not got a good bed like this back home. Probably would fit in the lift, too.' He stared at it and pressed his hands down onto the covers. 'If we had the power on.'

'Could try the next floor down?' Shelby replied from the doorway, keen on exploring further, knowing the stairwell carried on down.

'Aye, could do.' Roy eyed the bed again. 'You go on ahead. I'll keep looking on this level.'

'Sure, I'll come back up if I find something of interest.' Shelby left and headed towards the stairs. He hoped the next floor would provide a way out, or at least something to defend himself with.

After descending to the level below, the stairwell stopped completely, travelling no lower. Another narrow corridor stretched out in front of him in a similar layout to the floors above. Doorways lined both sides before it reached the lift shaft at the opposite end. The idea of finding another way out vanished now he stood on the last floor.

Facing the darkness alone and without a weapon, Shelby moved ahead, shining the torch through each doorway, opening any doors that were closed. On his right he found a small cupboard full of cleaning equipment, but it provided nothing of real use. To his left, Shelby was met by another closed door, though this one seemed wider. With a hard push on the handle, he opened it up and flashed his torch around, catching a glisten from several areas of the room.

He recognised the shelving units lined across the walls, much like the ones Roy had found upstairs. These, however, were filled with an assortment of weapons and labelled boxes of ammo. Realising what he had stumbled upon, Shelby picked up a pistol and pointed the torch at it. The black gun felt light to hold, with its grey magazines lying in a box underneath where he'd picked it up from.

He stared back at the doorway and listened out for any footsteps, quickly putting his torch down to load the gun. It took him a minute before he figured out how the ammo clipped up through the handle. It felt far different from the rifle he used back home.

Suddenly, the lights flickered on in the room, followed by the ones in the hallway, as Shelby loaded the handgun and pulled back the top. He kept silent, now hearing footsteps approach, knowing that if Roy found him with a gun in hand, it might cause an unwanted reaction. Shelby shoved the pistol into his coat pocket along with a few more of the ammunition clips before picking up the torch.

Turning towards the doorway, he called out, keeping one hand inside his pocket, resting on the gun.

'That you, Roy?'

Within seconds, Roy appeared in front of him with a broad grin. 'You did it then?' he asked, not grasping the number of weapons in front of him.

'The lights weren't me,' Shelby replied, assuming what Roy meant. 'I just found this place.' He switched his torch off. 'This could be what Hermann's looking for?'

'I mean…' Roy stepped in, his mouth ajar. 'Hermann said think bullets… but bigger. I don't see any particularly large bullets here, though these are quite hefty.' He picked up a long brass bullet underneath a huge dark green rifle that sat above it. 'Still, I've not seen anything of the sort. We'll get the others in here to shift it all out.'

Shelby moved his hand to the gun in his pocket. They were a long way underground, and he doubted anyone would hear. On the flip side, if this room contained what Hermann needed, they would all be heading home before the day had finished. He gripped the gun, knowing his own use might have expired.

'Hermann will be impressed either way, mate. You've certainly proved your worth.' Roy gave him a smile, moving towards the shelves of guns and turning away from him.

Shelby observed the man happily rummaging through the guns. Roy paid no attention to him standing near the doorway. Slowly pulling his hand out of his pocket, Shelby knew what he needed to do in the hopes of getting home quicker.

'Oh, and I stumbled on this,' Shelby said, drawing Roy's eyes to him. He pulled out the folded map he had found on one of the other floors. 'A map of this place, I assume.' He held it out.

'Huh, I see.' Roy moved over and took it from him. 'Armoury?'

'Doesn't look like it's talking about this room here, though.' Shelby peered around at the layout.

'Nope. This place is just for this bunker, it seems. Bettin' the main one has the bigger bullets Hermann mentioned. Likely back above ground.' Roy folded the map up into his pocket. 'Seems you really have been useful after all. Much more than some of the other lot.' He laughed and grabbed hold of the large scoped rifle from the top shelf and moved towards the door. 'Come on, back to the top. Let's see if this lift is working, eh.' Roy disappeared through the door.

After a few seconds, Shelby grabbed the closest box. Inside, the items reminded him of Kai and Mia, being two small balls of a dark green colour, though they seemed too weighty for kicking around. Small silver rings were clipped onto the sides of them. He stuffed the two balls into his pocket and caught up with Roy.

****

With the power back on, the lift now worked, allowing them to arrive swiftly back up to the top where they'd left Victor, who upon first glance couldn't be seen.

Roy and Shelby stepped out of the lift and followed the static noise to the centre of the room where Victor was sitting, happily fiddling with one of the control panels.

'Guessing we know who put the power back on then,' Roy said dryly.

'Guess we do,' Shelby replied, smiling at Victor, who had yet to notice their arrival.

'Though our exploring wasn't all for nought. Apparently, all it takes for Vic to get going is an old bit of tech. For me, though' – Roy dropped the end of the rifle he carried with a thump, catching Victor's attention – 'it's guns. So come on, how'd ya do it?'

Victor glanced at the large rifle before returning his eyes to the console in front of him.

'Followed the wires to a fuse box over there.' Victor pointed to the wall. 'No generators, though. Flicked some switches and everything booted up like new.' He pressed some buttons before turning up a dial. 'Just seeing if this radio works.'

'Do what you want with your tech stuff later. Now's not the time to listen to Ivan's drivel,' Roy replied. 'We've got a map of the place, so help me find what Hermann needs and you can spend all the time you want down here.' He lifted the rifle up and headed towards the corridor that led back to the surface.

'And you had to spend a couple of hours with him down there?' Victor turned to Shelby and nodded towards the ground. 'Poor sod.' He gave a small chuckle before standing up and going after Roy. Shelby followed a few paces behind them, thinking about the gun in his pocket and how noticeable it might be.

When all three of them arrived back at the top, it took a few minutes before they figured out that the other armoury resided in the hangar next door.

Outside, Shelby still kept his distance. The neighbouring hangar looked damaged, with a huge rip in the metal down one side. He searched for the trucks, finding them still in the same spot.

'Anyone looked in here yet?' Roy called out to a few of the other crew.

'Door ain't opening,' a woman replied.

'And what about that there?' Roy pointed at the ripped metal down the building's side. The comment drew only a blank stare from the woman.

The gap itself appeared dangerous, with splinters of metal sticking out of it. Judging from where Shelby stood, it seemed hardly wide enough for someone to squeeze through. All three of them moved up towards it with several other members of the crew now following.

'You're skinny and know what to look for,' Roy said, checking over Victor. 'Go on, lad.'

'Really?' Victor stopped walking.

'Aye, come on now. Just take it slow.' Roy nodded. 'No point us lot going in if it's empty now, is it? And you're far thinner than most here.'

The idea amused Shelby, letting the supposedly important person into an unchecked hangar alone. It did little to reassure him of his own safety.

Victor shook his head and removed the thick coat he wore. He slipped in and through the gap, avoiding the splinters of broken metal, and disappeared out of sight. Shelby glanced around him at the rest of the crew, who waited on Victor's return, some staring at him.

'This is it, guys,' Victor called out.

The crew looked at each other and began heading into the hangar, one by one. Shelby followed Roy through the gap, eager to avoid the gaze of others.

Once through, he found himself in a small office that opened up through a doorway into the rest of the hangar: one open room from floor to roof. Inside he spotted two vehicles at the back, behind the stacks of what Victor stood gawking at.

'Giant bullets,' Victor said, searching over them with his eyes. 'This has to be it.'

In front of him towered several large objects, in questionable condition.

'Bloody hell.' Roy widened his eyes at the absolute size of them. They were longer than the trucks they had arrived in.

'These are in fact missiles, far more explosive and powerful than any bullet could ever be,' Victor said, placing a hand on one.

'These too, perhaps,' a woman said, picking up a smaller one the size of her arm.

'Looks like we've got quite a selection then.' Roy eyed some short fat rounds stacked up beside a round barrel with thin legs.

'Guessing most of this goes together, though it ain't all in the best condition. And how are we supposed to get it out?'

He walked towards the front of the building, seeing the outline of a large door and chains hanging down both sides. He pulled down on one but not much happened.

'Give me a hand, then,' Roy growled, aggravated by all the eyes watching him. 'It's gotta open up one way or another.'

Two crew members jumped in to help, yanking the chain down and dragging the door up.

'I'm heading back underground for a bit if I'm done here,' Victor called out to Roy.

'Suit yourself.' Roy's voice was strained as he struggled to hold the door. 'Someone get a wedge to put under this. A spare truck, rubble or fucking anything, use your damn heads.'

Passing underneath, Victor gave a visible grin as Roy and the others fought to keep the door open. Shelby turned back to the missiles and wondered why they needed a genius to know what a giant bullet looked like, considering they were identical in shape.

Turning back to the front, he watched as Roy gave up on the wedge idea and instead started tying the chain up.

'Right, get the trucks brought around. We'll fill them up with what we can and head back to the ship once they're loaded. Some of you will be left here to prepare the next lot of loot to take back. The priority will be smaller weapons to start with,' Roy shouted, starting to head back towards Shelby.

'We now have to figure out how in the hell we'll be moving these big old bastards here.' He patted one of the missiles.

Shelby focused on Roy, knowing a few of the crew were staring at him. He should have escaped back with Victor underground.

CHAPTER 26 – ZARA

The bodies were still warm when they moved them. Eve mentioned the pair might have been on a certain route and began acting paranoid over others coming to investigate. Zara felt ill at stripping one of the two people who were now dead because of her. The Legions might have killed Trent, but she guessed the pair they had just killed were hardly responsible for it.

She took in a deep breath, adjusting the long black coat and Legion armour she now wore over her clothes. Then she picked up the assault rifle, believing the weapon posed more of a danger to herself than anyone else, having never used one before.

'Won't be long and you'll be home, my dear,' Eve said, searching over the pockets of the other body. 'Once you get across, ditch that helmet and coat, alright? Not sure what your side is like but here, if you get seen in Legion gear, there ain't no discussion. You're as good as dead.'

'I'll be sure to get rid of it once I'm across,' Zara assured her. 'It fits at least.' She held her arms out.

'Fits well. It'd convince me true enough.' Eve chuckled. 'How's the mask?'

'A little warm,' Zara mumbled, removing it at once. The Legion mask looked more like a helmet than a mask. It covered her entire head and was made from a mix of metal and plastic, with three ridges following along the top, from front to back. The eyes of it were sharp and glowed a faint yellow.

'Ever used that thing?' Eve nodded at the gun.

'Nope,' Zara replied, dropping the helmet to use both hands to explore the weapon.

'Me neither. Looks good, though, don't it?' Eve stared at it and moved towards the other body to pick up the second gun. 'This here is most likely the safety.' She pointed to the side of the gun. 'Same sorta position I've seen it in before. Stops it from shooting, which ain't no good for anyone.' She shook her head.

'Thanks,' Zara replied, uncertain of herself. She looked over the gun and switched the safety off. 'So what now?'

'Time for my distraction. I reckon if I cause one big enough, the Legion will come clawing at me. Should draw them away long enough for you to get across the bridge without any real attention being on ya.' Eve smiled. 'Thoughts on the plan?'

Zara struggled to think of any ideas.

'That sounds great.' Zara pushed a smile through her nerves. 'Thank you.'

Nodding in reply, Eve moved towards the brow of the hill they had lain on earlier. The sun now gave a clear view of the bridge. The ground dipped down from where they were, with a handful of trees ahead. Several Legions stood by the entrance to the bridge in the clearing. At the opposite side of the ravine, across the bridge, stood a large building with a giant symbol on its face: a circle with three swirls in a triangular shape over it, each swirl enclosed by two sharp prongs either side that met back in the centre.

'Now, we can't take too much longer or I'm betting they'll figure something's up.' Eve moved back down the hill.

'Eve?' Zara started walking behind her, anxious at what waited for her ahead. 'Are you sure you won't come with me?'

Eve stopped and turned to her, giving a sincere look. 'Oh, child, there ain't no place for me over there.'

'There is. Plenty of it. You could come back with me to the city. You've done so much for me. I'd be able to repay you for all of it.' Zara smiled.

'Getting you across is repayment enough.' Eve sighed. 'I'm old. I look it and I feel it. I had a chance to cross once and I crumbled at it. It's a little late now for me. Best last thing I can do is to help you get across.' She returned Zara's smile.

'I... What do you mean last?' Zara caught her words.

'Whatever noise I'm about to make, doubtful an old girl such as myself can outrun one of these Legions, let alone a dozen or so.' Eve lowered her head. 'Who knows, I could get lucky now I got one of their guns too.' Her eyes glinted before she stared at the assault rifle and laughed. 'Time to get a move on, Zara.' Eve patted her back.

Unsure what to say, Zara kept quiet. She knew a distraction was needed, and if they both travelled across, there would be no distraction at all.

Letting out a sigh, Zara leant in and hugged Eve. 'Thank you, Eve. Are you sure about this?'

'I made my choice a long time ago.' Eve closed her eyes. 'Might not have been the right one, but it's the one I live with.' She swallowed hard. 'Anyway.' She broke from the hug and turned to face the bridge, wiping a hand across her face. 'Finally gone and lost the plot, it seems.' She cackled. 'Let's get a move on already.'

Zara hugged Eve once more before they parted from each other. She gave her the old gas mask and Trent's bag, being unable to carry them with the Legion uniform.

Putting the Legion helmet back over her head, she took a deep breath. Zara grabbed her gun and crested the hill as Eve trotted away.

In the distance the bridge swayed, though no Legion soldiers were in sight. Zara stopped, unsettled by the lack of them. She knew Eve would provoke them with a distraction, but Eve had never specified what she intended to do. Her chest began to thump hard, unsure whether she had missed the signal.

Zara couldn't afford to lose her chance and walked down the hill, passing the last few trees before the clearing, the bridge growing closer.

A loud bang echoed on the opposite side of the clearing, scattering birds into the sky. Zara's eyes followed them up, drawing her attention to the peak of a mountain in the distance that reminded her of home.

Another gunshot brought Zara's mind back to reality. It must have been Eve, though there seemed to be a lack of reaction ahead at the bridge. She went to move out into the opening but recoiled at a voice to her left.

'Move on north-east,' a woman ordered into Zara's ear. The voice came from inside the helmet she wore.

Three figures in front of her came from nowhere. Zara bolted behind a tree and out of sight. She peeked around the trunk and watched two more Legions run across the bridge, joining up with the others who had disappeared into the treeline on the other side of the clearing. Zara gripped her gun, trying to control the uneasiness surging in the pit of her stomach. More gunshots fired, breaking the silence that failed to settle between them.

She peered around the tree again and found the bridge empty with no one around. Zara moved fast into the open and approached it, noticing the frayed rope and old wooden planks hanging over the sheer dark drop of the ravine.

Hearing a long burst of gunfire rattle off in the forest, Zara turned to face the sound.

'Send reinforcements, they're on the run,' a man's voice sounded from within the helmet.

Within a few seconds, she heard footsteps from the other side of the bridge. Zara twisted back to find a few more Legions running straight at her across it. She stepped back and dropped her gaze to the ground. The figures moved past without a word, disappearing into the treeline as she lifted her head. Zara let out a deep breath and turned again to the bridge.

A single Legion met Zara's gaze, wearing a rich burgundy coat and no helmet. The woman halted in front of her. The voices from within the mask made it difficult to concentrate.

'What are you doing?' the woman questioned sharply, cutting above the radio noise.

Words failed to come out of her mouth. Zara trembled under the uniform and moved her hand towards the trigger of her gun. She looked over the woman, who had fiery red hair, before staring back at the bridge only a few metres away. If she attempted to run across now, it would blow her cover.

The woman gestured towards the forest where the other soldiers were. Zara started moving back towards it, first at a jog but then more of a run to distance herself from the woman in red. Ahead of her were half a dozen Legion soldiers. They slowed to a halt upon entering the forest.

'Heading north-east still,' a voice said. 'Take it easy. We still aren't sure on numbers.'

In front of Zara, the group started to spread out among the trees, the shooting having ceased. The woman Zara had met by the bridge appeared from behind her, moving swiftly among the rest of the soldiers. She held what appeared to be a spear, with a long sharp spike at one end and three claws on the other.

Gunfire sounded ahead, making the group take cover. Zara attempted to calm herself from the rising dread, her heart feeling stuck in her throat. She looked back towards the bridge and then to the few Legion soldiers near her.

At the same moment, bullets sprayed out in her direction, shredding through a few tree trunks and hitting one of the Legions. Zara moved behind a tree, realising her masked helmet made her unrecognisable to Eve.

In an instant, the group returned fire in the direction of the shots. Zara lowered the gun to remove her helmet, but before doing so, someone shouted at her.

'Return fire.' A man to her left pointed. 'We're giving cover from the back here. You're with me.'

Clutching her gun, she gazed in the direction of the gunfire, thinking of Eve. Having to shoot at the woman who had got her this far was not a situation she thought to find herself in. Zara glanced around unable to find the red-haired woman.

She pulled up the gun and aimed down the sight towards where Eve must have been, the Legion soldiers all turned from her, pointing the same way.

'Covering fire!' the man to her side yelled as another Legion got shot. The man next to her ripped his helmet off and stared at her. 'What the hell are you doing?' he spat, his face a hot flush of red.

Zara's heart lurched. She turned, aimed and pulled the trigger of her gun at the man. The gun recoiled up, letting loose bullets that spat out into his chest and head. She spun to the soldiers in front of her and held the trigger down again, trying to keep the gun steady. The bullets flew out, piercing through the backs of a few more surrounding Legions before they started shifting to the opposite side of the trees.

'Enemy from behind!' a voice screeched over her earpiece. 'Class-1 uniform. We need more support. It's an ambush.'

Zara's gun stopped with a click. She hid behind a tree as bullets started flying towards her, splitting the bark.

Seconds later, the shooting stopped again. Zara took out her knife and ripped her helmet off, struggling to breathe in the heat.

'You,' a cold voice growled. The woman with fiery hair appeared from behind her. 'Are you a savage? Or some traitor?'

'Neither,' Zara said.

The sharp spear-like weapon the woman was gripping gave off a slight yellow glow. A sudden hard gunshot cut into the air, making both of them turn.

'Eve,' Zara mumbled under her breath.

The woman moved closer, gradually pushing the clawed end of her weapon towards Zara. The claw began to open, revealing a glowing tip, and wisps of smoke started rising from Zara's coat.

Before Zara had time to react, the woman stopped and frowned at her. 'You're the city girl.'

Another shot sounded. There was a splatter of blood and a cry as the red-headed woman's leg burst open, making her drop the weapon and fall onto the ground.

'Run!' Eve's voice screamed.

Still holding onto her knife, Zara grabbed her helmet and moved deeper into the forest towards where the shout had come from, the sound of more Legion soldiers moving across the bridge behind her.

CHAPTER 27 – SHELBY

Most of the crew left that evening with the trucks, taking weapons, oil and other items to the ship. Shelby attempted to leave with them to stay with the running vehicles, or at least get back to Hermann, but Roy ordered him to stay put.

After they left, Shelby made his way back underground to Victor, keen to escape the stare of the remaining crew members. The idea of Roy and the rest of them never returning flicked through his mind, but he guessed Victor would have been far too valuable to leave.

Victor sat where he had earlier that day, in front of a control panel, underneath several screens on the wall. Curious about what the man was concentrating on, Shelby sat a few metres away, not wanting to disturb him.

'Getting anywhere?' Shelby asked, glancing around the room. Old technology interested him if it proved functional, though his surrounding area back home lacked anything of the kind.

'Almost got it, I think. You used a radio before?' Victor replied.

'Yeah, it has people talking on it most of the time, right?' Shelby cast his mind back to the market in Lornsten where they often played out various bits of music. The thought made him fall silent, sudden memories of his family pouring back into his mind. He cleared his throat and took a deep breath, now thinking of the weapons downstairs.

'Indeed it does.' Victor nodded. 'And you can talk on it.'

A faint static noise sounded as Victor tampered with the controls, making Shelby sit up and lean in closer. Victor turned a dial, increasing the volume. The possibility of being able to speak to someone in Lornsten entered his mind. Most of the locals knew him and would have been able to let his family know he was alive. He stared at Victor, unsure how willing the man might be if he asked. Perhaps if he convinced him to leave the room for a moment, he might stand a chance.

'Let's see if we can find the frequency,' mumbled Victor. 'Might be able to make it feel like home in here.' He paused, looking towards Shelby. 'Well, for me anyway.'

Noise travelled from down the hall, prompting them both to turn. The chance of the sound being Roy seemed unlikely, considering how little time had passed since he and the others had left. Shelby's nerves spiked, his hand moving into a pocket and resting on the gun.

Two men entered the room and stood between Victor and Shelby. They were broad, tall and rough looking. Their eyes rested on Shelby before one started to talk.

'Roy mentioned before he left that there was a small armoury here. Weapons in good condition. Know where it is?' The man spoke slowly, his mouth hanging half-open with each word as he looked from Shelby to Victor.

Holding his gaze, Shelby hid his distress. Of course Roy had told them. An armoury stashed full of weapons, all in excellent condition. It would be the next thing they'd be after now they had found what Hermann wanted. Staying with Victor was a mistake.

'No idea, mate,' Victor replied, turning back to the control panels without giving them any attention.

Lifting his head in disbelief, Shelby gripped the gun tighter in his pocket, seeing both men turn towards him. A surge of adrenaline rushed through him in a mix of anger and desperation.

'I know where it is,' Shelby stated after a long stretch of silence. One hand still gripped the gun in his pocket.

'Lead the way then,' one of them replied hoarsely, holding his stare.

Shelby froze at the words. To accompany them further underground would be a mistake. He attempted to give instructions, his finger resting on the trigger of his pistol.

'It's over in that lift and down—'

One guy stepped closer towards him, bringing a stench of sweat to Shelby's nose.

'We asked you to lead the way, so lead.' The man gave a discerning smile, gesturing with one hand.

Shelby searched across the room for support, but Victor made himself appear too busy with the radio. Clenching his jaw and closing his eyes, Shelby wanted to scream at him.

Silence filled the room. The two men stood motionless in front of him. He scanned over them, noticing their weapons; one with a rifle over his back, and the other with a handgun holstered on his belt. Victor's cowardice made him feel utterly alone. The man unholstered his pistol and took another step towards him.

Standing up, Shelby removed his empty hand from the pocket and made his way over to the lift, deciding to leave his backpack by the chair. The doors opened at the press of the button. He stepped inside, believing his best bet now would be getting to the armoury before they did.

The lift was small, scarcely big enough for the three of them. He kept to one side and stared at the four buttons on the panel, pressing the lowest. The men got in and stood behind him.

It remained silent, besides a disturbing laugh both the men let out halfway down. Shelby kept focused on the door in front of him, feeling their eyes burning into the back of his skull. When the lift eventually stopped and opened, he stepped out and paced ahead to keep the distance between them, paranoid they might attack him at any moment.

'It's just down here,' Shelby said, striding even further ahead into the dimly lit hallway as he reached into his pocket again.

'Woah, murderer, what you going for there?' One of the men aimed his rifle at Shelby from down the hall. 'Go see what he's got in his pocket before we have some fun. I saw him move to it when we came in upstairs.'

The other bloke unholstered his handgun and approached Shelby with caution.

Shelby's heart crawled into his throat. He wasn't sure what to do. Giving up his only weapon would be suicide and wasn't an option.

The man pointed his weapon and spoke, grabbing Shelby's arm. 'Go on then, show us what you got.'

Staring from one man to the next, Shelby realised he had reached for the wrong pocket. The man pulled his hand out to reveal what Shelby held. It was one of the dark green balls he had picked up from the armoury earlier.

'And to think I thought he had a gun.' The man let go of Shelby's arm, and he and his companion both burst into laughter.

'Nah, he's no murderer, is he?' the man with the rifle teased. 'Bit a bad luck is all, killing our friend. Fell on ya weapon, did he?' The man with the rifle spat. 'What a load of bollocks.'

'Seems he collects toys like Victor, too.' The man closest to Shelby took the green ball from him, turning it over in his hand. 'No idea what it is but he ain't going to give us much of a fight with it unless he planned on throwing it at us.' He walked back over to the other man, who still aimed his rifle at Shelby. 'Bit of weight to it. Any idea?' He showed it to his mate, who stared, taking his eyes off his target.

Shelby kept frozen several metres ahead of them in the hallway. At the opportunity of distraction, he stepped back towards the armoury while the men looked over the heavy green ball.

'Not a clue,' the man replied to his mate before staring back at Shelby. 'Oi, what is it?' He gestured his gun at him.

'I… I don't know. Just picked it up from that town we were in,' Shelby lied, avoiding the fact it came from the armoury. 'From a jewellery shop, a place with gold and silver…' He tried recalling what Victor had said after remembering the ball had a small silver ring stuck on the side of it. 'Rings, too, necklaces...'

Both men stared at it, one with his back to Shelby, the other keeping his gun roughly aimed at him.

'The ring on top,' the guy with the rifle said. 'See it? Could be worth something?'

The other guy put his finger through the ring and pulled it out.

'Huh, it comes apart.' He frowned at the ring and then back at the ball in his other hand, touching the textured squares with his thumb. He turned it over, releasing a metal strip from between his fingers that made a faint clink when it hit the floor. Shelby took the chance, taking another few steps back, seeing them both glance down.

An explosion screeched and amplified, tearing outwards down the hallway, ripping through the walls and bodies that stood in its way. The two guys ahead of him were torn apart, taking the brunt of the impact. Shelby was knocked to the ground. His ears rang with pain. He found himself staring up at the ceiling, watching the lights flicker and break from the blast.

Dazed, he shoved off the rubble and flesh that had landed on him, trying to figure out what had happened. He attempted to push himself up off the ground but let out a cry and fell back, his head spinning in pain. Two of the fingers on his right hand were bent backwards, broken. The thick padded coat he wore was ripped down one side. He stopped moving and let the dust settle around him.

A noise ahead of him made him look up. One wall was in pieces and a large chunk of concrete had dropped off onto the floor.

Shelby forced himself over onto his knees, now realising someone might have heard the blast from above. He pulled himself up using the wall beside him, focusing on the broken corridor ahead. Body parts were mixed among the rubble, giving him a moment of relief. Cracks and holes covered the walls on either side of the hallway, but the structure still appeared to be standing.

Shelby stood up straight and stretched his back. He entered the armoury and grabbed one of the larger weapons. The ammo loaded into the underside of the front. It had a small metal aim on top, similar to the one on the pistol he had picked up. Shelby peeked out of the doorway, crouching, and aimed down towards the lift, waiting for someone to appear. His hand coursed with pain when gripping the trigger, making him swap over to his left. The light of the lift was visible through the doors, so he could tell it had remained downstairs with him.

****

Several minutes passed with the lift staying down on Shelby's level. He struggled to keep the gun aiming up ahead. A mixture of drowsiness and pain covered him. He felt the aches grow across his body.

He lowered the gun and stood up, groaning aloud at the pain jarring through his back and hand. Bringing his right arm up in front of him, he used his left hand to grab the two broken fingers. He closed his eyes and went to snap them back the other way, but gave up at the pain.

From his pocket, Shelby took out the other green ball and stared at it, attempting to distract his mind. The thing had almost killed him and had shredded the two guys surrounding it. He stared at the ring before placing the ball back into his pocket, and found a couple more in the armoury. Then he headed out into the hallway and turned right from the lift, deciding to use the stairs to the next floor where the beds were. Although no one had called the lift, Roy's rope still hung down one side of the shaft, and Shelby remained paranoid, knowing the crew could still use it.

Carefully entering up onto the next floor, Shelby aimed his gun ahead into the silence. A mirror caught his attention as he passed by one of the bathrooms. Dust and blood smothered him, accompanied by a massive rip on the right of his coat where something sharp had caught him in the blast. Shelby leant over a sink and twisted the tap, expecting nothing but a few drops of water to come out.

To his surprise, it came flowing through into the sink, though the smell was far from pleasant. Shelby washed it through his hair, face and stubble. He cleaned off any signs of blood before patting himself down to ensure he looked as normal as possible. Observing his right hand, Shelby tried again to snap the two broken fingers back into place. He gave an abrupt push without thinking, and this was followed by a loud click that forced him into a scream. Shelby felt unsure if it had helped, but the fingers sat back in their right place so at least no one would notice.

He picked up the rifle and headed to the next set of stairs to grab some food and decide on what to do next. Shelby thought going up on a full stomach before facing whatever awaited him made more sense than to face it starving. Hopefully it would just be Victor who waited for him, and bringing back a few snacks might help delay any questions.

CHAPTER 28 – LUTHER

The long mountain road narrowed to the width of a single car the further they travelled. Tarmac became broken and eventually the road turned to dirt. The city stood in the distance to the south with the mining district positioned between them. Luther always enjoyed the drive up, finding he could appreciate the cityscape without having to endure the people and noise within it.

Luther knew maintaining the route up the mountain had only been for the sake of Ivan, who hosted the city's radio station, Carbon Rocks. The man never ventured from his building, relentless in doing his daily shows and forecasts, so people delivered what he needed to him. Ivan also provided an extra layer of security for Luther, announcing sightings of unusual activity over the radio, whether good or bad.

Though Luther valued the man's position, it never lessened the irritating drone of his voice. He often wondered if Ivan looked more annoying than he sounded.

A large bump in the road brought Luther's attention back inside the car, where he watched Ruben keep a firm grasp on the wheel.

'Pull the bag from his head and remove the cloth,' Luther said, before once again staring out of the window.

The guard beside Jetson in the back yanked the bag off, revealing a sweaty pallid face. He pulled the cloth out from his mouth.

'You liar,' Jetson griped, his voice rising. 'You two-faced—'

'Ugh, stick the cloth back in his mouth, will you? I can't stand his tone.' Luther shook his head, glancing back at the man. 'You've lost the privilege to talk now. Watch your manners when I give you the chance again.' He turned to admire the view of the mountain above, with its snowy tops catching the sun, as the guard shoved the cloth back into Jetson's mouth.

'This is far enough, I'd say. Maybe halfway? Ivan is still a few miles ahead,' Luther said to Ruben.

The car pulled over towards the edge of the mountain in a spot where the ground widened to several metres. Ruben stepped outside along with Luther, while the guard pulled Jetson from the back, still gagged, his hands cuffed behind him. A light breeze rustled the trees and bushes, disturbing the silence. Luther gestured for the guard to bring Jetson up to the edge of the cliff side.

'Take the rag from his mouth and get him on his knees,' Luther ordered.

In one swift motion, the guard forced Jetson onto his knees and removed the rag before stepping back.

'Pathetic,' Jetson said coldly, staring up at Luther.

'Woah, Jetson, buddy, this is all part of the plan. Good man for going along with it.' Luther smiled, shifting his eyes from him to the city. 'Beautiful, isn't it?'

'Oh, really? And what's this plan of yours?' Jetson pointedly asked. 'This isn't the prison.' He glanced around. 'What I did was for the city, you know that. Why didn't you explain it? How does this make sense to you?'

Luther's tone was light. 'It makes sense to me. You'll be living up here with Ivan for a bit, helping him when he needs it and, most importantly, keeping to yourself.'

'What? For how long?' Jetson asked, narrowing his eyes.

'Forever?' Luther replied with a shrug.

'What? I can't do that. What would be the point? And why have we stopped here?'

Luther kept quiet, mulling over his thoughts before finally answering. 'Well, you see, the issue here isn't really to do with your little traitorous act.'

'What? Then what is it? Project Carbon? I've not told a soul, I swear. No one knows of that besides us, Hermann and whoever you rounded up for the ship.' There was disbelief in Jetson's voice.

'Really?' Luther took out his gun and pulled the trigger. With a sudden bang, a bullet pierced through the side of the guard's head.

'What the fuck are you doing?' Jetson screamed. He failed to get to his feet as the body slumped over beside him.

'That's on your conscience.' Luther stared at Jetson before turning to Ruben, who stood motionless by the front of the car.

'He didn't know the details, just names,' Jetson cried out.

'Names are enough. Last thing I need is to be dragged down to your level and be named a traitor.'

'Look, can we please get back in the car?' Jetson edged away from the guard's body, still on his knees. He looked back down the road.

'Tired of asking questions already?' Luther frowned and looked over the golds of his gun in the sunlight.

'I swear what I did was for the good of the city. This was just an honest mistake. I told you. I've forged good relationships,' Jetson pleaded. 'I'm an asset to the city. Now, can we please just move on from this? Drop me at Ivan's. I've done as you said, admitted to things I need not admit to.' Jetson tried to get up from his knees again but fell back onto them.

'You really are missing the point here, aren't you?' Luther shook his head. 'I don't take threats casually.'

'Threats?' Jetson shook his head. 'What threats?'

'Really?' Luther raised his brow. 'The oilfields. You were happy to mention them before, so surely you haven't forgotten now?'

'Uh, yes, the oilfields, yes. That wasn't a threat, though, no, just simply a mention. You hear things, you know, and I've not said anything to anyone. Water under the bridge and all.' Jetson tried to assure him with a smile.

'Huh, have you not thought about why I want the weapons I sent Hermann to find?' Luther returned the smile, looking back out at the city.

'I thought… for the city. Against the Legion?' Jetson shook his head.

'Well, in part... Though, oil. Something you've always failed to negotiate for.' Luther sighed.

'Oil? You can't.' Jetson scowled.

'I can and will.' He paused, raising his gun against the light. 'You don't really believe you're going to Ivan's, do you?'

'Please, you can't. I swea—'

'Oh, the stories you could tell with Ivan over the radio. You're a liability, Jetson.' He gave a sincere look towards him. 'I've always fancied a hand at foreign relations. Two birds with one stone, wouldn't you say?'

Luther smiled and shot Jetson through the centre of his forehead. The echo faded into the wind. Luther took in a breath of fresh air and holstered his gun. He stared at the slumped body before kicking it over the edge and down into the mountainside.

'Ruben.' Luther signalled to the guard's body. Ruben pushed it over the edge. Luther wondered what Ruben thought of this whole ordeal. His face remained blank, revealing nothing.

'Fancy moving up in the world, Ruben?' Luther smiled. 'I need those posters of the male engineer, Trent, drawn up so we can spread them across the city like Jetson did with the girl. Think you can take charge of that?'

'Of course,' Ruben replied with a nod.

'You can sound more excited than that, you know.' Luther glanced over the edge. 'Ah, I should have taken those cuffs from him.'

'No one will find the bodies,' Ruben replied.

'More concerned about losing the cuffs, if I'm honest. Anyway, Ruben, I need someone to be acting security chief, too, while I sort out handling these foreign relations.' He kept his eye on the man, hoping to see a reaction, but Ruben's face was still expressionless. 'A pay rise comes with it, you know – a hefty one,' he added, intent on seeing him perk up.

'Luther, sir, I – thank you.' Ruben's face lit up with what appeared to be a genuine smile and he shook Luther's hand. 'I'll do exactly what you ask of me, though I may need time to adjust. Thank you.'

Those were the exact words Luther needed to hear. 'That's more like it.' He smiled too, giving Ruben a pat on the back. 'You'll be able to move into the capitol building. Let me work out the details with the others on the committee first before I announce the decision. Anyway, it's time we got going so we can sort out this mess.' Luther moved to the back of the car and opened the door.

The smile seemed to be holding on Ruben's face as he opened the driver's door.

'Oh, Luther, sir, I was thinking about what happened here. Jetson tried to escape and killed the guard before I managed to kill him. Keeps your hands clean and out of the picture if anyone asks. I'll notify the guard's family, too, of the event but will leave Jetson's name out. It also gives a reason for my promotion?' He sat down in the driver's seat and closed the door.

'I couldn't have planned it better myself. We'll make something of you yet.' Luther observed him with a mixture of spite and envy. 'The next few weeks will be quite the task when Hermann returns… Say, have you ever seen Ivan?' Luther asked, moving his mind on to another subject.

'Can't say I have or would want to,' replied Ruben. 'Probably looks worse than he sounds.'

'Agreed.' Luther laughed.

'What made you think of that?' Ruben asked.

'Just, I don't think anyone's actually seen the guy,' Luther replied.

Ruben nodded towards the mountain peak. 'Can always pop by if you want?'

'That's a no. You hate the bloke more than I do, and I can't have you killing such a treasure of our city.' Luther grinned. 'How else would we know what the weather might be?'

'I won't disagree with that.' Ruben widened his eyes before turning the car around and starting the long drive down the mountain.

CHAPTER 29 – ZARA

The luscious greenery surrounding the bridge disappeared into a decaying forest. Zara kept up with Eve, following her and keeping ahead of any Legions. They were yet to speak about what had happened, knowing that in their small moments of rest, keeping silent was far more important.

Further east, they reached a large abandoned building that sat alone between the trees. The barbed metal fence surrounding the place had held its ground well, having only collapsed in a handful of areas.

They crossed over and into the fenced zone, Zara trailing close behind Eve. Even though there was little to stop them crossing it, Zara let out a sigh of relief at passing the fence, feeling safer on the other side of it.

'What happened?' Eve asked, following the building around the corner.

'I managed—'

Something slammed nearby, making them stop. Eve pulled out her handgun, gesturing for Zara to do the same.

Both moved slowly around the next corner. An entrance came into view, a huge crack spanning across the glass doors. Through it, a desk stood alone.

'Could be a place to stay,' Eve whispered, placing her hand on the door and giving it a shove. Nothing happened. Zara pressed her shoulder up against it and pushed too, thinking it might be stiff. The door was locked. She dropped her helmet before pressing her foot up against the glass and giving it a kick.

Another crack appeared across the door. Both of them looked around and Eve gave her a nod. Zara kicked hard, making the door shatter. She fell onto the ground and gave a brief but painful smile at her success.

Eve returned the smile, then grabbed her bag as they heard footsteps approaching. Zara seized her helmet and passed through the smashed door behind her. They crouched down behind the desk inside the entrance.

Seconds later, three figures appeared, carefully approaching the shattered doorway. Two men and a woman, looking tattered and rough, each held a weapon, though Zara struggled to make out what weapons they were. She hid back around the corner and listened.

'Seems clear to me,' the woman said.

'It does,' one of the men replied. 'Besides the glass.'

'Glass does that. Too much tension and it'll just smash. That or could be the temperature.' The third man eyed the door frame, now void of glass.

'Heat makes it break, not the cold,' the woman replied.

'How do you know?' the third man answered. 'The cold could do just the same.'

'Well, I don't think it's been too hot or too cold,' the other man said as the voices began to fade.

Zara glanced out to see if they were moving off.

'If anyone went inside, we'd know about it,' the woman said, sounding unconcerned.

Eve and Zara looked at each other, before they both turned towards the darkened corridor.

The silhouette of a man aimed his rifle at them. He stepped closer, glaring down at Zara. 'Drop what you got.'

Hearing the man's voice, the three outside turned and entered through the broken glass door, surrounding the desk.

'Well, well, well… Looks like we got ourselves a lost little Legion.' The woman grinned.

CHAPTER 30 – SHELBY

Shelby pressed the top button in the lift, crouching and taking aim with his rifle at the closing doors. Before leaving, he had checked over his weapons and tested them, discovering the rifle to be fully automatic instead of the usual bolt-action one he used at home.

Adrenaline coursed through him at the thought that he might be killed within the next few seconds. He imagined the rest of the crew standing by the door, waiting for him to appear.

The lift stopped, reaching the top floor, and opened its doors. The empty control room faced him; his backpack was still visible by the chair where he'd left it. Shelby stepped out with caution. Only Victor sat in the room, still fiddling with the radio. He lowered the rifle and hid it behind one of the desks before approaching him.

'Got it working then?' Shelby asked, attempting to sound calm. A few muffled voices could be heard amid the static noise.

'Well, it isn't Carbon Rocks… It seems to be picking up something else, maybe a conversation? It's been going on for a few minutes now, but I can't for the life of me figure out what they're talking about.' Victor glanced at Shelby, his eyes going to the tear in his jacket.

'Sorry if they gave you a rough time,' he said grimly. 'They've tried it on with me a few times, too, but I had Hermann to keep them under control.' He moved more of the controls on the panel. 'Sorry I couldn't do much.'

'Nothing you *could* do,' Shelby replied soberly, his anger towards him turning into unease.

'I'm actually surprised they didn't kill you,' Victor said, looking at Shelby again. 'Anyway, here, want to try a hand at the radio?' he added, smiling. 'Pretty sure we can talk on it now.' Victor bumped the volume up. 'Could even join the conversation, too, if we can make out what these people are saying.'

The radio crackled with the volume as the distorted voices came and went. '...levels regular... readings reg... across the board...'

Victor looked at Shelby and shuffled towards an old microphone sticking up from the console.

'Maybe it's an old recording?' guessed Shelby, unsure what to say.

'Nah, it's definitely live.' Victor screwed up his face and pushed up his spectacles. 'Any ideas what they're on about?'

Once again, Shelby felt out of his depth. 'They mentioned reading, I think, so maybe books? Would they read across the radio?'

'Could be.' Victor nodded and pressed down a button to speak. 'What we reading then, guys?' he interrupted cheerfully over the radio.

The distorted voices stopped, leaving Victor with radio silence.

'What happened?' Shelby asked. Victor looked over the console.

'Not sure. The signal was rubbish to begin with, I guess. Might have just dropped.' Victor tinkered with the controls before giving up. 'Well, that was short-lived. Another time, perhaps.' Victor sighed. 'Still, least it works for the most part. Worth taking for sure.'

'I could always have a look. Used one or two radios back in Lornsten.' Shelby smiled, eager to get it working.

'Ah, this one is a touch more complicated, sorry.'

Nodding, Shelby reached into his coat and pulled out a packet of crisps. 'I brought this up for you.' He handed Victor the packet. 'They're a bit chewy, but the flavour seems good.'

Victor opened them delicately and put one in his mouth.

'They taste a bit...' He squinted as he chewed. 'Strong. Strong but nice.' Victor smiled and took a handful. 'Thank you. Anyway, I suppose it's time to pack some of this up and take it to the top. Having it ready for Roy when he returns means we can get out of here quicker, which is good for both of us.'

Shelby grew uncomfortable with going back up, unsure who else might have known what the two blokes were up to.

'Didn't Roy say he'd ask Hermann if they wanted this stuff? Perhaps we should wait. Otherwise it might mean dismantling it for no reason.' Staying down with the radio intact seemed like Shelby's best option.

'Eh, he did, but I know Luther well enough,' Victor replied, now standing up and taking another handful of crisps.

'Is he an expert on this stuff like yourself then?' Shelby asked, eager to delay rejoining the group.

'Not really. I mean, he has an interest in some of it, but only if it helps him with his job.' Victor leant over the desk. 'He's a bit of a prick, really.'

You're more like him than you think, Shelby thought, realising that soon enough, Roy would return and want to head down to the armoury.

'Should I help with the armoury stuff?' Shelby queried, keen to empty the place below before anyone else took the chance.

'Really?' Victor raised his brow, seemingly offended by the question. 'Look, you're up here now. Forget about them. Don't go doing something stupid, alright? Trust Hermann's word. He's a good bloke underneath. Before you know it, we'll be back on the ship and on our way home.' Victor began unplugging the consoles and screens. 'Now help me wrap some of these leads up so we don't trip.'

Unless he wanted to confess, Shelby had little ground to argue his idea. Victor appeared to dislike the crew, but proved hardly a man to trust when confronted.

'Sure.' Shelby moved around behind the console units, trying to think up a plan. Escaping on foot still felt like a mistake. The returning trucks were certainly his best bet. He flinched at the pain that struck across his broken fingers.

'You alright?' Victor poked his head up from one of the consoles.

'Yeah, yeah, I'm good. Caught my hand on something.' Shelby forced a chuckle, searching for a wire to follow.

****

A few hours passed as they moved screens, computers and console boards into a pile in the two hangars above. The pain in Shelby's hand still pulsed with each item he carried. Constant aches plagued his body, though helped keep him awake in his exhausted state. He glimpsed one of his arms bruising yellow, but the coat he wore thankfully covered most of it.

One other person had been roped in by Victor – a rough skinny woman with sharp blue eyes. Shelby tried to keep a watch on her, paranoid she might somehow find out about the men below. His lack of energy eventually overcame his nerves as the three of them moved and passed things up the ladder to the surface.

The room they were clearing looked empty compared to when they had first arrived, with only the desks remaining. The crew at the top appeared to be growing increasingly agitated at the lack of Roy and the others returning.

Shelby followed Victor up again. They each carried an old screen out of the hanger with the bunker and into the one with the missiles. The piles of old technology and weaponry kept growing in size. Shelby doubted they could transport all the gear in one run if he and the crew were to board the trucks, too.

'Anyone seen Bogdan?' a guy asked inside the missile hangar. Shelby woke himself from his drowsy trance.

'Likely with Dareen,' someone replied.

'Well, they better hurry back cos we ain't waiting around for them when Roy arrives,' the guy spat, chucking down a few guns onto the pile by the large missiles.

Thumping started within Shelby's throat as he realised who they might be talking about. He kept his eyes in front, noticing how uncomfortably warm it had become in his coat. Placing the monitor beside Victor's, he hurried back and kept close to him and the woman.

Engines sounded in the distance, making those outside the hangar door gather up and walk towards it. A few moments later, headlights entered the compound and a truck pulled up in front of the building, the sun making it difficult to recognise who stepped out.

A figure jumped from the driver's side. A thick ginger beard accompanied a thick accent. 'Found much more then?' Roy headed towards the group in the hangar.

Churning in Shelby's stomach made him feel ill. He was unsure whether to be relieved at Roy's arrival.

'Eh, not too much. These small launchers here, some more guns, and this… metal shit Victor and the murderer keep bringing up,' Erma, one of the group leaders, said, giving both Shelby and Victor a dirty glance.

Pretending not to notice, Shelby stopped to stretch his back, staring at three trucks now parked outside the hangar.

'That metal shit is more valuable than you'd think,' Roy answered her, moving towards the large missiles. 'What about these big bastards?' He patted the missiles stacked up. 'I see they're already on wheels.' He looked at the long trailer they rested on. 'Bring in a truck, would you?' Roy called out.

'They're on wheels, yeah,' Erma replied, walking with him. 'Nothing to attach them to or with, though.'

'Well, then, it looks like we'll be back for a third trip, so plenty of time to figure it out. Hermann is eager on getting them, even after I explained the difficulties of it.' Roy bit his tongue. 'This is what he's after.'

Groans and cursing erupted at the news.

'I was against it, I assure you,' Roy continued. 'But like Hermann said, to come all this way and not get exactly what we were after would be foolish, especially considering the price he's paying us. We may as well make another trip while we figure this out. It's all on you now, like it is with me.'

'Alright for Hermann to say,' a woman grumbled. 'He's still rolling around on that ship and always knew where we were headed.'

Roy let out a loud sigh. 'Look, the sooner we get this done, the sooner we can go.' He turned to pick up some weapons. 'So let's get it loaded already. I'd rather we just get on with this for now and figure things out along the way. I'm not too keen on being here either.'

'Here? You keep going back to the ship. We're the ones stuck here, not you,' a bloke shouted.

'Sooner we load it, the sooner we leave. You're currently included in that,' Roy snapped. 'So, get on with it, will ya, and don't forget you're being paid for all this,' he growled, picking up several guns.

Shelby stood in silence, still anxious that attention might be drawn to him somehow, now that the crew were all moving to pick up something. The third truck backed into the hangar, moving close to the missiles.

Everyone began moving in and out, loading the other two. Roy walked over to Victor, who was carefully placing the screens onto the back of one of them. Shelby remained inside, attempting to round up some wires and keep out of the way.

'I take it that this stuff all works?' Roy asked Victor, moving past Shelby and back out to the truck.

'Sure does. Most of it's in the other hangar next door, but some parts I've separated and put in here, due to being—' A loud crack sounded from behind him. 'Fragile.'

Victor turned from Roy to find one of the crew had fallen over with a monitor and was sitting on the ground with it, the screen smashed. The woman on the floor stared wide-eyed at him.

'Fragile...' Roy repeated slowly as he leant in to stare at the screen. A bullet was stuck in the metal back of it.

Spinning his head, Roy turned to Victor, who stood in front of him, his mouth and eyes wide open and a hand trying to cover the red stain spreading across him. He dropped to the floor, gasping for breath. Fear flickered to anger across Roy's face. He glanced around, looking for whoever had shot the bullet, but before he got the chance to say or do anything, two gunshots echoed into the sky.

'West!' Roy shouted. 'Get to cover!' he screamed, running behind the back of the truck.

'Help...' Victor gasped, clawing the ground where he'd fallen. Another shot thudded into him, causing him to stop moving. The sound followed up into the air a few seconds later.

Still crouching inside the hangar door, Shelby dropped the wires and grabbed a gun from the pile, making sure it was loaded. He peered out towards Roy, who was kneeling beside the truck. Behind the man, Shelby saw more movement on the opposite side of the compound. His heart raced as he had the urge to run for one of the trucks.

'ROY!' Shelby yelled, his voice straining. 'The tower.'

A handful of the crew had also spotted the figures moving.

'To the east,' a man shouted. 'Roy, get here now!'

'The Eastern Legion,' a woman called out. 'We need to leave.'

After running into the hangar, Roy crouched down beside Shelby. 'Shelby and you two.' He pointed to a man and woman beside each other. 'Cover fire for the rest. We'll get into the trucks and start them up. Jump onto the back when you can.' Roy picked up an assault rifle and loaded it. 'These fuckers won't let us leave alive so we best not wait around.' He ran out to the vehicle without giving the signal to cover fire.

The other two started shooting before Shelby finally joined in. A stream of bullets flew out of the hangar as the trucks started to move. The third truck from inside drove across their line of sight and sped off west, ignoring the bullets. The other two trucks followed close behind the third, leaving Shelby and the couple behind.

'WAIT!' the woman screamed, trying to catch up, before dropping to the ground. The man fired at the truck, screaming.

Shelby watched, realising he needed to act fast if he intended to survive. He moved further inside the hangar and out of the tear that stretched down its side, before sprinting out and across into the neighbouring hangar with the bunker. The man followed. Shelby jumped down onto the ladder and through the hatch. Gunfire, screeching, and an immense rumble sounded before an explosion went off.

'Close what you can behind you,' Shelby said, jumping down from the ladder.

The man slammed shut what remained of the hatch door and dropped down after him. They headed to the empty control room, where Shelby entered the lift to press the middle floor button, then jumped back out of it before the doors closed on him. He grabbed a chair and started to pull the doors back open, eventually wrenching them apart with the help of the other man. Finding the fuse box Victor had shown him earlier, Shelby smashed it with the end of his rifle, turning the lights off. Before his eyes adjusted, he got out a torch and untied the rope still left by Roy, chucking it down the shaft.

'There're metal cables in the middle,' Shelby said in a hushed tone, slinging the rifle over his shoulder and grabbing his bag that had been left in the room. He dropped a chair into the shaft and leant out to grasp the cable, letting himself slide downwards. The pain in his hand made him grunt as he gripped tighter to slow his descent, a dry mucky substance from the cable collecting around his fingers.

He could hear the other man close above him as he reached the bottom. Shelby noticed the other chair thrown down by Victor still on top of the lift. Using the second chair to stand on, he wedged the other one between the lift doors above them and pushed hard to open them.

'Bring the chair up and grab the rope,' Shelby whispered, lifting himself through with the old chair. The bloke climbed up behind him, taking the other chair up with him, the rope thrown over one shoulder. Shelby pulled him up into the corridor.

'This is the only way in.' Shelby looked at the lift doors that remained partially open before moving down the corridor.

'Take it in turns to watch it?' the man said.

'Both watch,' Shelby replied. 'If we last long enough, we'll take it in turns.'

They both lay down at the end of the hallway, aiming their guns in silence and listening for any movement above.

****

A few hours passed in silence between Shelby and the other man. Both still aimed down the hall towards the lift shaft. Shelby kept feeling his eyelids close and his stomach rumble. The hallway remained in darkness, a good enough sign that those above never found the bunker or the fuse box.

'Gone?' Shelby spoke in a hushed tone.

'I'd guess,' the man replied.

'Hungry?' Shelby asked.

'What do you think?' the man said briskly.

'Follow me.' Shelby lowered his gun and walked down the hall towards the food storage room. The man followed, keeping at a slight distance with his gun still raised at the door.

'Here. Plenty of it. Never seen half this stuff.' Shelby pulled his torch out and flashed it around. The man stared at the amount of food and lowered his gun to find his own torch.

'Blimey,' he said almost in awe, before he started rummaging.

'Grab what you want and follow me.' Shelby seized a few packets of crisps and headed back out of the room.

The man followed with a handful of food. They entered the lounge area. Shelby dropped his food on the floor before going over to one side of a settee.

'Here, take the other end and we'll line it up with the lift.'

The man put his food down and lifted the other end, and together they moved it across the hallway.

'Better,' Shelby said in a cheery tone, happier to sit on something soft.

Silence settled itself. Shelby dwelt on his thoughts. He was alone – except for this other guy, who he didn't exactly trust – and without a vehicle. As well as that, there were the attackers. Were they still outside?

After a few minutes, the man stopped eating, making Shelby aware of the noise he had been making. He tried to glance at the bloke without staring, knowing how most of the crew wished him dead. The quietness unsettled him. In the darkness, he made out the man's pale complexion and pointed chin. On one side a scar ran down the length of his cheek. *He's the tracker. Jason's mate.*

'Well, what the fuck do we do now?' the tracker asked.

Swallowing the food in his mouth, Shelby replied, 'Well... could head back to the ship?' He hardly knew what to say, but to him it seemed like the best next step to take, and now the safest and quickest route home, figuring whoever made it back would want to leave immediately.

'The ship?' The tracker raised his voice. 'What fucking ship?!' He stood up. 'They're not going to wait around for us, you idiot. They may never have made it back.'

The sudden spike of anger made Shelby grip the handgun still in his coat pocket.

'For all we know they could be dead. I mean, just like we'll be. You realise we're fucked, right? Please tell me you know that?' He didn't wait for an answer and kept shouting.

'You don't know that.' Shelby struck in between the man's words. 'They might have gotten away and could be coming back. After all, Hermann didn't get what he wanted, did he? He might force them to return, and we'll be right here in possession of what they're after.'

The tracker went quiet. 'That's true.' He paused. 'But we could always try and bargain our way out with the Legion. Tell them what we were here for. That might work. Or that we were forced. Yeah, like you were. You're the murderer, aren't you? I could be from where you are, yes. Why, that could work.' He yawned. 'Information for safety, yeah.'

Relieved that the shouting had stopped, Shelby soaked in the man's words, keeping an ear out for any noise above.

'We going to do that then, yeah?' The tracker tried to muster up the energy he'd just lost. 'We're gonna say that, yeah?'

'Sure,' Shelby replied, wanting to keep him quiet. The last thing he needed to do was give the man another reason to kill him. 'There are some beds on the floor below this one. You could get some shut-eye while I watch the door. I know this place well, so I'll draw us up a plan for when you wake?'

The tracker studied him in the darkness. 'Yeah, I'm pretty tired. Yeah, and get food for me and put it in our bag,' he said, standing up.

He went to walk away before turning back and snatching his gun that leant against the settee. 'You got one job.' He spoke coldly, but Shelby felt happy to see the back of him heading down the stairwell.

When the steps faded, Shelby leant against the soft back of the settee and relaxed his neck. What the tracker wanted sounded like a terrible plan and not something Shelby intended on doing. Attempting a deal with those who had attacked felt like a sure way of getting captured or killed.

He stared longingly at the corridor ahead, the darkness infinite. Home entered his mind once again. He wished he could see his children. Back in Lornsten, most strangers he met were mannered at least, even if some weren't friendly, but the crew from the ship were all ill-behaved killers, besides Victor. His mind drifted to Victor's body lying outside. Half a day back, the man was happily working on the radio and had even attempted to cheer Shelby up.

Shelby's heart dropped. He bolted up and aimed his rifle at the stairs. Two floors below remained the remnants of the two men from the group, who had blown themselves up. A hot flush came over him at the thought of his companion finding what remained of the bodies. It was undeniable the tracker would assume his involvement.

He picked up his bag and rushed down the hallway, fearful the man might come up to confront or kill him, seeing how irrational he could quickly become. Shelby climbed up the metal lift cable, making more noise than he had hoped he would, his bag and gun clanging against it. The pain in his right hand almost forced him to scream, while tears escaped from his eyes as he attempted to keep silent.

Finally, he pulled himself up and over the ledge into the control room, exhausted and in pain. He went to rest for a second but a sudden mix of shots and flashes echoed up the shaft, prompting Shelby to turn and cover his ears. The noise bounced around the metal walls.

'MURDERER!' the tracker repeatedly screamed, shooting a flurry of bullets again.

It fell silent. Shelby knew better than to risk looking over the edge. He glanced around the near-empty control room for something to block the way. The shooting and screaming started again, making him cover his ears. When the gunfire stopped, his ears still rang with pain.

The silence began to freak him out. He pushed a desk hard through the gap between the lift doors. The weight of it abruptly lifted as gravity took hold of it. It dropped over and down the shaft, with Shelby tripping behind it to the floor. Pain struck through his hand and back as he scrambled to move away from the edge. The desk scraped and plummeted down the shaft, a loud crash sounding when it hit the bottom.

Everything went silent. Shelby got to his feet, checking over his mask, guns and bag, before heading through the corridor and out of the hatch. He moved out of the hangar, straining to listen for any sound, but the compound remained deathly silent.

To his left lay the remains of a flipped truck. To the right, towards the neighbouring hangar, Shelby noticed the pile of weapons, tech and missiles were missing, along with Victor's body. He approached the hangar until something caught his attention further ahead.

On the opposite side of the military base, a large yellow plume of haze engulfed everything and was heading straight for him. He took out the tube from his inside pocket and pulled it up through the back of his coat; it proved easier than anticipated. He loosened the straps on the mask, connected the tube and placed the mask over his head, tightening the elastic. He picked up his gun and backpack, keeping still while the cloud closed in and surrounded him. Outrunning it would have been impossible.

Shelby took in a deep breath, hoping Victor had done his job with the mask correctly. His eyes watered a little at the haze since the mask only covered his nose and mouth.

After a minute, Shelby started to move, trusting the mask more, though he could only see a few feet ahead of him. Victor had mentioned how the mist ate people alive from the inside out, but so far, he felt nothing of the sort and decided his best bet would be to head for the ship. The chances of reaching it before it left might be slim, since the crew had left on trucks, but he had little choice. He wasn't sure the crew would return here, even if Hermann ordered it.

The hangar. Shelby remembered that the missile hangar contained a few vehicles towards the back. He went in, keeping to one side due to the reduced visibility. After a minute, he came upon the back wall and moved out to see if any of the vehicles remained.

The shape of a small truck appeared in front of him. Shelby rushed to it, still aware that the tracker might try to follow. He opened the door and went to step in, then saw the slashed tyres. Letting go of the door, he carried on moving, finding another vehicle beside it. A pang of desperation ran through him when he saw the tyres of this truck had been cut open too. He walked further on, but found nothing. Shelby returned to the small truck, glancing into the back of it.

A bicycle lay across it, and to his surprise, the tyres appeared untouched. He picked it up at once and got on, feeling his time running out if he intended to catch the ship. Thankfully, he had used bicycles back at home before getting the horse and cart.

Cycling out of the hangar, Shelby made his escape from the compound, and headed towards the ship.

****

A handful of hours passed before Shelby neared the coast. His body throbbed at the constant pedalling. The haze had lifted, allowing him to take clearer breaths and see further ahead.

The sea came into view, and with it, a rowing boat on the shore where the road plunged into the ocean. Shelby made his way to the small boat, trying to see the ship out at sea. The air had cleared, yet there appeared to be no ship in sight. *Fuck.*

He stretched his head towards the sky. The ship was gone. Shelby looked back down, a new wave of panic setting in at the heightening chance of his home being raided and his children killed.

His mind raced through dozens of ideas until one caught his attention. A radio. If he got his hands on a radio, he could warn Lornsten and, in turn, his family about the incoming danger. Shelby looked around and found what he needed: a truck parked up to his left.

Jumping into the driver's seat, he twisted the small key, making the vehicle roar into life. He looked eastwards at other buildings off in the distance. He presumed his best bet of finding a working radio resided in the remains of any town nearby. Whatever the cost, he would protect his family.

EPILOGUE

The low hum of machinery could be heard coming from underground. The yellow haze floated steadily in place, remaining still and dense. Through it, dead trees and foliage led down to cracks in the earth that grew deeper and wider until they reached a broad circular crater. The yellow haze sat over it all, small gusts of wind stealing off the upper layer and pushing it towards the west.

Gunfire sounded in the distance, followed by a screech and an immense rumble. An explosion followed, before the humming of machinery stole back its place over silence.

The Dark Array series will continue in *Disarray*.

****

Also coming soon is *The Art of Displaced*.

ACKNOWLEDGEMENTS

Thank you to everyone who helped give me support and feedback for this book. Without you, writing this novel would have taken a whole lot longer and been a far messier process. A special thanks to Sara for her amazing artwork that has brought this series to life, Tim for the incredible soundtrack, and Chloe for her excellent mask designs.

ABOUT THE AUTHOR

Dan Hook is a graduate from the Open University, successfully gaining his BA (hons) Open degree in-between his building work and writing. When not being called upon to fix computers, he enjoys relaxing on the Sussex coast to soak in the views.

If you want to keep up to date with his latest projects, you can find him over on Twitter at:

www.twitter.com/danhook

Or his own website:

www.danhook.co.uk

CPSIA information can be obtained
at www.ICGtesting.com
Printed in the USA
LVHW012028170820
663417LV00009B/1301